David grabbed both her wrists . . .

pinned her hands above her head and swiftly shoved one knee between her legs, completely hemming her in with no way out.

"This look submissive to you darlin'?" he growled.

They were both breathing hard, their lips almost touching.

"For your information I'm a third-degree black belt in karate," she said.

"Bring it on. I'm fifth degree."

"You don't threaten me." She gulped, belying her own bravado.

His gaze locked onto hers.

She raised her chin. She was so close her body heat set him on fire.

They stood there a long moment, neither of them blinking, neither wanting to be the first to back down. He forced himself not to think about how nice she smelled or how her chest rose and fell in cadence with his own raspy breathing or how much he wanted to kiss her at that very moment.

"This novel has chuckles aplenty. . . . The sexual tension is hot and funny and at the same time sweet."

—ContemporaryRomanceWriters.com
on *License to Thrill*

"Passionate . . . amusing . . . fast-moving. . . . An impossible to put down read."

—ARomanceReview.com on *License to Thrill*

ALSO BY LORI WILDE

License to Thrill

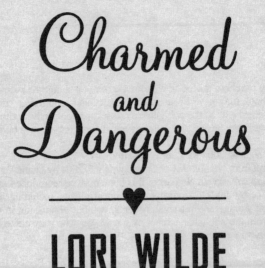

Charmed
and
Dangerous

LORI WILDE

WARNER
FOREVER

NEW YORK   BOSTON

Copyright © 2004 by Laurie Vanzura
Excerpt from *Mission: Irresistible* copyright © 2004 by Laurie Vanzura

Warner Forever is a registered trademark of Warner Books, Inc.

Cover art and design by Shasti O'Leary Soudant
Book design by Giorgetta Bell McRee

Warner Books

Time Warner Book Group
1271 Avenue of the Americas
New York, NY 10020
Visit our Web site at www.twbookmark.com

Printed in the United States of America

First Paperback Printing: July 2004

10   9   8   7   6   5   4   3   2   1

To my father, Fred Blalock, who nurtured my love of reading and mentored my budding writing talent. And to my mother, Francis Maxine Reid Blalock, who gave me the iron-will to succeed. Thank you. I love you both more than words can say.

Acknowledgment

Many thanks are in order for my wonderful editor Michele Bidelspach for sending me back to the drawing board after the first draft wasn't quite as good as it could have been. Thank you, Michele, for challenging me to dig deeper.

Charmed
and
Dangerous

Prologue

❤

North Central Texas
Christmas Day, eighteen years ago

$\mathcal{I}$T WAS TURNING out to be the worst day of Maddie Cooper's nine-year-old life.

For one thing she hadn't gotten the super cool purple-and-white Nikes she'd wanted for Christmas. Instead she wound up with a stupid half-a-heart necklace that matched the one her identical twin sister wore. Why was Mama always trying to turn her into a prissy girly-girl like Cassie?

For another thing, she'd wanted to go running in Granddad's cow pasture so she could pout by herself, but oh, no, Mama said she had to let Cassie come along.

As if her lazybones twin could even run. How was a girl supposed to become a famous track and field Olympic athlete if she couldn't practice in peace?

And then came the icing on the cupcake.

"Maddie, make sure you take good care of Cassie," Mama called from the back porch. She stood shivering in her see-through lace blouse, black leather mini-skirt and spike-heeled boots because she and Daddy were going to a party.

"How come I always gotta look after Cassie and she don't ever have to look after me?"

"You know why," her mother chided.

Yeah. She knew why. Because if left on her own, Cassie did dumb stuff like taping peacock feathers to her arms and jumping off the roof to see if she could fly.

Maddie marched through the pasture. Her breath coming out in frosty white puffs. Cassie trailed along behind her, humming some goofy *Sesame Street* song. Gramma had bundled them up like marshmallows in their matching goose down coats and knit scarves. The only difference between them was Cassie wore rubber boots while Maddie had on her well-worn Pumas.

"Look," Cassie said. "The stock pond's frozen."

"Stay away from there." Maddie stopped beside an oak tree, took off her coat and then placed a palm flat against the trunk to keep her balance while she stretched. "Gramma says there's nothing more dangerous than an iced-over stock pond in Texas. It never freezes solid enough to hold your weight."

"Aw, pah." Cassie waved a hand and toddled out onto the slick surface. "Look at me! I'm skating."

Maddie rolled her eyes and refused to glance over. She was too busy limbering up her hamstrings and being mad. "Get off the pond, Cassie."

"You're not the boss of me."

"Mama told me to take care of you. That makes me the boss of you."

"Pfftt." Cassie gave her the raspberry.

"Get off the ice."

"Stop telling me what to do. Look, look, I'm in the Ice Capades."

"I'm not watching." Maddie folded her arms over her chest and turned to face the opposite direction.

"Good. Fine. Don't watch."

"I won't."

"You're boring anyway. I wish you weren't my sister."

"Me too!"

Maddie took off running, her sneakers slapping against the ground. Anger poked her hard in the ribs and that stupid necklace bounced off her chest and smacked her in the chin. She fisted her hand around the chain, snapped it from her neck and flung the heart into a clump of prickly yucca.

She ran until she got a stitch in her side. By then she was on the opposite side of the pasture. She heard a scary cracking noise. Loud as Granddad's rifle when he shot doves.

"Maddie!" Cassie screamed. And then she heard a splash.

"Cassie?" Maddie whirled around, scanning the distant pond. Her heart went boom-boom-boom in her ears.

No sign of her sister.

"Cassie!" Her frantic shout echoed back to her.

She didn't remember much about what happened next. She hurtled toward the pond, spying the gaping hole in the middle of the ice, but no Cassie. Not knowing what else to do, she sprinted to the house for Granddad and Gramma.

Granddad fished Cassie from the water. Her lips were blue and her skin was the color of snow and she wasn't breathing. Granddad blew air in Cassie's mouth until the ambulance came.

The next time Maddie saw her twin she was lying oh-so-still in a hospital bed. A machine was helping her breathe and other awful looking tubes poked out of her.

Mama sat in a chair by Cassie's bed, holding her hand and crying. Daddy smelled like beer and his eyes were red. He kept walking back and forth and running his hands through his hair. Neither of her parents spoke to her. Maddie knew this was all her fault.

Why wouldn't Cassie wake up?

A doctor came into the room. He said Cassie might never wake up. Mama and Daddy stayed at the hospital. Granddad and Gramma took Maddie back to their house.

They put her to bed with hugs and kisses. They told her she wasn't to blame, but she didn't believe them. It was all her fault. Mama told her to take good care of her sister and she hadn't. She should have made Cassie get off the ice. She shouldn't have yelled at her. She shouldn't have run away.

What if Cassie never woke up? What if her sister died?

She sobbed low in her throat and reached up to touch the half-a-heart necklace to remind her she was one part of a twin set and realized the necklace was gone. She'd thrown it away.

Terror grabbed her stomach and Maddie thought she was going to throw up. Desperate to find the necklace, she crawled out of bed. She put on her coat, took her granddad's flashlight from its place by the back door and sneaked out into the pitch-black, ice-cold night.

She searched the pasture for what seemed like hours, digging through every clump of yucca she could find, getting poked through her gloves by the sharp leaves. Her teeth chattered from the cold. Her toes were numb. But she didn't care. When at last she found the necklace, Maddie let out a gasp of relief and burst into tears.

Dropping to her knees on the frozen earth, she tilted her face upward, beseeching the midnight sky.

"Dear God," she prayed and clutched the necklace to her heart. "I didn't mean those ugly things I said to Cassie. I love her. If you please just let her wake up, I swear I won't never ever let her get hurt again!"

Chapter
ONE

FBI SPECIAL AGENT David Marshall loved a good fight and he played to win.

Always

His personal credo: *He who hesitates is lost.* And David hated losing more than anything.

Whenever a situation called for action, he immediately seized control and bluffed his way through the consequences. Usually victoriously. He'd learned at an early age you had to battle hard against life or die. He had also discovered, that for the good of the cause, you occasionally had to bend a few rules.

But once in a while, one of his less prudent rule bending episodes came back to bite him viciously in the ass.

Like now.

Where in the hell was Cassie Cooper?

For the tenth time in as many minutes, David checked his wristwatch.

With an impatient snort, he sank his fists on his hips and scanned the rendezvous spot. Forest Park on the

Trinity River, fourth picnic bench at the seven-mile marker of the jogging trail, eight A.M. sharp.

It was now eight-thirteen.

Had Cassie gotten mixed up about their meeting place? It was highly possible. The woman personified dumb blonde jokes.

Which was why the art theft task force had rejected using her as an informant. Even though Cassie was a public relations specialist at the Kimbell Art Museum and they knew Peyton Shriver had marked her as his next sweetheart victim.

Realizing that Cassie was the best lead he'd had on Shriver in years, David had taken matters into his own hands. He'd gone behind his boss's back and recruited her. No one except he and Cassie knew about her involvement in the case. Not even the men he had shadowing her. His men believed they were simply tailing her because she was Peyton's new girlfriend. Because of this, all their previous contact except for the initial meeting had been via phone or e-mail. He would deal with the fallout of his unorthodox police methods once he had Shriver securely in handcuffs. It was always easier to get Jim Barnes's forgiveness than his permission.

For ten years he'd been doggedly pursuing Shriver. The time had come to end this battle of wills. With Cassie's help, he'd known he was going to win it.

Come hell or high water he was determined to see justice served.

But last night his surveillance team had delivered bad news. They'd observed Shriver meeting with a world-class scumbag by the name of Jocko Blanco. The creep was a tattooed, pock-faced skinhead with a rap sheet as thick as a telephone book and a history of violent behavior.

Shriver might be a heartbreaking cad and an unrepentant thief, but he'd never physically harmed any of his victims. In fact, his courtly behavior was legendary. Blanco on the other hand was as dangerous as dynamite near an open flame.

Upon hearing the news about Blanco and Shriver hooking up, his first thought had been totally selfish. Yes! Two criminals for the price of one. That would show his boss he'd been right to make an end run around authority by involving Cassie Cooper.

But then his irritating conscience had voiced its opinion: *You can't keep her on the case.*

As eager as she might be to help him bring down Shriver, frivolous Cassie was no match for the likes of Jocko Blanco.

Regretfully, he had to terminate Cassie's mission. No matter how much he lusted to see Shriver cooling his heels in the slammer, he couldn't justify jeopardizing her life.

David shoved a hand through his hair and paced to the edge of the embankment on the opposite side of the jogging trail. He stared down at the thin ribbon of river several hundred feet below and then he swung his gaze through the rest of the vacant park.

Not too many people out and about this early on a damp, blustery February day. A couple of joggers off in the distance, an elderly man letting his dog take a leak on the trashcan near the park entrance, but no one else.

A heart-stopping thought occurred to him. What if Shriver had discovered Cassie was spying on him for the

FBI? What if he had actually hired Blanco to bump her off?

Icy chills shot up his spine.

"Dammit, Cassie." He glowered, royally pissed off at himself.

He shouldn't have arranged a meeting. Instead of setting up the rendezvous, he should have just told her over the phone he was pulling her off the case. But he'd needed the tape she'd recorded of Shriver bragging about his exploits. Besides, David thought it only fair he break the news to her in person.

Where in the hell *was* Cassie?

He glanced at his watch again. Eight-fifteen.

Mindlessly, he reached to pat the breast pocket of his London Fog trench coat in search of the cigarettes that were no longer there.

It had been almost a year since he'd kicked the butts but in times of stress the old nicotine hankering still lingered. He'd given up the cigs not long after his ex-fiancée Keeley dumped him. Not because he still had a thing for her and was trying to win her back. No, that ship had sailed. In fact, she married an orthodontist not two months after they had broken up. Nope, he'd quit smoking simply to prove her wrong.

"Face it, David," Keeley told him the day she'd dramatically yanked off her engagement ring and tossed it in his face. "Your obsessive need to tempt fate and win at all costs is going to be the death of you. And I refuse to hang around and watch it happen."

"I don't have an obsessive need to tempt fate," he'd protested.

"Ha! Look, you can't even stop smoking long enough

to have this conversation with me," she'd crowed. "What's puffing on a cancer stick, if not tempting fate?"

So he had quit smoking. He was at least going to win that argument.

But although he was loath to admit it, maybe Keeley had a point. If Cassie's subversive involvement ended up botching the investigation, his boss would have his head.

And his job.

Shriver would get away and David would lose.

Shit.

At that moment, a woman jogger appeared from under the train trestle. She was too far away for David to see her facial features, but his baser male instincts homed in on the luscious body striding rhythmically toward him.

Boobs bouncing in spite of the sports bra, blond ponytail swishing, hips rolling forward.

Mama mia, come to Papa.

And then she drew close enough for him to recognize.

Cassie. Thank God. Relief rolled over him.

He stared at her.

And she ran right by him without a second glance.

Dumbfounded, David's jaw dropped as he gazed after her retreating figure.

What in hell . . . ?

He quickly looked in the direction from which she'd come to see if anyone was following her. Nobody. Hadn't she seen him standing there?

Perplexed, David trotted after her. "Hold up," he called.

She swiveled her head, saw he was following and started running faster.

Dammit. What game was the woman playing?

"Stop," he commanded, even as he sped up to cover

the increasing distance between them. Damn, but she was in some kind of shape. Who knew?

He was running flat out by the time he caught her. He grabbed her by the elbow and spun her around to face him. They were standing on the edge of the embankment, both panting hard, their gazes locked.

Before David could suck in his breath long enough to speak, she whipped a can of mace from the pocket of her sweat top.

She was quick, but David was quicker.

"Oh no you don't," he said and clamped his hand over her pepper-spray-clutching fist before she had time to depress the nozzle. He wrenched the can away from her. "What's the matter with you?"

"Hands off, buddy," she commanded and jerked backward.

The force of her momentum was so strong she teetered unbalanced on the edge, a look of shock passing over her face.

"Oh," she cried, her arms windmilling wildly. "Oh."

Reaching for her, David grabbed at the first thing he could get his hands on. He ended up snatching the front of her workout pants, attempting to reel her in like an unruly tarpon.

She flailed. The material of her pants stretched out, exposing her naked skin, and David swiftly learned that not only was she wearing pink satin G-string undies, but that she was also a natural blond.

He blinked, his mind momentarily numbed with the breathtaking view.

"Hi-ya!" she yelled and aimed a foot at his crotch.

He dodged her kick but the movement sent him reeling off balance too.

Gravity took over and plunged them both headlong toward the river.

"Oh, crap," David muttered, finally realizing she wasn't Cassie. This spunky woman could be none other than her identical twin sister, Maddie.

The big man had an even bigger gun.

Maddie felt the hard delineation under his coat as they rolled down the wet, rocky knoll together. Her heart practically hammered out of her chest. He was going to rape her, shoot her and throw her in the river for fish bait. She just knew it.

For years, she'd been running in Forest Park unscathed, but as the cautious type who believed in always being prepared, she had an ongoing contingency plan.

Mace 'em in the face, kick 'em in the nuts, haul ass.

What had gone wrong?

Well, for starters the guy outweighed her by a good eighty pounds, but even so he was quicker than a cobra.

Do something now. Fight back. You can't die and leave Cassie alone.

As they rolled downhill, Maddie made a feral sound low in her throat and clawed at his face. Too bad she kept her fingernails clipped short. As soon as she had a chance, she'd go for the car keys in her pants pocket and gouge his eyes out.

"Ouch, damn, hell," he cursed. "Quit that."

They came to a stop just short of the water, his big body crushing hers into the muddy riverbank.

"Get off me you rapist pervert." She slapped at his chest and tried not to panic when her hand smacked against his shoulder holster.

Lungs heaving with the effort of drawing in air, he

grabbed her wrists and pinned her hands above her head while straddling her. Uselessly, she tried to buck him off, but his weight held her prisoner.

"Maddie," he roared. "That's enough!"

She froze and stared into his potent dark eyes. A spark of sexual awareness, so intense it left her stunned, surged between them.

"How . . . how," she stammered. "Do you know my name?"

"I thought you were Cassie," he said.

"Oh." She blinked at him, letting this information sink in. "Let me guess, you two were playing some kind of kinky sex game in the park and it got out of hand?"

"What?" He frowned.

"Cassie's into all that red hot pursuit stuff. You must be her new boyfriend."

"No, I'm not."

They were pressed chest to chest, their lips almost touching. He had an unusually complicated mouth. The outer shape was angular and uncompromising, like some sort of hardware store tool, but at the same time the actual flesh of his lips appeared smooth, soft and inviting. His mouth, she decided, had a personality all its own.

"Then who are you?" Maddie snapped, almost as mad at herself as she was at him.

"David Marshall. FBI."

FBI? At least that explained the gun. What kind of trouble was her twin in now?

Cassie had told Maddie to meet her in the park at eight-fifteen because she had big news to share. Maddie had scheduled her morning run to coincide with the rendezvous. But her twin wasn't at the appointed spot and this bearish man claiming to be with the FBI was. The whole thing smelled fishier than the Trinity River.

"Let me see some identification," she said.

"Only if you promise not to knee me in the groin when I turn you loose."

"All right," she agreed warily, even though she had no intention of keeping her promise if she felt threatened in the slightest.

He released her hands and pushed up on his knees. Maddie lay on her back, head cocked, watching his every move and making sure he didn't go for his gun. Just because he said he was FBI, didn't mean he *was* FBI.

As she studied his face, she realized he was rather good-looking in a rugged, unkempt sort of way. He was tall and muscular with a granite jaw and chiseled cheekbones that oddly enough, lent him a sensitive air. He wore his sandy brown hair clipped short and spiked up. She kind of liked the kingfisher thing he had going on, not that she was really noticing. His nose was neither too big nor too small for his face, but it crooked slightly to the left at the bridge as if he'd used it once or twice to stop an irate fist.

He got to his feet and held out his hand to help her up. She hesitated.

He just kept standing there, hand outstretched.

Reluctantly, she accepted his offer of assistance and he hauled her to a standing position. Once on her feet, she immediately turned away from him.

"Hold on," he said, his skin still branding hers.

"What is it?" she snapped.

"You've got mud on your clothing."

And then, before she knew what he was doing, he reached out and briskly brushed off her bottom.

The touch of his palm against the smooth stretchy Lycra of her workout pants sent a shower of sexual sparks scorching up her backside. Maddie swallowed hard against the storm of sensation flooding her body.

Seriously dangerous stuff.

"There you go." He released her arm. "All dusted clean."

She gulped and her stomach lurched because her butt kept tingling long after his hand was gone. "Your badge?" she said, determined not to let him distract her.

"I'm getting to it." He removed his badge from his coat pocket and flashed it in front of her face.

She held out her palm.

"You wanna hold it?"

"Yes."

He rolled his eyes, but handed it to her. She traced a finger across the emblem. The badge winked goldly at her in the shaft of hopeful sunlight struggling through the cloud covering. It looked real enough, but she wasn't taking any chances. She'd heard about psychos who posed as law enforcement authorities and committed crimes.

"You won't mind if I call the local FBI division and check you out?"

"For crying out loud, woman." He snatched his badge from her hand. "I am who I say I am."

"Don't get testy, bub. You were the one who attacked me."

"Excuse me?" he raised his voice and glared. "Who pulled out the pepper spray and who tried to kick me in the family jewels?"

"You chased me down," she protested.

"After I asked you nicely to stop and you ignored me."

"Because you were a weird guy alone in the park."

"Weird? *You're* calling *me* weird?" He jerked a thumb at himself.

"Ya-huh."

He was studying her as intently as she was studying him, his gaze practically burning a hole through her bottom lip. What did he think of her mouth? Did he find it as interesting as she found his? Her heart was tripping a gazillion beats a minute and a bizarre sensation twisted her stomach.

Good grief! What had come over her?

He moistened his lips and swallowed. "You're nuttier than your sister, you know that?"

"My sister is not nutty," Maddie declared defensively. Impulsive, yes. Irresponsible, well at times. Impractical, that was a given. But he had no right to call Cassie nutty.

"She's a frickin' sack of cashews and tardy to boot. She was supposed to meet me here at eight o'clock and it is now . . ." He paused to glance at his watch. "Eight-twenty-five."

"Why were you meeting her?"

He hesitated.

She could see that he didn't want to tell her any more than he had to. "Well?" she demanded.

"Your twin was working for me. We were attempting to get the goods on an international art thief named Peyton Shriver."

"Get outta here."

"I am deadly serious."

"Cassie? Working for the FBI?"

An uneasy expression that she could not decipher crossed his face. "In an unofficial capacity."

"What exactly does that mean?" Maddie narrowed her eyes. She didn't like the sound of this. Not one bit.

"Look," he said, changing the subject and confirming her suspicion that something wasn't on the up and up. "Have you heard from your sister this morning? I've tried repeatedly to call her. Do you have any idea where she's at?"

"How was Cassie helping you catch this art thief?" Maddie asked, switching the subject right back again. He'd have to be slicker than that if he wanted to pull the wool over her eyes.

"Shriver had pegged Cassie as his next mark and he was courting her hot and heavy."

Maddie shook her head. "I'm not totally following you. If you know who and where the guy is, why don't you just arrest him?"

"Lack of concrete evidence. We need to catch him in the act. Plus, we suspect an influential art broker is backing his little forays and we want to nail that guy too. Your sister is helping me tighten the noose. Now where is she?"

"Exactly how is she doing this?"

He sighed. "You're not going to tell me where Cassie might be until I disclose everything, are you?"

"You got that right."

He growled softly and the sound was so electric it seemed to push right under her skin. Maddie forced herself not to shudder with perverse delight. What was it about this guy that simultaneously repelled yet attracted her?

"Okay, here's the deal."

Maddie could tell he begrudged having to fill her in. Well, too bad. If he wanted information from her, he'd have to pony up with some of his own.

The wind gusted cold and she felt her nipples bead beneath her sweat top. David was staring at her chest but trying to pretend he wasn't.

"You wanna go sit in my car?" He gestured up the hill toward the parking lot. The breeze tousled his already spiky hair, giving him a roguish look.

She shook her head and crossed her arms over her chest.

"I promise I won't bite."

Her natural cautiousness outweighed her desire for warmth. "I'm fine. Your story?"

"I've been tracking Shriver for years, but he's pretty damned slick."

"Slicker than you obviously." Maddie knew she was aggravating him, but she couldn't seem to help herself. Call it retribution for the way his rugged good looks provoked her heretic hormones.

David glared. "Do you want to hear this or not?"

"Go on."

"Peyton Shriver is thirty-eight, a native of Liverpool, England," he said. "His father was a petty criminal who fell in with a dangerous crowd, got involved in armed robbery and ended up a lifer. His mother was an alcoholic who was run down by a truck on her way home from the liquor store when Shriver was ten."

"Poor kid."

"Save your sympathy. Shriver's aunt Josephine took him in. She lived in New York City and she'd married into money. She didn't have any kids of her own and she doted on her charming nephew. When Josephine died, her husband cut Shriver off without a cent. Desperate for a way to support the lifestyle he'd come to enjoy, he launched a series of sweetheart scams, focusing mainly on older women."

"What's that got to do with my sister?"

"Hold on. I'm getting to that. There was one victim in particular. Her family once had a great deal of money, but the fortune had been squandered over the years. She had planned on funding her retirement with the last remaining family heirloom, a Rembrandt worth close to a million dollars. Shriver romanced her, then waltzed away with the painting."

Something in his expression, something in the way his body tensed told Maddie this case meant more to him than just business. He'd flattened out his lips, fisted his hands and broadened his stance, as if secretly readying himself for a fight.

Had he known the woman with the Rembrandt? Was his pursuit of Shriver as much about revenge as duty?

"After that theft, Shriver dropped out of sight for several years," David said.

"Living off the money from the Rembrandt," Maddie guessed.

He nodded. "A few months ago a new spate of art thefts bearing Shriver's unique pretty boy signature—but focusing mainly on museum employees rather than rich women with private collections as before—began cropping up all over Europe. The FBI has been working closely with Interpol and we've tracked Shriver to Fort Worth. He's been casing the Kimbell and he started a relationship with Cassie."

"He's using her," Maddie said flatly.

"Yes."

"But you're using her too."

"Okay," he admitted. "But I only approached her because Shriver is completely nonviolent. He's never hurt any of the women he's charmed."

"What about those other women? Why didn't you recruit them? Why single out my sister?"

"None of the other victims would testify against him and Cassie was not only willing, but eager to help."

"Why am I not surprised," Maddie muttered under her breath.

"With Cassie's assistance, I had a good chance of foiling the robbery and finally putting Shriver away for a very long time."

"Had?" His tone made her nervous.

David cleared his throat. "Yesterday I discovered an old friend of Shriver's had blown into town."

"Yeah?"

"The guy's name is Jocko Blanco. He's also a thief, among other things."

"What sort of other things?" she asked, even though she was afraid to hear the answer.

"Armed robbery, gun running, drug smuggling. You name it, he's done it."

"Even physical violence?" Maddie croaked.

He paused. "I'm afraid so."

She felt the blood drain from her face and her head spun dizzily.

"Don't panic," David said. "I was meeting Cassie to pull her off the case and offer her police protection."

"But she hasn't shown up." Maddie swept a hand at the empty park, the old familiar dread flooding through her body.

"No, she hasn't."

She gulped. This wasn't good news. Not good at all.

David's cell phone drolly played the theme from *Dragnet*.

"Do you think it could be Cassie?" Maddie asked. "Does she have your cell phone number?"

"She does." He yanked the phone from his coat pocket and glanced at the small display screen. "But it's not her." He flipped the phone open. "Marshall here."

She studied him while he listened to the voice on the other end of the conversation. His countenance changing from dangerous rebel slouch to full-on badass cop posture. He pressed his mouth into a hard, uncompromising line. His gray eyes turned as moody as the heavy clouds brooding overhead. He swore viciously and kicked at a rock.

Alarmed, Maddie backed up, distancing herself.

"I'll be right there," he barked into the receiver and then switched off the phone before jamming it back into his pocket.

"What is it?" she asked, knowing in her heart of hearts something was terribly wrong. She imagined a dozen what if scenarios, each more grisly than the last and all of them involving Cassie's safety. She sank her fingers into David's forearm and squeezed tight. "Tell me the truth. What's happened?"

He met her gaze with an uncompromising stare. "Some time during the early morning hours, Peyton Shriver used your sister's security clearance to break into the Kimbell Art Museum, override the alarm system and steal a Cézanne worth four million dollars."

Chapter

♥

TWO

WITH SINGLE-MINDED purpose, David spun on his heel and scrambled up the embankment toward his car. That bastard Shriver had trumped him again.

"But the game's not over yet, you sonofabitch," David muttered under his breath. "Not by a long shot."

His neck flamed hot with anger. He had to get to the museum and find out exactly what had gone wrong. Cassie was supposed to give him a heads up if she suspected Shriver was about to make his move. But she hadn't.

Why not?

He didn't like the answers his gut flung at him. There were two obvious choices. Either Cassie was in deep danger or she'd thrown her lot in with Shriver. He could easily see flamboyant Cassie entertaining some *Thomas Crown Affair* fantasy about the guy. After all, Shriver was quite the rakish charmer.

Either scenario spelled mucho trouble.

"Hey wait, where you goin'?" Maddie scurried along beside him.

"To the Kimbell," he said, without looking over at her. The stubborn woman possessed the potential to become a royal pain-in-the-ass and he wasn't going to encourage her.

"What about my sister?"

"What about her?" he asked, slapping back the guilt digging into his conscience. He had no use for regrets. He made a decision, committed to a course of action and accepted the drawbacks. Only weak men second-guessed themselves.

"Where is she?"

"How should I know?"

"I'm coming with you."

"Don't you have to go to work or something?"

"I own my own gym. I'll call my manager and have her arrange for someone else to teach my exercise classes."

"You can't come."

"Why not?"

"I'm too busy to mess around with you."

"You owe me," she said, puffing up the hill beside him, matching his stride step for step.

"How do you figure?"

He hesitated just long enough to glare at her and wished he hadn't. The determined set of her jaw caused him to think wickedly inappropriate thoughts. Like what would she do if he hooked a finger under that tenacious little chin, tilted her face up to meet his and kissed her hard?

She'd probably sock you in the breadbasket.

Probably.

"You shoved me off a cliff."

"That was an accident."

"You involved Cassie with a criminal."

"What's that got to do with you?"

"We're twins."

"And . . . ?"

Maddie tossed her head and her ponytail flicked provocatively from shoulder to shoulder. "Obviously, you don't understand the bond. We're exceedingly close."

"If you two are so chummy, how come Cassie didn't tell you she was working for me?"

She blinked. "I suppose you swore her to secrecy."

"Nope." This time she frowned. David could see it was bugging the hell out of her that her twin hadn't confided in her. "I do know one thing about Cassie."

"And what is that?" Maddie asked suspiciously.

"She was raring to prove herself to somebody and after making your acquaintance, I'm guessing that somebody is you."

"What's that supposed to mean?" Her emerald green eyes flared a warning.

"I don't have time for this." He stalked toward the Impala. "She's your sister, you figure it out."

"Wait, wait, wait." She placed a restraining hand on his shoulder.

"What?" He wanted to brush her off but he was afraid of what might happen to his libido if he touched her. Disconcerted, he stepped back and she voluntarily removed her hand.

"I've been abrupt," she said. "I'm just worried about my sister. Please forgive me."

"You're forgiven." He punched the alarm control on

his keypad and his car chirped twice indicating the doors were unlocked.

"Great." She hurried around to the passenger side.

"Oh, no, no, no." He quickly reactivated the locks just as she reached for the handle.

"You're still not taking me with you?"

"That's right." He unlocked the driver's side the old-fashioned way and slid behind the wheel, but before he could get the door shut and the car started, Maddie flew over to jam her body between him and the door. She wrapped her fingers around the steering wheel, anchoring herself to his vehicle.

"You're fast," he said.

"And don't you forget it."

"Physical talents aside, you're staying here." He keyed the ignition and the engine rumbled to life.

"You're a rude, rude man."

"Bingo. Now get out of the way if you don't want me to back over you."

"Okay, you asked for it. I didn't want to have to resort to dirty tactics, but you've forced my hand."

"Are you threatening me?" He narrowed his eyes and met her gaze. Damn if a thrill of sexual excitement didn't blast straight through his groin. Nothing tickled him more than a worthy opponent.

"Yes I am."

"Bring it on."

"I will."

"I think you're bluffing."

"I never bluff."

He eyed her for a long moment. "What do you have up your sleeve?"

"I'll got to the media. Tell them that you involved a

private citizen in your cops-and-robbers game and now she's missing."

"She's not missing."

Maddie waved a hand at the empty park. "You see her anywhere?"

"She's a flake. Maybe she just forgot."

"You know better than that," she chided. "Admit it, you screwed up, David Marshall. You placed my sister's life in peril when you recruited her to spy on your art thief."

She was right. And he loathed her rightness. He couldn't allow her to go to the media. They would be all over this story like hot on chili peppers.

And then his boss would be all over him.

He couldn't let Shriver win. No way, no how. Better to tolerate this smart-mouthed pop tart than ruin years of detective work.

"Take me with you or I go to the news stations," she reiterated.

"You wouldn't dare." He felt obligated to call her bluff one more time, test her commitment before giving her the green light.

"When it comes to my twin sister, I'll dare anything." The look on her face told him that she was dead serious. He admired her devotion to her sibling while at the same time he cursed it.

"This is not the optimal way to get in good with me." He glowered, doing his best to quell her with a withering glance.

"I could care less about getting in good with you." She defiantly thrust out her chest, which just happened to be at his eye level.

Trying hard not to notice what a truly exceptional pair

of ta-tas she possessed and fantasizing about how they
would look out of that sports bra and in a low cut va-va-
va-voom dress, David clenched his jaw and unlocked the
passenger door.

"Get in."

"Thank you." Tossing her head, she pranced around
the car and climbed inside. David slammed the Impala
into reverse and plowed out of the parking space, tires
squealing as he burned rubber.

Fuck! He hated this. Bested twice in one morning.

David made Maddie wait in the employee lounge of
the Kimbell Art Museum while he and his team assessed
the crime scene. She was none too happy about it.

Before they got out of the car, he'd threatened to handcuff her to the steering wheel if she didn't agree to obey
his orders. The 'I've-reached-the-limits-of-my-patience-
don't-push-me-one-more-millimeter' expression on his
face told her that he meant every word.

And then, just to rub his power in her face, he'd positioned one of the museum security guards in the doorway
to keep her from wandering off and doing a little investigating of her own. Jeez. You'd think he didn't trust her.

Stuck with the situation, she had called her assistant
and asked her to find a replacement instructor for the remainder of the week. She had no idea how long it was
going to take to resolve this thing with Cassie, but it was
better to be prepared for the worst.

She spent the remainder of the time calling all of
Cassie's friends to see if they knew where she was, pacing the lounge and imagining the most terrible things
when no one had heard from her. What if Shriver had
taken Cassie hostage? What if this Blanco person had

hurt her sister and she was lying helpless somewhere calling Maddie's name?

She reached up to finger the half-a-heart necklace she
never took off. *Hang on, Cassie. Never fear. I'll find you.*

"Maddie."

She glanced over to see David standing in the doorway
looking grim. Immediately, she was at his side. "What is
it?"

"I sent a man over to Cassie's apartment."

"Was she there?" Maddie bit down hard on her bottom
lip. Don't worry, don't panic, until there's something to
panic about.

He shook his head. "The place was turned upside
down."

"Ransacked?"

"No. It looked more like she had packed in a hurry."

"What are you saying?"

"You might want to prepare yourself for the possibility that Cassie has switched sides and become Shriver's
accomplice."

Maddie shook her head. "No way."

"I'm going to search her locker. I thought you might
want to be present," he said quietly.

For the first time since she'd met him, Maddie saw a
look of compassion in his eyes. His sympathy scared her
more than his aggressiveness. He was being way too nice.
Why?

"Let's go," she said.

They stepped into the corridor together and that's
when she saw the extent of his entourage. A half-dozen
Fort Worth cops, a couple of plainclothes detectives, the
mayor, the police chief, the museum curator and two
other FBI agents.

Oh boy.

The curator gave her a pink plastic shopping bag decorated with black-and-white Picassos. "For Cassie's things," he said as if she were already dead.

The dull throbbing in Maddie's heart ratcheted into a sharp, steady hammering as they waited for a security guard to break into Cassie's locker. When the officer got it open and her locker had been dusted for prints, he stepped aside and let David at it.

Maddie held the bag outstretched while David removed items from Cassie's locker. He studied each object intently and then dropped them one by one into the open bag.

Hairspray, extra hold. Eyelash curlers. A wand of mascara. Lancôme Firecracker Red nail polish. Curling iron. Cinnamon flavored Altoids. A blue cashmere cardigan. A package of shrimp-flavored ramen noodles and an empty box of Godiva chocolates.

Maddie pressed Cassie's sweater to her nose, inhaling the scent of her twin before reluctantly dropping the cardigan into the bag. Her sister was in trouble. Really deep trouble. Wherever she was, Cassie desperately needed her.

David passed Maddie a photograph. It was a picture of Cassie and a very handsome dark-haired man of about forty at Billy Bob's in the Stockyards. Cassie's arm was draped over the guy's shoulder. They were standing in front of a mechanical bull, longneck beers in hand and mugging tipsily for the camera.

Maddie caught her breath, raised her head and met David's gaze. "Peyton Shriver?"

He nodded. "They certainly look like a couple."

"Appearances can be deceiving and besides, didn't you encourage her to fan a romance with him?"

"I didn't mean for her to fall in love."

"She didn't." Maddie glared. "You got her into this, I can't believe you're going against her."

"I'm not going against her, I'm simply following the evidence."

"If by some wild, ridiculous stretch of the imagination Cassie did fall for Shriver, then it's all your fault," she accused. "You've got to assume responsibility for getting her involved."

David turned away, leaving her with the frustrating urge to kick him in the seat of his obstinate pants. He kept digging through the locker.

A copy of *Vogue*. Two hair clips. Four ballpoint pens.

"Ah-ha."

Maddie jerked her head around to peer over his shoulder to see what he was ah-ha-ing about. It was a travel brochure for Grand Cayman Island.

"What?" she snapped. She didn't like his self-satisfied expression. Men. They were so predictable. Gloating when they were certain they were right.

"The smoking gun."

"Since when is a travel brochure considered a smoking gun?"

"Since the world's biggest dealer in stolen art lives in Grand Cayman and he just happens to be very friendly with Peyton Shriver."

"Oh come on, that's quite a stretch, don't you think?" she said, even as fear tightened her gut. "I bet a lot of people have travel brochures to Grand Cayman in their locker."

"But those people don't work in a museum where a

Cézanne just got heisted, nor are they dating art thieves," David said.

He was right and she knew it, but Maddie still couldn't accept the fact that Cassie might be a willing participant in a crime.

He touched her arm. "I know it's difficult sometimes, to accept the truth."

She gritted her teeth. She didn't want or need his pity. What did he know about the truth? All he cared about was bringing Shriver in.

"You're a cop. You should know a travel brochure proves nothing."

"It's a step in a treacherous direction."

The people behind them were murmuring, discussing the significance of David's find, but Maddie paid them no mind. Her attention was on the man standing to her left. The man with the penetrating dark gray eyes.

Eyes, that if he were on your side, could comfort you. Eyes that said, *You can always rely on me.* But if he wasn't on your side, if you were his enemy, those mercurial gray eyes issued an entirely different message: *Do wrong and I'll make sure you pay.*

Maddie shivered. She had no doubt that he could back up either message. He wasn't a guy you'd want to tangle with in a dark alley.

Or even a well lit one for that matter.

She shifted her weight, her anxiety escalating with each passing moment.

David's cell phone did the *Dragnet* thing. He answered with a terse, "Marshall."

She tensed and leaned forward, straining to hear the voice on the other end. She couldn't make out much of what he was saying but she did hear Cassie's name bandied about.

"Good work," he said and switched off the phone.

She raised her head. His eyes glowed with the thrill of his job. The man was a bloodhound through and through. Pick up a scent and he was off on the chase.

"What is it?"

He took a deep breath and she saw him trying to curb his excitement for her benefit. "Shriver and your sister caught the six-oh-five to Atlanta on Delta Air Lines. From there, they took a connecting flight to Grand Cayman."

Her heart slipped into her Nikes. "That still doesn't mean Cassie went willingly."

David steepled his fingertips. "I know this is hard for you to deal with, but you've got to accept the possibility your sister is a fugitive from the law. I know it's an ugly thought. I know you don't want to believe it. But Shriver has a Svengali effect on women. He can make them do almost anything for him."

"If you knew that about him, then why did you ask Cassie to work for you?"

"Shriver had already marked her as his next victim. She'd started dating him before I ever asked for her help."

"You could have warned her. Given her a chance to break things off with him." Maddie studied his uncompromising grimace. "But you weren't about to do that. Admit it. Nailing Shriver is an obsession with you. You don't care about the cost."

He shrugged but didn't deny her accusation. The jackass.

"Cassie did not fall in love with him," she said adamantly. "You don't know my sister."

Flighty though her twin might be, Cassie was honest to a fault, had never stolen so much as a gumball in her life and no man, no matter how charming, could cause her to commit a crime.

"Like it or not, here's something else you're going to have to be prepared to deal with," David said. "So just brace yourself."

She notched her chin up and met his challenging stare. "What's that?"

"If Cassie is involved with the theft of the Cézanne in any way, shape or form, when I catch her, I'm going to bring her to justice right along with Shriver. No excuses. No exceptions. Got it?"

Chapter
THREE

$\mathcal{W}$HAT WAS IT with women?

David lined up behind a handful of business travelers at the ticket kiosk outside the Delta Air Lines counter at DFW airport. Why did they invariably fall for charming bad boys? Did they honestly think they could rehabilitate such men with their undying love? Or did they just get off on the thrill of danger? What had caused Cassie to throw her life away over the likes of Peyton Shriver?

He pondered these questions because he wasn't too keen on examining his role in Cassie's turncoat behavior. David rejected guilt as a useless emotion.

"David!"

He raised his head, saw Maddie barreling across the terminal toward him. He had the distinct impression she wasn't here to see him off.

She was dressed in a short denim skirt, a Hawaiian floral print blouse, a floppy, red straw hat and matching strappy, high-heeled sandals. The flirty ensemble looked like something Cassie would wear. She pulled a wheeled carry-on bag behind her and, over her arm, a denim jacket.

She was dolled up like Miss Hawaiian Tropics. Why? It was fifty degrees outside.

Helplessly, he found his gaze drawn down the length of her long, lean muscular legs to the tips of her toes painted a cheeky pink.

Uh-oh. This didn't look good. Not good at all.

"Wait up," she called to him.

He moved to one side to let the other travelers go ahead through the checkpoint. He needed to get rid of her. Now. His flight left in twenty minutes and he was determined to be on it.

"Thank heavens," she said, not even breathing hard although she'd sprinted to reach him. "I was afraid I was going to miss our plane."

"Our plane?"

"I'm going to Grand Cayman with you," she said brightly. "Do you like my outfit? I thought if I looked like a tourist I'd blend in better."

David stared, unable to believe she'd just invited herself along on his investigation. This was one pushy dame. He peered into her eyes and spied a determination so staunch he'd seen it in only one other place.

The mirror.

"You're not coming with me."

"I have to. You're convinced my sister is in league with Shriver but I know better. Cassie might be a ditz and I'll grant you, at times she's impulsive and misguided and easily distracted, but she's got a heart of gold and you simply cannot put her in jail. I won't allow it."

"You won't allow it?" He smirked, amused. Her vehemence was almost cute.

"I don't mean to be aggressive, but I've already fig-ured out you don't do subtle. One way or the other, I have to get your attention. Cassie is not in on this heist with Shriver."

"And you're not the least bit prejudiced."

"I know my sister."

"Your loyalty is commendable, but it's clear you have a huge blind spot where your twin is concerned. Look at the evidence. Cassie has romanticized Shriver and she's picturing herself living some kind of outlaw, movie star lifestyle."

Okay, so he *was* sorry he'd ever recruited Cassie. But he wasn't going to let Maddie dream up some fanciful scenario that ignored the truth in favor of exonerating her sister. If he expressed regret, she might seize upon that as a loophole she could exploit.

Maddie shook her head. "You're wrong. Shriver has kidnapped her. I feel it in my bones."

"All I want is to see justice done. If Shriver kidnapped your sister, then you'll be the first to receive an apology. In the meantime, you're delaying me from my flight. If you'll excuse me." He turned back toward the security scanners.

She marched right along behind him. He stopped and she plowed into his back. He took her by the wrist and pulled her around to face him.

"You cannot come to Grand Cayman with me. Got it? The matter is not open for discussion."

"It's a free country, bub, I can go anywhere I want."

"And I could have you arrested for interfering with an officer of the law."

"You wouldn't dare." She jerked her wrist away from

him and sank her hands on her hips. Her steely-eyed gaze challenged him to make good on his threat.

Dammit. Why did he have to admire her spunk and the open way she defied him? No covert sneaking around for this woman. If she was half this feisty in the bedroom, look out.

Ah, but then a slight quiver of her lower lip gave her away. She wasn't nearly as self-confident as she wanted him to believe, but she was sure giving it hell.

"Look," he relented. "I understand your concern for your sister. I promise I'll give Cassie the benefit of the doubt."

"I'm coming with you," she repeated, enunciating each word clearly as if speaking to a particularly slow child.

"You're not."

"I am."

"Please don't make me go over there and ask those security guards to detain you. Neither one of us needs the hassle."

She didn't say anything for a long moment. Finally she sucked in a deep breath and whispered, "Okay, fine, have it your way."

Maddie spun around, but her heel must have caught on something. She teetered precariously, then stumbled against him, reaching out with both hands to grab his jacket lapel to keep from falling.

The brim of her hat smashed him in the chin. Her firm, high breasts grazed his arm.

At the feel of her palms against his chest, instant heat pricked his groin. His body's inappropriate response to their physical contact irritated him. He battled against his lust.

It was so weird that she turned him on when her identical twin sister did not. What was that all about?

"Sorry," she mumbled, quickly righting herself, and then without another word turned and sashayed off.

Watching her go, he was unsettled to discover he felt disappointed and it took him a minute or two to figure out why. It was because she'd given up so easily. He'd been looking forward to more of a fight.

Flustered, he shouldered his carry-on and moved once again toward the scanners. The line had grown longer since his encounter with Maddie. Impatiently, he glanced at his watch. He had less than ten minutes to board the plane.

He shifted his weight from foot to foot and rolled his eyes when a lady with tons of gold jewelry kept setting off the alarm. Finally, his turn came.

Just as he went to remove his duty weapon from his shoulder holster and check it in, an armed security guard tapped him on the collarbone. "Excuse me, sir, if you could just step over here."

What now?

He followed the guard to a small, enclosed area where two uniformed Dallas police officers stood, guns drawn.

What in hell . . . ?

"Hands on your head," one of the policemen said.

"I'm FBI." David raised his arms. He knew they were only doing their job and he tried hard not to lose his temper. "I'm on the trail of a suspect and it's imperative I make my flight."

"The lady who reported you carrying a concealed weapon said you would claim that." The second officer moved around David and relieved him of his gun.

"Lady? What lady?"

"The one you've been harassing."

"What!"

"No sudden movements," the first officer said.

"I've got my ID right here." David made a motion to go for his badge. "I can prove I'm FBI."

"I said don't move!" the first officer trilled and pointed his weapon right at David's head.

"Where's your ID?" the second officer asked.

"Right breast pocket."

The man patted him down. "Nothing here."

"Try the other pocket." David felt like an idiot standing with his palms pressed against the back of his head, his elbows sticking out, getting frisked by Officer Overzealous.

Where was his badge? Had he left it in his car? But he couldn't have done that. The badge was as much of an extension of himself as his arm or his leg. He didn't forget it and he didn't lose it.

"Not here."

"It's there somewhere," he said through clenched teeth. "Look again."

"Last call for flight 234 to Atlanta," came the announcement over the speaker system.

Shit. He was going to miss the plane.

Then, all at once, David realized what had happened.

Maddie Cooper.

If he hadn't been so distracted by his body's very physical reaction to her, he would have caught on sooner. Her clumsy stumble against him had been no accident.

The unprincipled wench had picked his pocket and stolen his badge.

*   *   *

Cassie Cooper sprawled in a lounge chair outside the Hyatt Regency on Seven Mile Beach in Grand Cayman. She was sipping a piña colada and enjoying the afternoon sun and the salty ocean breeze blowing over her bikinied body. This sure was a great change of pace from damp, dreary Fort Worth in February.

Not three feet away, Peyton lay on a massage table beneath a cabana getting a Swedish massage from a tanned island girl.

Taking a long pull on her straw, Cassie twirled the pink paper parasol in her drink and marveled at her opulent surroundings. She still couldn't believe she'd convinced Peyton to bring her with him.

Mentally, she patted herself on the back. She was quite the little actress.

When David Marshall called her last night to set up a rendezvous she'd sensed something was up, even though he'd acted nonchalant.

For one thing, he'd asked her to bring all the evidence she'd gathered over the past few weeks to the meeting.

For another thing, ever since her accident as a kid when she had spent three months in a coma, she occasionally experienced a weird sort of hotness at the very base of her brain. The sensation almost always preceded an unexpected turn of events. While she'd been talking to David, her brain had started its familiar sizzle.

And she had just known, for whatever reason, David was going to pull the plug on her role as his informant.

She couldn't allow him to dump her. Not now. Not when she'd worked so hard. As they'd talked, a spontaneous plan spun in her head. A plan destined to make her the toast of the art world and the darling of the FBI.

A plan to prove to Maddie that she could not only take

care of herself, but thrive in the process. A plan to show everyone that she was as tough and strong and smart as her twin.

And Cassie had come up with the perfect obstacle to keep David preoccupied while she carried out her strategy. That was when she had phoned Maddie and asked her to meet her in Forest Park at eight-fifteen. She knew David would mistake Maddie for her. She also knew Maddie would give him hell. Especially if he told her that he had recruited Cassie to work for the FBI.

She grinned and rubbed her palms together just thinking about those two at each other's throats. What would be really nice was if for once Maddie got into trouble and had to turn to David for help. That way the tension between them just might turn into something delectable.

Once she had that problem solved, Cassie had jumped in with both feet, simply trusting that everything would work out the way she wanted.

Boldly, she had gone to Peyton and told him everything. How she had been working with the FBI to catch him, how she knew of his scheme to use her security clearance to get into the Kimbell and steal paintings.

At first, Peyton tried to deny it, but then she'd smoothly lied and told him she didn't care if he was an art thief or that he'd been using her.

She professed her love for him regardless of his past. She wanted to be his girlfriend and if he would take her with him, she would use her friendship with the curator at the Museo del Prado in Madrid to help him make off with a fortune. She had detailed a robbery so daring he'd quickly grown excited at the possibilities.

Greed had him agreeing to include her in his escapades. He'd fallen for her lie, hook, line and sinker.

And here she was, an FBI operative, about to catch one of the world's most elusive art thieves.

Okay, so technically she was no longer working for the FBI since David had been about to pull her off the case, but Cassie was certain once he realized the lengths she'd gone to in order to stay in good with Shriver, he would apologize for not having more faith in her.

"Happy, luv?" Peyton called to her from the massage table.

"Terribly."

God, she was a sucker for a British accent. Cassie grinned and ignored the twinge of guilt.

She had to keep reminding herself Peyton was a notorious criminal who had conned over a dozen hapless women with his suave bullshit. If she didn't keep that bit of information at the front of her mind, she would end up thinking about how gorgeous his blue eyes were and how cute he looked with his thick ebony hair tousled so boyishly by the tropical breeze.

She sighed and took a caviar canapé off the silver tray presented to her by a tuxedoed waiter. If it weren't for Peyton's nasty habit of taking expensive things that didn't belong to him, he would be the perfect man. He certainly knew how to live the good life.

Don't forget your real goal. This is about proving you can stand on your own two feet. This is about showing Maddie you don't need her hovering over you.

Still, it was a shame about Peyton.

Cassie stretched and wriggled her toes. She'd just painted them a lovely shade of Wanton Sunset.

However, there was one teeny little flaw with her plan. How was she going to let David know what she was up to without arousing Peyton's suspicions?

She couldn't just pick up a phone and blurt it out. She had packed in such a hurry she'd forgotten her wallet. She only had her clothes and her passport. She was living it up on the grace of Peyton's largess. She couldn't even call from the hotel phone. They'd charge it to his account.

But Cassie didn't want the hunky FBI man thinking she had fallen under Peyton's spell and become his cohort in crime. One way or the other, she would find a way to send David clues.

"So," she said, sliding her sunglasses back up on her nose and trying her best to act cool and nonchalant, as if she didn't really care about his answer. "What do you have planned for the Cézanne, darling?"

Peyton smirked. "Don't worry your pretty little head over it. The details are in the bag."

"My, you are efficient." She managed to control her curiosity, knowing if she pushed too hard, too quickly, Peyton would kite her like a hot check. Being a spy was a tricky proposition.

"I've got a present for you," Peyton said, and then grimaced as the masseuse plowed her knuckles over his shoulder blade.

"Oh?" Cassie grinned. She loved unexpected gifts.

Peyton shooed the masseuse away, sat up and swung his legs over the edge of the massage table. He slid to the sand, slipped his feet into black rubber flip-flops and held out his hand to her.

"Let's take a walk."

Parking her piña colada on the small table beside her lounge chair, Cassie squinted up at him. He was backlit by the sun and the cabana cast a dark shadow over his face, giving him an ominous appearance. The breeze picked up, raising the hairs on her forearm and illogically her heart stuttered.

"Cassie?" His hand was still extended.

"Uh-huh?" She felt dizzy, from either the sun or his presence. Maybe both. Suddenly, she was very nervous.

Peyton inclined his head toward the beach. "Let's take a walk."

"Okay." She forced herself to smile brightly.

She sank her palm, still damp and cool from the condensation of her glass, into his hard, hot hand. His grip seemed unnecessarily firm. She gulped.

Did he suspect something? Was he on to her?

You're imagining things. Don't start assuming the worst. That's Maddie's job.

If Maddie could only see her now! Her sister would have a shit fit.

Eventually, she was going to have to get a message to her too.

Cassie ignored the annoying thought. She curled her bare toes into the warm sand as they walked, allowing Peyton to guide her closer to the ocean.

Watch out! He could try something funny. Pull you into the water and take you under. Maddie's ultra-cautious voice echoed in her head.

Pooh. Cassie shoved the irritating noise aside.

After they'd traveled several yards up the beach away from the other sun worshipers, Peyton stopped walking. He took both of her hands in his and gazed deeply into her eyes.

"I've never met a woman quite like you," Peyton murmured.

Cassie felt herself blush. "Why, thank you."

"And I want to trust you."

"You can," she lied glibly.

And the Oscar goes to Cassie Cooper. For her mesmerizing role as art museum public relations gal turned special agent for the FBI.

"How far would you go to prove your devotion to me?" he asked, his eyes growing deeper, darker.

Gulp.

She swallowed the lump in her throat. What had seemed like a fool-proof plot last night in Forth Worth, Texas, was starting to look like a not-so-brilliant plan on the clean white sand of Seven Mile Beach.

"What do you mean?"

"I have to know that I can trust you with my life."

"You can trust me."

"I'm afraid I need more reassurance than just your word."

"What's it gonna take?"

"I was hoping you would ask me that question." He let go of her left hand and fumbled in the pocket of his swim trunks.

When he produced a small black velvet box, Cassie thought she might swoon or throw up or start laughing maniacally. This wasn't her first proposal and all three reactions were within the realm of possibility.

He cracked the box open, revealing a dramatic two-carat marquis-cut diamond engagement ring.

Her knees quivered and she had to hold on to his arm to keep from toppling over.

"Marry me, Cassie."

"Marry you?" her voice wobbled, as tremulous as her legs.

"I know it's sudden, but I'm as crazy for you as you are for me," Peyton purred. "Together, we'll make an awesome team, traveling the world, stealing our treasures, living the high life."

"Uh-huh." She breathed.

"And besides . . ." His grin was wicked. "A wife can't be forced to testify against her husband."

Oh, ho. Here was the real reason for his impromptu proposal. The diamond winked, beckoning her to gamble everything for her ultimate goal.

What the hell? Why not say yes? Before she had to actually prove herself by marrying him, she intended on seeing his handsome butt locked up behind bars.

Mores the pity.

"Yes, Peyton," she said and met his gaze head on. "I'll marry you."

He slipped the ring on her left hand, then pulled her into his arms and kissed her hard and long. When he released her at last, he pressed his mouth against her ear.

"But it has to happen tonight," he whispered. "I've made all the arrangements. If you are truly on my side, then you must marry me at dusk at my friend's estate on Dead Man's Bay."

Chapter
FOUR

"Miss," THE FLIGHT attendant glowered at Maddie. "I'm going to have to ask you to stop pacing and take your seat. You're making the other passengers nervous."

"Sorry," Maddie mumbled and returned to her cramped seat at the back of the plane. Her hefty, ruddy-faced seatmate shot his eyes heavenward and polished off his third bloody Mary before lumbering to his feet and letting her squeeze in next to the window.

She hated flying. For that matter, she hated traveling. She was a creature of comfort and missed her habits. Her short-lived Olympic career had been a royal pain in the keister, shuttling from tournament to tournament on buses, in planes, taking the train.

The only reason she had stuck with it as long as she had was because being an Olympian made her feel strong and in control of her life at a time when she'd desperately needed all the strength she could muster to look after her calamity-courting twin.

She needed double that strength now.

Her gut told her David Marshall wasn't going to relent in his position against Cassie. It was her gut that had instigated the backup plan to filch his FBI badge and then sic security on him as a gun-toting loony.

That was why she had worn Cassie's ridiculous high heels and her outlandish straw hat. The heels had been an excuse to lose her balance. The hat had been to camouflage his view of her larcenous hands.

And it had worked.

Her intention had been to get David detained long enough for her to make the flight and for him to miss it. Once she'd turned him in to security, she had slipped over to a different terminal to check in and had gone on to board the plane.

She knew David could unsnarl the tangle she'd wrapped him in pretty quickly, but all she'd needed was a head start. If she could get to Grand Cayman before he did, she would have a few precious hours in which to find Cassie. She intended on rescuing her sister from Shriver and bringing her home before the hard-assed Officer Marshall got his hands on her.

By the time David caught up with them, Maddie would have hired the best lawyer she could afford. She would even take out a second mortgage on her condo if she had to. Anything for her sister.

The brightness of the sun reflecting off the field of white clouds floating below the plane's wing hurt her eyes. And the weary, dogged sound of the engines made her feel oddly alone. She burrowed in her handbag for her drugstore sunglasses, slipped them on and wondered if David was already on another flight.

David Marshall. Mister My-Way-or-the-Highway.

Hmmph. Imagine. That irritating man telling her she

couldn't go search for her own sister. Like he and what army were going to stop her?

She would have given a month's pay to be a fly on the wall when he had tried to flash his badge for airport security and found it gone. She grinned at the idea, but then she immediately felt contrite for taking pleasure in his misfortune.

She wasn't a malicious person. She'd only absconded with his ID badge because there had been no other way around him. She'd given him a legitimate chance to take her along and he had refused.

Idly, she wondered about him. Was he married? He didn't wear a ring. But who cared? It wasn't as if she was interested in him. He was far too annoying and bossy and pigheaded. The guy had the personality of a steamroller. Plus, he actually seemed to enjoy locking horns with her.

Who needed that kind of aggravation? Certainly not she. Cassie created enough commotion in her life.

"Ladies and gentlemen, we're making our approach to George Town and the pilot has switched on the seat belt sign. Please remain seated for the duration of the flight," the flight attendant announced over the intercom.

Fifteen minutes later they were on the ground. Relieved to be out of the sky, Maddie retrieved her carry-on from the overhead bin, thankful she didn't have to go through baggage claim.

She had packed lightly on the outside hope she would be bringing Cassie home in record time and also because she had an innate distrust of baggage handlers. She'd once seen one of those hidden camera investigative news programs where they had secretly videotaped sticky-fingered ramp workers rummaging through suitcases.

One tasteless employee had even stolen a female passenger's panties. Creepy.

Once inside the terminal however, she paused in confusion, not knowing what to do next. She was uncomfortable at not having hotel reservations or an itinerary to follow. She never traveled without detailing every eventuality.

She spied a sign directing her to ground transportation and followed the arrows out of the concourse. So far so good, but where did she go from here?

Argh.

She was miserable at this spur-of-the-moment stuff. Where was Cassie when you really needed her?

A balmy breeze licked her skin and the air lay heavy with the provocative scent of ocean and coconut and sugarcane. She stood waiting for inspiration to strike.

And then there he was.

David Marshall hailing a cab not twenty feet away.

Impossible! How had he gotten to Grand Cayman ahead of her?

Apparently, her sneak attack hadn't worked. Well, never mind, she had a new plan. Stick to him like glue.

"David!" She hollered and waved, but the slamming of the car door must have drowned her out. Either that or he was purposefully ignoring her.

Not that she could blame him for being angry, but she'd be damned if she'd let him out of her sight.

His cab pulled away from the curb.

Maddie rushed to the taxi stand and flung herself into the back seat of the next vehicle in line. The dark-skinned, dimple-chinned driver turned to beam at her over his shoulder.

"Where to Miss?" the man asked in an odd accent that was both British and island lyrical.

She gestured frantically at David's taxi careening through traffic. "Follow that car!"

David checked into a low budget motel several streets back from Seven Mile Beach. The FBI frowned on agents squandering their expense accounts on high-end beach resorts.

Then again, they also frowned on their agents recruiting citizens as informants when they'd specifically been told not to. Especially when those informants went renegade and turned into suspects. They also weren't thrilled with agents who got pickpocketed by a suspect's identical twin sister.

At the thought of Maddie, David blew out his breath. He was still steamed over her stunt at the airport. It was damned unsettling having his badge stolen by a beguiling woman so distracting he hadn't even noticed she had pinched his identity.

For about the ninety-ninth time since it happened, he ground his teeth at his own stupidity.

Luckily for him a federal air marshal, who'd once worked with David, had been transporting a prisoner through the terminal. The marshal had spied him getting frisked by the Dallas PD and he'd intervened, vouching for him.

Contrite over detaining an FBI agent, security had gotten David on an American Airlines flight leaving for Grand Cayman thirty minutes after the Delta flight. Actually, it turned out to be a better deal. The Delta flight stopped in Atlanta, whereas the American flight went straight through.

But dwelling on his glaring *faux pas* wasn't going to help him catch Shriver. And thinking about Maddie would only agitate him. He had to focus on the task at hand and forget about her.

David had no sooner accepted his key from the desk clerk, returned his credit card to his wallet and bent to pick up his carry-on when he caught sight of a very familiar pair of jaunty red sandals.

Oh no.

He groaned inwardly. He wasn't in the mood for this.

His gaze roved from cute feet to shapely ankles and on up divinely curved calves. He appreciated the tanned knees, the firm thighs and those rounded hips. He visually traversed her flat belly, narrow waist and nicely rounded chest before reluctantly finding himself face-to-face with Maddie Cooper.

"Get an eyeful?" She sank her hands on her hips and glared.

Audacious woman.

He was the one who should be glaring. David shrugged. Hell, he was only human and she was some tall, cool drink of water. Nothing wrong with looking. If she didn't want him to stare, she should wear a snow parka.

"I should have known," he said.

"Known what?"

"That you weren't the type of woman to give up without a fight."

In spite of himself, David found his respect inching up a rung or two. She'd followed him, tracked him down and he'd never once suspected she was behind him. He made a mental note never to underestimate her again.

"This is where you're staying?" She scanned the lobby of the bare-bones accommodations.

He shrugged. "I'm a government employee."

"I'm not exactly flush with cash myself," she said. "I'll stay here too."

"You know Peyton and your sister are probably living it up at the Hyatt."

That pissed her off. He could tell by the way her eyes flashed a brilliant emerald green and how she drew herself up tall and squared her shoulders. She could have been a swimsuit model with her height and that amazing figure.

"Think what you will, Agent Marshall, but I know my sister. Which is why I'm here. To make sure you don't falsely imprison her."

Man, but she sure had an unerring talent for ticking a guy off.

She turned her attention to the desk clerk who'd been openly eavesdropping. "I'll take a room for the night, please."

The thin young man flashed her a row of white teeth and held out his palm for her credit card. David had seen enough. He had to leave before he said something he would regret. He picked up his suitcase and headed for his room.

"Wait," she called. "Wait for me."

He ignored her.

Five minutes later an angry rapping sounded at his door. He'd just taken off his coat and tie and was unbuttoning his shirt.

"What?" he demanded, flinging open the door, his fingers twisting at the second button.

"That was rude of you," Maddie said. "Running off and leaving me when I asked you to wait."

"I thought we'd already established the fact that I'm a rude guy."

She forced a smile. "Call me optimistic, but I had high hopes for your rehabilitation."

"Don't you get it, lady?" he snapped. "I don't want you along."

"It's not about what you want." She blithely trailed over the threshold. "It's about what's going to happen."

"Excuse me?" he bellowed.

She couldn't have picked a more inflammatory tactic, waltzing into *his* room, trying to take control of *his* investigation. She must be a glutton for punishment. What was the matter with her? Was she one of those women who liked to be spanked?

Well, it was time to turn the tables. He took an intimidating step toward her and undid another button. He wanted to see how long it would take her to run from the room.

He undid another button and then another.

His ploy failed.

She pretended not to notice what he was up to and instead sauntered over to the sliding glass door. She opened the curtain, freeing bright late afternoon sunlight into the room.

Then she spun on her heels to face him. "You're going to make me your partner on this investigation."

He snorted.

"What's so funny?"

"I don't know what schoolgirl fantasies you've got bouncing around in your head, but this isn't a James Bond movie, kiddo." He undid the next to the last button and took another step closer. "And I can't make you an honorary member of the FBI."

"You recruited Cassie to work for you. Why not me?"

"That was different."

"How was it different?"

"I get it," he said. "Severe case of sibling rivalry. You're jealous."

"I'm not jealous," she denied and her voice went up just enough to let him know he'd nailed her insecurity dead on. "Why would I be jealous of my twin sister?"

"Because she's not afraid to grab life by the throat and live and you are." He undid the last button and now he was standing just a hand's breadth away.

Anxiously, she sucked her bottom lip between her teeth.

Something about that nervous yet unintentionally sexy gesture gave him a funny feeling in the pit of his stomach.

"Who says I'm scared of life? I'm not scared. I hopped on a plane and flew to Grand Cayman without a day's notice, didn't I?"

"Yes, and it's making you a nervous wreck."

"I'm not a nervous wreck."

"Then how come your thumbnail is gnawed to the quick and you've got a Rolaids wrapper dangling out of your purse?"

Frowning, she tucked the errant wrapper back inside her shoulder bag and then jerked her ravaged thumb behind her.

"Well, it doesn't matter. You're following Shriver and I'm following my sister so we're always going to end up in the same place. Wouldn't it just be easier for you to let me in on what's going on?"

He could tell she was trying not to look at his chest but every so often she would sneak a peek at the expanse of skin revealed beneath his open shirt. She raised a hand to her cheek and he saw she was blushing pink.

Gotcha.

"Are you trying to blackmail me?" he asked, stripping off his shirt and tossing it onto the bed.

"No more than you're trying to intimidate me."

"Am I?"

"Aren't you?"

"Question is, do you like it?" he asked.

The air in the room seemed miserably hot even though he'd twisted up the controls on the air conditioner when he'd walked in. Or maybe it was the heat of his blood rushing through his veins.

"Nobody likes being intimidated."

"Don't be so sure of that. Ever heard of a submissive?"

"I'm not a submissive," she denied. "Far from it."

"You sure? You entered a man's room while he was getting undressed."

"That doesn't make me submissive. If anything, I'd say I was dominant."

"You dominating me?" The notion was so foreign, so utterly ridiculous that David burst out laughing.

His derision incensed her. She stabbed an index finger in his direction. "Maybe you're the one who's longing to be submissive."

"Oh yeah?" Swiftly he covered the remaining distance between them.

She backpedaled until she ran smack dab into the wall. David grabbed both her wrists, pinned her hands above her head and swiftly shoved one knee between her legs, completely hemming her in with no way out.

"This look like submissive to you, darlin'?" he growled.

They were both breathing hard, their lips almost touching.

"For your information I'm a third degree black belt in karate," she said.

"Bring it on. I'm fifth degree."

"You don't threaten me." She gulped, belying her own bravado.

He saw the column of her throat muscles pump hard and he knew he'd succeeded in intimidating her, but still she held her ground. She might be scared, but she was too damned proud to run away.

Dammit. Why did her bravery in the face of her fear turn him on so frickin' much? He was one sick puppy.

His gaze locked onto hers.

She raised her chin. She was so close her body heat set him on fire.

They stood there a long moment, neither of them blinking, neither wanting to be the first to back down. He forced himself not to think about how nice she smelled or how her chest rose and fell in cadence with his own raspy breathing or how much he wanted to kiss her at that very moment.

If he kept thinking like this, he'd be rock hard in a matter of seconds. He was halfway there already.

"Yep," she said, "I'll be out there on my own, no protection, no gun, a woman traveling alone. You know I'm gonna be pretty well defenseless."

"You're about as defenseless as a porcupine."

But even as he denied her vulnerability, he felt his

guardian instincts charge to the forefront of his emotions. He'd always possessed this need to defend the underdog. It was one of the reasons he'd become a cop. Unbelievable how this irksome woman had figured that out about him.

How had she known the one thing he simply could not refuse was a damsel in distress? She didn't seem the type to take advantage of her femininity but here she was suddenly giving him a wide-eyed, helpless look. He knew he shouldn't fall for it, but damn his hide, he did.

"You're going to plague the living crap out of me until I agree to take you along."

"Pretty much." She nodded.

Sighing, he let her go and stepped back. "I can't trust you."

"Why not?"

"I can't have you trying to one up me again like you did at the airport. And speaking of that, give my badge back." He held out his hand.

She fished in her purse, found his badge and passed it over to him. "I won't try to one up you again. I promise."

"Oh, that makes all the difference in the world," he said sarcastically.

"I'll swear on a bible." She raised her left hand while splaying her right hand over her heart. "Got a bible? Betcha the Gideons left one in the bedside table, they're reliable that way."

"No need to be a smart-ass. This isn't a court of law, you don't have to swear on a bible."

"Then how are you going to know you can trust me?"

"Swearing on a bible won't make me trust you."

"I never break a solemn vow."

The expression in her eyes told him that she meant

every word. He decided to surrender, mainly because he knew if he didn't he would end up spending more time fighting her than chasing after Shriver and Cassie. But he also gave in because she seemed so earnest and a little desperate.

Besides, if she was with him, he could control her. Out there on her own she was a wild card and he couldn't afford to let her run amok and screw up his investigation.

"All right," he said after a long moment. "You can come."

Her shoulders sagged visibly at her hard-won victory. She blew out her breath with an adorable sound that made him feel warm and protective inside. Ah hell, he liked her.

"Thank you," she said, and headed for an overstuffed chair in the corner. He noticed her hand quivered ever so slightly as she lowered herself down. A cloud of dust motes drifted up. "Now let's establish some ground rules."

"Ground rules?" he echoed.

How cute. She still had the illusion that she had some measure of power in this crazy relationship. Mindboggling. Give the woman an inch and she took the entire freeway.

"I promised not to one up you, but now you've got to promise me something."

"Like what?"

"No more using sex as a weapon." She nodded from his shirt to his bare chest. The heat of her gaze scorched his flesh.

"Excuse me?"

"You heard what I said."

"Wait a minute. Simply because I took my shirt off you think I was using sex as a weapon?"

"Don't forget calling me submissive and then pinning me to the wall with your knee to try and prove your point."

"How could I forget that?" He wriggled his eyebrows suggestively.

"Ah, ah." She pointed a finger. "See there, you're doing it again."

"You call eyebrow wriggling a sexual weapon?"

"It's innuendo."

"No, it's not."

"Oh, give it up. You know what you're doing and I know what you're doing and as long as we're working together I won't stand for any more of your masculine intimidation tactics. Got it?"

She was like an impudent kid, trespassing on a farmer's land, cockily waving a red flag at the bull in the pasture.

He could have replied in a thousand different ways, each and every response designed to put her firmly in her place, but somehow David managed to restrain his tongue.

Maddie was worried about her sister and even though he fought against the guilt, he felt responsible for what had happened. He had known Shriver had a spellbinding effect on women. He had also recognized Cassie was gullible and yet he'd enlisted her anyway. He'd used her hunger for excitement to fulfill his own needs.

Man, it hurt when your selfish decisions came back to bite your butt.

"No more using sex as a weapon," he agreed.

Maddie looked surprised at his capitulation. "Thank

you. Now could you, um, cover up?" She waved a hand at his naked chest.

Grinning, he slowly leaned over, making sure she got an extra good view of his muscles and plucked his shirt off the bed.

"Any other rules I should be aware of?" He might as well know what her rules were so he could systematically set about breaking them.

"That's all for now, but you should prepare yourself for future rules as they arise."

He slipped on the shirt but didn't move to do up the buttons. He could tell she was still struggling hard against her desire to look at him. You couldn't deny it. They had sexual chemistry, no matter how unwanted it might be on both their parts.

"I can't promise you anything. I'll be fair with you, but that's all I can offer. Take it or leave it."

"I suppose I'll have to take it." She hopped up from the chair and edged toward the door, giving him a wide berth.

Good. He'd rattled her at last.

"Wait just a minute." He reached out and touched her elbow. She sucked in an audible breath.

"Yes?" her voice was soft, but her skin was softer.

"I have a few ground rules of my own."

"Oh?"

"When it comes to this investigation, you have to obey me without question."

"I can't agree to that."

"Then I can't take you along."

"But what if you tell me to do something detrimental to either Cassie or myself?"

"I'm afraid you're just going to have to trust me," he said, feeling her muscles tense beneath his touch.

"Trusting a stranger isn't my strong suit."

"Mine either, kiddo." He thrust his hands deep in the pockets of his trousers. "But for the foreseeable future, I'd say we're stuck with each other."

Chapter

♥

FIVE

"WHERE ARE WE going?" Maddie shouted an hour later as she sat in the passenger seat of the no-frills subcompact car David had rented.

The bargain basement vehicle didn't have air conditioning so they had all four windows rolled down. Her hair lashed her face like a hundred tiny whips. Her skin stung and she felt as if she was sitting in a NASA wind tunnel.

"To see Shriver's fence," David answered.

"Who is that?" she asked, battling valiantly to smooth her hair down.

"Name's Cory Philpot. He was raised in New York high society. He and Shriver have known each other for years," David hollered.

Maddie was still feeling unnerved from their encounter in his motel room. She thought about the way David had used his bare chest as a weapon of intimidation. How he'd speared his knee to the wall between her spread legs. How he'd pinned her arms over her head.

Her stomach went quivery all over again.

He seemed much larger than he actually was. Even though his body wasn't the least bit bulky, he had a bearish quality about him. Maybe it was the wide shoulders or the broad chest. Maybe it was the way he managed to come off gruff and cuddly all at the same time.

Or maybe it was his uncommon combination of brute strength, cocky self-confidence, dogged determination and pure animal magnetism. He was deeply intense at times, while at other moments he seemed cynical and flippant. She liked the contrast but she did not know why.

Usually, she went for quiet, brainy guys who analyzed everything to death just as she did. She'd only been in love once and that had been during her senior year in high school.

Lance was a wild, reckless guy who ditched her for being too cautious. He'd even had the audacity to ask her why she couldn't be more like Cassie. Imagine! She'd told herself never again. She made it a habit to stay away from dangerous guys like the one sitting beside her.

The sun hunkered on the horizon, a big orange smoldering ball. The mingled smells of pungent fish, aromatic frangipani and sweet tropical fruits defined the aroma of Grand Cayman. They drove down the waterfront road passing quaint restaurants, souvenir shops and financial institution after financial institution after financial institution.

"What's with all the banks?" she asked, abandoning the struggle to tame her hair.

"Offshore accounts, laundered mob money, tax evaders. The Caymans are a great place to stash cash you don't want other people knowing about."

"I see."

David leaned back in the seat in a casual but oddly alert posture, like a male lion guarding his pride. One arm lay draped over the steering wheel, his other elbow rested against the window. Maddie tilted her head and surreptitiously studied his profile.

The wind tousled his short, golden brown hair. It gave him a relaxed, simple look and stirred a surprising appetite inside her. An appetite she tried to pass off as hunger. She hadn't eaten anything all day except two handfuls of roasted almonds on the plane.

Without meaning to, Maddie found herself wondering what it would feel like to run her fingers through that thick, unruly hair. What would his heated skin taste like against her tongue?

Her errant thoughts spun dizzily, wildly as she pondered how his warm body would feel straddling hers, moving over her, supplying them both with stark physical pleasure.

Beneath her skin, a strange hotness extended, throbbing outward. Something about him, something mysterious yet fundamentally masculine, called to her. But Maddie was determined to ignore the summons.

Her hormones did not easily influence her. Unlike her earthy twin, she had never been a slave to either her libido or her impulses. So why now was her brain sending her body a dozen frantic messages all centered on sating her sexual desires?

The uncharacteristic bent of her thoughts alarmed her and she quickly jerked her gaze away from his face, but not before he caught her giving him the once over.

Jeez, she'd practically been drooling.

His eyes narrowed, his thick lashes lowered as he

swept a glance at her lap. Maddie looked down. Her denim skirt had ridden up, revealing a yard of thigh.

One eyebrow quirked on his forehead and he grinned like a man with a dirty secret. The faint laugh lines at the corners of his eyes deepened, making him somehow—impossibly—even more good-looking.

Damn him.

Maddie tugged her skirt down as far as it would go, which unfortunately wasn't far enough to extinguish the heat burning her cheeks.

Both sets of 'em.

"Eyes on the road, Mister."

"I could say the same thing to you." David chuckled. "I caught you checking me out."

Disgruntled with her unruly hormones, Maddie snapped her head around, stared purposefully out the passenger window and wondered why she was having such a hard time breathing normally.

The sun slipped below the horizon. All along the waterfront festive lights flicked on. Bonfires blazed on the beach. Yachts on dinner cruises bobbed in the harbor. People strolled the sidewalks in brightly colored casual wear. Grand Cayman was a nice island. Too bad she wasn't here to have a nice time.

"Where is this place?" she asked.

"Dead Man's Cove, tip of the North Shore."

"Quaint name," she said dryly.

"The Caymans have a bit of a pirate past."

"So I've gathered. What are we going to do when we get there?"

"I'm not sure."

"What does that mean?"

"We'll play it by ear."

"Do you think Shriver is there? With Cassie? Fencing the Cézanne?"

Was her sister okay? Was Shriver treating her right? Was she getting enough to eat?

David shrugged. "Your guess is as good as mine."

"Wow, you're a real fount of information."

"Detective work isn't an exact science."

"So tell me, is there anything you do know?"

"I know you're a nosy pain-in-the-ass," he said and glared at her.

"Watch the road," she said and automatically braced the flat of both hands against the dashboard.

She hated it when drivers took their attention off the road. Her sister was the world's worst. Cassie could talk on the cell phone, eat a bagel and apply mascara all the while hurtling down the freeway at seventy miles an hour. Maddie shuddered just thinking about it.

David might have muttered "bossy wench" but she could have misunderstood him. In actuality, he probably said something far less complimentary. You never knew about men.

Silence descended, broken only by the sound of Maddie's rumbling stomach.

"You hungry?" he asked.

"Yes."

"We don't have time for a restaurant. Fast food in the car suit you?"

"Anything." She nodded. As any athlete, she wasn't much for greasy fries and burgers but under the circumstances she'd take what she could get.

"Ah, the ubiquitous burger franchise," he said, wheeling the car through the drive-through. "What'll you have?"

"A salad. Fat-free Italian dressing. Hold the croutons."

"It'll be kinda hard to eat a salad in the car. I'll get you a burger." He pulled up to the order box. "Two cheeseburgers, a couple of orders of fries, two chocolate shakes and an apple pie," he said into the intercom. To Maddie he asked, "You want an apple pie?"

"I want a salad."

"Just one apple pie," he cheerfully told the anonymous female voice taking his order.

"That'll be twelve fifty-eight, sir. Please drive around."

Maddie plucked a twenty from her purse and held it out to him.

He waved her off. "My treat."

"If you planned on telling me what to eat, why did you ask what I wanted?"

"Because I've figured something out about you," he said, paying for their order and handing her the sack of burgers.

The food smelled so good Maddie feared she might start salivating. He took their chocolate shakes from the cashier and slipped them into the console cup holders.

"Oh, yeah?"

"Yeah."

"What's that?"

"You're the type of woman who does what's good for her whether she likes it or not. You toe the line so you can take care of everyone else. But secretly, you're just waiting for an excuse to let down your guard and do something wild like your adventurous sister."

"Ooooh, you've got my number, all right." She waved both hands in the air. "I've just been dreaming of a man who would come along and force-feed me junk food. Yeah, buddy, it doesn't get any wilder than that."

"Rome wasn't built in a day."

He chuckled and the deep sound wrapped around her like a comfortable hug. He was teasing her and damn, if she wasn't enjoying it. Why did she feel charmed by him? She should be irritated, aggravated, annoyed. Instead her insides went all whooshy.

This wouldn't do. Not at all.

"What's that crack supposed to mean?" she asked in a quarrelsome tone. She would pick a fight with him if she had to. Anything to eradicate this warm, soft fuzzy sensation arrowing through her heart every time he glanced her way.

"You gotta start small."

"I get it. Today it's hamburgers, tomorrow the world."

"Something like that."

"You're so full of bullshit. Obviously, you've confused me with my sister if you're thinking I'm just waiting for some big strong man to come along and tell me what to do."

"Now, now. Don't disparage your sister. She might be in trouble, but she's a good woman. She just falls for the wrong kind of guys. You're lucky you have a sibling."

He smiled and his teeth flashed white in the illumination of the neon lights. The lighting softened his rugged features and the tender look in his eyes took her by surprise. Maybe he wasn't such a hard-ass after all. Could this tough guy be like the delightfully delicious sabras cactus? Prickly on the outside but sweet and soft on the inside. Her pulse skittered off kilter.

So why the armor-plated exterior? What was he so

afraid of? He gestured toward the sack. "Pass me one of the burgers, will you?"

She moved the sack out of his reach, tucking it against the right side of her body. "Nope."

"No?"

"I've got your number too, mister."

His grin widened. "Let's hear it."

"You're one of those guys who's so focused on winning that you try to shut down your tender feelings by channeling your energy into blasting your way through any given situation."

"Now why would I do that?"

"Because if you're winning that means you're in control. Because if—horrors—you're not busy telling other people what to do, that means someone could be taking advantage of you. You view soft emotions as a weakness and nothing terrifies you more than being seen as weak."

"You think?" David asked lightly, but Maddie noticed he'd lost his teasing smile. Ah-ha! Apparently it was quite a different story when the pop psychology was on the other ego.

"I think."

"Well, I think you're one of those women who doesn't appreciate having their shortcomings pointed out to them, so in order not to have to face said shortcomings, they grasp at very thin straws and lash out at the person who observed their flaw in the first place."

"You think that was lashing out?"

"Uh-huh."

"Buddy, you don't wanna see me lashing out."

"I guess it would depend on what kind of lashing we're talking about. A physical tongue lashing is quite a different animal from a verbal tongue lashing."

"There you go with the sexual innuendo again."

"But you're so fun to tease."

"Maybe we should examine the reason you feel compelled to tease me, if indeed it is, as you claim, teasing."

"Maybe we should leave the psychoanalysis to the professionals," he said.

"I'll go for that."

"Could I have my supper now, please?"

She relented. He had asked nicely. She unwrapped his burger and handed it over.

The next few minutes passed quietly as they concentrated on fueling their bodies. The farther north they traveled, the more rugged the terrain grew. Smooth sandy beaches gave way to dense scrub, rocky thickets and sedge swamps. Just when Maddie was beginning to think that David had no earthly idea where he was going, the beaches reappeared.

After finishing her food, Maddie wiped her hands on a napkin and stuffed it, along with the greasy wrapper, back into the paper bag.

Well-kept bungalows graduated to pricier digs until they found themselves in Cayman Kai where the manor houses were lavish and the condos exclusive. David followed a string of cars down the road to Dead Man's Cove.

"Looks like someone is having one heck of a chichi party," she said, impressed with the assortment of Jaguars, Porsches and Mercedes-Benzes.

The line of cars slowed as they turned into the private drive of a very swanky plantation-style house surrounded by coconut groves. The cars were stopping at a checkpoint manned by a uniformed security guard.

David backed the car up and narrowly missed running

into a Viper. He slipped their outclassed rental into drive and eased past the party house.

"What's going on?" Maddie asked.

"Change in plans."

"You mean we're not just going to walk up to the front door, ring the bell and say, Hey dude, you fencing Shriver's stolen Cézanne?"

"That was never my plan." He sounded irritated.

"What was your plan?"

"I agreed to bring you along, basically to keep you from screwing up my investigation. I did not agree to play twenty questions. Now hush," he said, scanning the waterfront.

"What are you looking for?"

"What did I just say about asking nosy questions? Weren't you listening? Or are you just bad at taking instructions?"

"That last part. Now what is it that you're looking for?"

"A secluded place to stash the car. Satisfied?"

"See? How hard was that."

"Woman, you try a man's patience," he growled under his breath and ran his fingers through his hair, as agitated as an air traffic controller on the heaviest travel day of the year.

She realized then that he saw her as nothing more than an annoyance he'd been forced to tolerate. She felt at once snubbed and defiant.

Who cares what he thinks about you? The only thing that matters is finding Cassie and bringing her home in one piece.

David switched off the headlights and edged down a narrow dirt lane leading to a public beach not far from

Philpot's house. He pulled the car off the road and cut the engine.

"Stay put," he said, and got out of the car.

"No way. I'm coming with you."

She popped from the passenger seat and found herself ankle deep in fine white sand. It sucked at her high-heeled sandals, dragging her down with each step. The damned shoes were ridiculously useless. How did Cassie walk in the things?

"Why am I not the least bit surprised," he muttered.

Maddie slipped off the shoes, looped the straps over her fingers and hurried after him. They trudged through the sand, headed toward Philpot's mansion. Music filtered through the air. She identified it as some schmaltzy tune by The Carpenters frequently played at weddings.

"Not much of a party song," she commented.

But David wasn't paying any attention to her. He was like a bloodhound tracking a raccoon. His eyes were narrowed, his posture tense, his attention focused on Philpot's place. They couldn't see much of that section of the beach from where they walked, cloaked as it was by the coconut grove.

But as they crept nearer, Maddie spotted a makeshift altar set up on the beach, along with dozens of folding chairs and flaming tiki torches.

"I think it's a wedding," Maddie whispered.

"We're in luck," David said. "They'll be so busy with the wedding, no one will notice us. Now if fate is really smiling, Peyton Shriver will be among the guests."

"And Cassie," Maddie supplied, anxious for this single-minded FBI agent not to forget her sister.

"Get down," David said roughly and dropped to a crouch. He tugged on the hem of her skirt.

The brush of his knuckles against her thigh was slight, but it was enough contact to send her pulse staggering against her throat. Deliberately struggling to ignore the sizzle of awareness he'd generated, she squatted beside him in the sand.

"Now what?" she asked.

Through the trunks of the trees they could see a robed minister standing at the altar and two other guys, presumably the groom and the best man, positioned in front of him, but from this distance, Maddie couldn't make out their features.

"We go closer."

"Through the coconut grove?" Anxiously, she glanced up at the trees with their thick, heavy fruit looming above them in the deepening twilight.

"Sure, why not." David moved forward

"Wait, wait." She grabbed on to his belt loop.

"What is it?" He turned and glared at her.

"Are you always this testy?"

"Only when being pestered by some pesky female. What is it?" he repeated.

"I read a guidebook about Grand Cayman on the flight over."

"And . . . ?"

"The article warned to watch out for falling coconuts."

"For crying out loud. What are the odds of getting beaned by a coconut in the next five minutes?"

"Good enough that they bothered to mention it in a guidebook."

"Well, I guarantee you'll get beaned if you keep visualizing it. Fret about something enough and it'll eventually happen."

"See there, you prove my point. That's a perfectly good reason to keep out."

"It's a perfectly good reason not to visualize falling coconuts."

"I can't help but visualize them." She worried her necklace with her fingers.

"Fine, stay here if you want." David dived into the grove, wasting no time in ditching her.

Maddie hesitated, alternating between eyeing the coconuts dangling above and the FBI agent sneaking through the trees. Her innate sense of caution warred with her allegiance to her sister.

Stay or go?

Hang back and wait? Or take your chances and plunge ahead?

Risk your noggin or Cassie's life?

Tick-tock.

David was halfway through the grove when she realized loyalty trumped safety.

"Okay, all right, wait up, I'm coming," she whispered loudly.

"Shhh. I think I hear the wedding march." He stopped and cocked his head to listen.

She clamped her lips shut and nervously duck-walked behind him as quickly as she could. It wasn't easy, navigating the moist sand and the coconut trees in that position.

When Maddie heard the deadly whoosh-thunk of a descending coconut to the left of her, she almost peed in her pants.

Yikes!

The second whoosh-thunk, closer even than the first sent her stomach into spasms and her heart rate into hyperdrive. She felt like she was in the video game Frogger she and Cassie used to play as kids.

She scuttled faster and by the time she reached David, she felt edgy, overheated and even a bit faint. She cowered beside him, arms wrapped over her head, eyes squeezed closed. Her pulse stepped up its shallow, flighty beat.

David reached out and laid a hand across her shoulder. "I want you to prepare yourself," he murmured.

"Prepare myself to die by coconut?" Maddie asked, peering over her shoulder and praying she wouldn't see any angry island gods hurling ripe fruit at her.

He took her chin between his fingers and thumb and turned her head toward the beach. "Look at the bride."

"Yeah, okay, I see her."

She squinted at the woman in white walking rather stiffly down the green Astroturf laid out as an aisle. Maddie was a tad nearsighted, but glasses got in the way of sports and she'd never gotten the hang of poking plastic contact lenses into her eyes.

"You don't recognize her?"

"Should I?"

"It's your twin sister and unless I'm mistaken the groom is Peyton Shriver."

Before she could shriek, "What?" David clamped one hand over her mouth and snaked his other hand around her waist, pulling her down flush against his warm body.

"I told you she ran off with him voluntarily," he whispered.

Maddie tensed and she struggled to break free from his overbearing grasp. She had to get to Cassie and stop that wedding now, but David wasn't about to turn her loose. She aimed an elbow at his ribs and jabbed hard.

"Ouch, that hurt. Stop fighting me."

"Turn me loose," she mumbled around the salty taste of his skin.

"Only if you promise not to go ballistic."

Yeah okay, she would promise anything in order to get David to let her go, but that didn't mean she would sit here idly by and allow her sister to marry that sleazebag art thief.

Slowly he released her and then slipped his gun from its shoulder holster.

"Stay well behind me, or I'll handcuff you to a tree," he threatened.

"I think you're bluffing."

"Just try me."

Something in his tone of voice, told her he meant every word. The last thing she wanted was to be handcuffed to one of those coconut trees.

They both looked toward the beach. Her sister—if indeed the bride was Cassie—reached the altar and the music stopped.

"Dearly beloved," she heard the minister say.

She couldn't heed David's warning; she had to speak out. She didn't care if he got mad and handcuffed her to a coconut tree, she'd take her chances. She had to stop her twin from making a horrible mistake.

"Cassie, no!" she screamed. "Don't do it!"

David was on his feet, staying low, gun held at his side. Maddie was on his heels. They were at the edge of the grove when she glanced up and saw it, a coconut dangling precariously from the tree right above them.

Don't visualize it falling.

But she couldn't help herself. She was a worst-case scenario gal ever since that ill-fated Christmas day eighteen years ago. The harder she tried not to see the coconut cracking into David's skull, the more vividly she pictured it.

The coconut was going to fall.

She knew it as surely as she knew the sun would rise. In order to prevent David from getting assassinated by one badass milk fruit, she had to act now.

Without hesitation, Maddie lunged for his feet and knocked him on his back.

"What in the hell are you doing?" he yelled, just as the coconut dropped.

The hard green shell missed David, but lightly clipped the back of Maddie's skull.

Thwack!

Sharp waves of pain mulched her brain. She saw a million shimmering stars—yellow, white, blue—and smelled a dozen strange odors. She tried to stand but her knees were noodles and she wobbled precariously, grateful she'd taken off those deadly sandals.

"You saved my life," David murmured, staring from Maddie to the coconut and back again, obviously not realizing she'd been bushwhacked.

She blinked repeatedly and bit down hard on her bottom lip to keep from passing out. The pain was pretty intense, but she couldn't black out, she had to stop Cassie from getting married. She pushed her palm against the back of her head and willed the earth to stop spinning so fast.

"Maddie?" David knelt beside her. "Did you get hit?"

She tried to nod but it hurt too much.

"Can you hear me?"

"Uh-huh."

"Are you all right?"

Squinting she peered at David. How come there were two of him? He wasn't a twin. "Stop moving."

"I'm not moving."

There was something she was supposed to be thinking about. What was it?

Oh yeah. Cassie.

She swung her gaze toward the beach, saw Cassie and some guy holding hands and running through the tide toward a dune buggy parked on the sand.

"They're getting away." She gestured.

David jumped up and started to run to the beach but he hesitated and glanced back over his shoulder at her. She saw the internal conflict play across his face.

Stay and make sure she was okay, or go after his quarry?

She was afraid to trust him, but she had no real choice. "Go. Stop them. Save my sister."

"You're sure you're okay?"

"Yes. I'm fine. Go!"

He nodded, turned and sprinted off.

And that's when Maddie passed out cold.

Chapter

SIX

$\mathcal{D}$AVID RAN UP the beach, his heart thumping with adrenaline, his brain pounding out a single message. Stop Shriver. Stop Shriver. Stop Shriver.

But he was too late. The flasher lights of the dune buggy winked on and off as it disappeared over a faraway sand dune.

The well-dressed wedding guests gasped and scattered, knocking over folding chairs and shoving each other. The minister ducked behind the altar. One woman screamed. That's when David realized he was running with his gun drawn.

"Don't be alarmed, ladies and gentlemen," he said and held up his badge. "FBI." He pointed at the nearest man. "You, call an ambulance. My partner's been hurt."

His partner? Why had he said that?

He hurried to the grove, his gut knotting tighter with each step. He realized he was giving Cory Philpot plenty of time to hide the Cézanne if he did indeed possess it, but David couldn't afford to care about that right now. Maddie needed him.

It was dark in the grove and it took him a moment to see her body stretched out on the sand.

"Maddie?" he said softly. Anxiety grabbed his gut and squeezed hard.

He holstered his gun and knelt beside her. She looked so peaceful that at first he thought she was sleeping. He reached out to brush a lock of hair from her face and was startled to find her skin cool to the touch. He scooped her into his arms. She lay limp, not moving. Her breathing was shallow, but steady.

When she didn't respond, fear jammed his heart tight against his Adam's apple.

Please God, let her be okay.

"Maddie, can you hear me?"

Nothing.

Where in hell was that ambulance?

He cradled her in the crook of his arm and stared down into her face. In repose, she was especially beautiful, no worry lines furrowing her brow, no tension about her lips. A wisp of blonde hair curled against her cheekbone. He studied the curve of her chin, the sweet shape of her mouth, the slope of her cheek.

He had no idea what possessed him. Perhaps it was the fairy tale myth of the sleeping damsel brought to life by a kiss. Perhaps it was a desperate maneuver spurred by the guilt and fear he was determined to deny. Perhaps it was simply gut instinct.

He lowered his head and kissed her.

The minute his lips touched hers, she responded. Her mouth softened, grew warmer and her eyelashes fluttered lightly.

He felt her tongue gently probe his lips and she murmured a soft sound that turned him inside out.

Now that she had responded, he knew he should break the kiss, pull away, but she shifted into him and wrapped her arms around his neck, drawing him closer.

Ah, hell, he was just a man.

She tasted of heat and honey and heaven. She moved her lips against his, drinking him in. He heard his own heartbeat in his ears thumping loud and solid.

Stop this. Now.

But somehow the tables had turned and she was the one doing the kissing, giving him a momentous taste of her femininity. Her scent made him dizzy with desire.

This was so wrong on so many levels. He tried to pull back, but she held on like a cockleburr.

"Maddie," he mumbled around her kisses, "are you awake?"

She didn't answer; she just kept kissing him.

He gently shook her shoulders.

She continued pressing her lips against his chin, his cheek, his nose, wherever her mouth landed. Her eyes were closed, her response totally automatic. Even though she was technically conscious, she was still wandering in a foggy, mental never-never land.

"Sweetheart, can you hear me?"

She nuzzled his neck. She smelled like Christmas morning, full of wonder and surprise.

Stop thinking like this, he commanded himself.

"Mmm," she murmured.

"Wake up."

She licked his throat, her hot, wicked tongue scaring the living daylights out of him. How much damage had that coconut done to the pleasure center of her brain. Had it somehow flipped on her sexual switch?

He gulped and cautiously ran his fingers over her head in search of a bump. She purred like a kitten and arched her back into him. He found a small knot just above her left ear.

Ho boy. What now?

He tried to disentangle himself and ease away. It was difficult, considering he wanted nothing more than to kiss her right back, but he wasn't the kind of guy who would exploit the situation, no matter how tempting. He liked his women to know exactly what they were doing when he made love to them.

"Come on," he coaxed. "That's enough of that. No more kissing. Wake up now." Gently he slapped her cheeks, hoping to rouse her to full waking consciousness.

Without warning, Maddie sat bolt upright, doubled her fists and punched him squarely in the solar plexus.

Peyton didn't stop until they were several miles away from Dead Man's Cove. He parked the dune buggy not far from the Rum Point ferry landing, and then he turned to clamp a hand over Cassie's wrist.

"What in bloody hell just happened back there?" he yelled.

"I don't know." Cassie wasn't lying. When she'd heard Maddie cry out her name she had been as surprised and confused as Peyton. How on earth had her sister managed to track her to Grand Cayman?

And when David had come running from the coconut grove with his gun drawn, well, her heart had just about stopped.

Undoubtedly, David and Maddie would have misinterpreted the wedding. They probably thought she loved Shriver and had decided to become Bonnie to his Clyde. Not that she could blame them from drawing those conclusions. The evidence was pretty damning.

As unsettling as their appearance was, she was really glad they'd shown up when they did, otherwise, she would be Mrs. Peyton Shriver right now.

Peyton grabbed her chin and forced her to look at him. "Look me in the face, Cassie, and tell me the truth. Are you still working for David Marshall?"

"N . . . n . . . no," she stammered, her gaze locked with his. She'd never seen Peyton act so macho and forceful. It was more of a turn-on than scary.

Easy, Cassie, no matter how sexy, he's still a thief.

His grip twisted like a vise against her wrist.

"Ow," she cried out. "You're hurting me."

Okay, she was officially not turned on anymore.

"The truth." Peyton didn't release her.

"I'm not working for him. I promise." She grimaced, her hand throbbing from the pressure of his clench.

"Then how did he find us here? How come he shows up just in the nick of time to prevent us from getting married?"

"I don't know. I swear on my mother's life. Please, Peyton, you're really hurting me."

He let her go and sat back in the dune buggy. "Maybe it was Philpot," he mused. "Double-crossing me. Trying to collect the reward the Kimbell is putting up."

"Or Jocko Blanco," she pointed out. "You just double-crossed him and he's bound to be looking for revenge."

Peyton shook his head. "Blanco would never rat me

out to the feds. He'd just hunt me down and snap off my digits."

Cassie didn't ask him to elaborate on which digits.

"If it wasn't you who betrayed me, it has to be Philpot." Peyton nodded.

"It wasn't me, but maybe it wasn't Philpot either. Maybe David is just a good detective."

"Not bloody likely." Peyton laughed. "He's been trying to catch me for ten years. Ever since I scammed his dear old auntie. The man couldn't find his arse with both hands in a house of mirrors. No, someone ratted me out."

"It wasn't me," she insisted.

"I guess I have a decision to make." Peyton gave her a hard speculative stare.

"A decision?" she echoed.

"Whether to trust you and take you with me or leave you here for David Marshall to find. If you're telling me the truth, then he'll arrest you. The man is a bulldog. He won't care that you fell in love with me. To him you're as guilty as I am."

Cassie gulped. She was just starting to realize the trouble she was in. If she went with Shriver, David would be convinced she was in on the theft of the Cézanne. She would lose her job, and very likely go to prison when he caught up with them. If she stayed behind, Peyton would get away with the painting. She would probably still lose her job and she would not get what she wanted most in the world, to prove to Maddie that she was competent and capable and could stand on her own two feet.

What to do?

She wasn't one to vacillate. She had to convince Peyton to take her with him. The only way this whole scenario was going to have a happy resolution was if she set a trap for both Peyton and Jerome Levy, the art broker who had commissioned the theft of the Cézanne.

What she needed was a plan. A big, bold plan so foolhardy it just might work. She also needed a way to let Maddie and David know that she was still working the case from the inside.

But what and how?

She had to be very careful. She could not arouse Peyton's suspicions.

The ferry docked.

"There's my ride," he said.

"Don't you mean *our* ride?" she dared.

Peyton studied her. Cassie did her best to look sad and vulnerable and sexy all at the same time.

"Don't make this goodbye," she said, wracking her brain for a clue to leave behind that Maddie would understand. If her twin was convinced of her innocence, Cassie knew she would move heaven and earth to prove it to David.

"Give me one good reason why I shouldn't leave you."

"Because I know something you don't."

"And that is?" Peyton crossed his arms over his chest in a go-ahead-prove-yourself pose.

"The Prado is in the process of installing a new state-of-the-art security system. Even if my friendship with the curator can get us in the door, we might not be able to bypass the alarm like you planned. It depends on how far along they are in implementing the new method."

"So your convincing argument is that you're basically useless to me?"

"Not exactly."

"What exactly?"

"I happen to know whose system they copied right down to the same security code."

"Whose?"

She shook her head. "How stupid do I look? You take me with you, then I'll let you in on my little secret."

He cocked his head and eyed her speculatively. "Why didn't you tell me this before?"

"Because I wasn't sure I could trust you not to dump me once I'd served my purpose."

"The ace up your sleeve, ay?"

"Something like that."

Peyton laughed. "Cassie luv, you're some piece of work."

"So you'll take me with you?" She caught her breath and waited. He took so long answering she thought she might black out from breathlessness.

"I hope I don't end up regretting this," he said, "but come on."

He hopped from the dune buggy and held his hand out to her. She grabbed the train of her wedding gown so she wouldn't trip over it and gave him her other hand.

Leave a clue for Maddie. Think, think, think.

All at once the answer hit and Cassie knew exactly the right thing to leave behind for her sister to find.

"David, speak to me." Maddie hovered over him, clenching and unclenching her fists.

David lay on the ground, doubled over and gasping for air.

"I'm so sorry. I didn't mean to punch you. I don't know why I punched you. Autonomic reflex I'm guessing. You were kissing me and in my dazed state I thought you were a stranger trying to accost me. By the way, why were you kissing me?"

Unable to draw in air, he simply shook his head.

"Could you step out of the way, miss?"

Maddie glanced up to see two burly paramedics coming through the trees with a stretcher. She rose to her feet. The men hustled over, unceremoniously picked David up and dumped him onto the stretcher.

"Not . . . me," he wheezed.

"What did you say?" asked the paramedic, tilting his head toward David's mouth.

"Her." David waved a hand at Maddie.

Both paramedics turned to look at her. She shrugged. Yes, she'd taken a knock to the head, but she wasn't about to go to the hospital. Not when Cassie was still AWOL.

With her index finger she drew a circle in the air near her temple. "Coconut must have knocked him loopy," she said. "Don't listen to him. He doesn't know what he's saying."

The paramedics nodded and started hauling him away.

"Dammit, Maddie," David said, coming up from the stretcher in one lumbering movement. Apparently he'd gotten his breath back. "You get on this stretcher right now." He pointed at the gurney, looking like a disgruntled father chastising his child.

That attitude wasn't going to wash with her. "No."

"You got hit on the head."

"It's nothing. I don't even have a headache."

"Liar."

How did he know she was lying? Her head hurt like the dickens but she was not going to the hospital. She couldn't show weakness. Especially not now. Not when her twin sister had disappeared again. Not in front of this strength-is-everything FBI agent.

"I'm fine," she insisted.

"So no one goes to the hospital?" one paramedic asked.

"She does." David jerked a thumb at Maddie at the same time she said, "He goes."

"You both look fine to me," said the second paramedic.

"She got hit on the head by a coconut and she was unconscious for several minutes," David said.

"I thought you said he got hit by the coconut." The first paramedic raised his eyebrows at Maddie.

"Okay, so I lied, but I'm not going to the hospital." She shifted her gaze to David. "And you can't make me."

"Fine, great, go ahead, suffer the consequences of a concussion." He threw his hands up in the air, pivoted on his heel and stormed away.

"Hey, wait, where are you going?" Maddie took off after him, leaving the paramedics standing there perplexed.

"To do my job," he called over his shoulder.

"I'm coming with you." She scurried to catch up.

"Of course you are," he said, his voice heavy with sarcasm. "Heaven forbid you trust me to perform my duties. You would rather risk your health than have a little faith in me."

"It's nothing personal."

They were walking abreast down the beach toward Philpot's house. The guests had scattered but the altar remained and the tiki torches still burned. It looked romantic in a rather wistful sort of way.

"Sure as hell feels personal," he grumbled.

Maddie put a hand on his arm to stop him. She tried not to notice how strong his biceps were or how her fingers seemed to sizzle against his arm. "Where do we go from here?"

"I'm going to call the local police for help searching Philpot's house and locating the dune buggy."

"Because of the wedding you're more convinced than ever that Cassie is a part of this, aren't you?"

His eyes met hers. His gaze was not unkind. "How can you continue to deny her obvious involvement?"

"She's my sister. I just know."

"Tell me, Maddie, what would it take for me to earn such blind loyalty from you?"

The question knocked her off guard. "Don't ever let me down," she blurted.

He stared at her and their gazes fused. An invisible, high-energy current passed between them. Something unspoken but so real Maddie felt the pressure in the very center of her body.

"Good to know," he said at last. "Good to know."

Two hours later after David and the Grand Cayman police had thoroughly searched Philpot's mansion and found not even a hint of the Cézanne, David received a call from another contingency of police officers who had been searching the island for Shriver and Cassie.

They were standing in Philpot's living room, Maddie struggling to pretend her head wasn't still throbbing from the coconut. David hung up the phone and turned to her. "They found the dune buggy at Rum Point Landing."

Maddie plastered a palm against her throat. "And Cassie?"

He shook his head. "No sign of her."

"What now?"

"We're going to head on over to the dune buggy, see if we can find some clues."

Maddie noticed he said *we*. For some crazy reason her heart did a somersault.

"I'm ready," she said. "Let's go."

It took them only ten minutes to reach Rum Point Landing. David met with the police officer who'd found the dune buggy while Maddie gazed out at the ocean. *Cassie, where are you? Are you okay?* She sent her questions into the ether, hoping her twin would pick up the telepathy.

David touched her shoulder lightly. "Beautiful night."

"Yes."

"You want to help me go over the dune buggy?"

"Wouldn't that be breaking protocol? What if I found incriminating evidence and destroyed it?"

"Would you do that?" he asked.

"I might," she admitted.

He looked more than disappointed in her answer. He shook his head. "Then you better just sit on the dock and wait for me."

She'd just banished herself and she couldn't say why she'd done it. With a lump in her throat, she plunked down on the dock while David pulled on a pair of latex gloves. He took the flashlight one of the officers had given him and began processing the dune buggy for evidence.

Hugging her knees to her chest, she watched him work in the limited illumination from his flashlight. He looked so stern, so serious. He studiously pored over the vehicle, plodding, methodical, not missing a thing. She could tell he was damned good at his job and that didn't bode well for her sister.

"Maddie," he said.

"Yes?"

He held something in the palm of his hand. "Could you come here a minute?"

She rose to her feet, dusting off her bottom with both hands and half-heartedly ambled over. Maybe if she walked slowly enough his discovery would evaporate into thin air.

No such luck.

"What is it?" she asked once she'd reached him. She sounded quarrelsome and she knew it.

"Does this belong to your sister?" He shone the light on his palm and a small cross earring with a ruby in the center glistened up at her.

She caught her breath. She had bought those earrings for Cassie on their twenty-second birthday the year they had lived in Madrid.

With the uncanny intuition of a twin, she knew the earring was a clue Cassie had intentionally left behind for her to find. She also understood that if her sister had left a clue, it meant she was under Shriver's control and not free to get away or call her for help.

Or, she could have just lost the earring.

But Maddie didn't believe that, not for a second.

"Well?" David asked.

"It's hers." Should she tell him the rest? Maddie mulled over her choices. Should she mention her suspicions to David or should she keep quiet and go after Cassie on her own?

"And . . . ?" He cocked his head, looked at her expectantly. He seemed to know she was holding out on him.

"There is no and."

"I can read it on your face, Maddie. What aren't you telling me?"

Her gaze met his and she knew he wasn't going to let her get away with not talking. She might as well tell him.

That's right, his eyes coaxed. Give it up.

Knowing she really didn't have much of a choice, Maddie confessed. "Shriver's taking her to Madrid."

Chapter

SEVEN

With the help of the Grand Cayman police, David gained access to Shriver's hotel room at the Hyatt Regency on Seven Mile Beach. It was a quarter past eleven when he and Maddie stepped into the room.

David had one thing on his mind—find out where Shriver had gone. He felt like he was rapidly losing control of the investigation and he hated feeling stymied. The fiasco at Dead Man's Bay had dinged his ego. Shriver had been within his grasp and he'd let him get away. He had to do something, anything, to regain his sense of power.

The room was a wreck with the bedcovers strewn across the floor, dresser drawers pulled out and the closet door wide open. Someone had left in a big rush.

Maddie took one look at the room, slumped into a nearby chair and dropped her head in her hands.

Poor woman. She was exhausted. Dark circles ringed her eyes and she kept rubbing her temple. He knew she had a pounding headache from the coconut, but he also knew there was no way she would admit it.

She was tough. He'd grant her that.

Concern for her softened his heart. He had an uncharacteristically sentimental urge to draw her into his arms and promise her that everything would be all right.

Knock it off, Marshall. No getting sloppy over a suspect's sister.

"Why do you believe Cassie and Shriver might have gone to Madrid?" he asked more to distract himself than anything else and sauntered into the bathroom.

The shower curtain was half-in, half-out of the tub, and there was water on the floor. Shriver hadn't been gone long. Two hours. Three, tops. He and Cassie might even still be on the island. The local authorities were checking departing flights for him.

"Cassie loves Madrid." Maddie's voice sounded heavy, defeated. "We lived there for a year when we were in college. She worked at the Museo del Prado."

"What?" David poked his head out of the bathroom. "What was that last part?"

"Cassie worked at the Prado."

"She knows the museum inside out?"

"Yes."

David exhaled loudly. Ho boy, this tidbit of information had all the earmarks of big trouble.

"I know what you're thinking." Maddie stood and marched over to square off with him. The pulse in her neck thumped. Like an ace poker player he was beginning to recognize her tell. Whenever she was gearing up to give him a hard time that pulse point danced.

"Reading minds now, are we?"

She sank her hands on her hips. "You're thinking she and Shriver are going to rob the Prado."

"I never said that." Her feistiness amused him. Too bad their timing was off. If they'd met under different circumstances he would be chasing her hot and heavy.

"My sister is not a thief."

"Much as I like a good fight, we've been over this ground before. Besides, I've got work to do. If you'll excuse me." He moved past her, his arm barely brushing hers.

That light touch should have been nothing.

Instead, it was everything.

Flesh against flesh. Heat against heat. Scent against scent. He'd never been more aware of anything in his entire life than the brief whisper of her skin scorching his. Holy cow, he had it bad and that wasn't good.

Mentally, he shook himself and stalked over to the bedside table looking for anything to divert his attention from his damnable attraction to the woman staring after him.

Did she feel it too?

He didn't trust himself to look at her. If he saw the same desire written across her face, he would want her even more.

And he couldn't have her.

At least not yet. Not as long as her sister was a robbery suspect.

He tried to concentrate on searching for clues but his ears were highly attuned to the sound of her breathing. Was it his imagination or was she raspy with desire?

David glanced down at the notepad resting on the table and noticed there were indentations in the paper from where someone had written on the top sheet and then ripped it off.

"Do you have a pencil?" he asked.

"Yes, I think so. Hang on." She dug in her shoulder bag, extracted a mechanical pencil and rolled down the lead for him. "Here."

Their fingers connected when she passed the pencil over and he tried to ignore the inferno blasting up his arm but the blistering sensation was like ignoring the sun.

Never mind. Do your job.

He took the pencil and rubbed the lead across the indentations.

"Let me see." Maddie stood next to him, trying to peer over his shoulder. Her warm breath stirred the hairs on the nape of his neck and he felt himself stiffen like a starched shirt at a Chinese laundry.

"Jeez, woman," he barked. "Give me some breathing room."

"Okay, sorry." She held her palms up in a gesture of surrender and thankfully, stepped away.

David glanced at the paper in his hand. The pencil rubbing revealed not only the address of the Louvre museum, but also flight information to Paris.

"Well? What does it say?"

"I'm afraid this blows your Madrid theory all to hell."

"How's that?"

He passed her the paper.

"They're headed for Paris?" Maddie frowned. She seemed confused and for once David wasn't excited about being right.

"It looks like the earring your sister left behind wasn't a clue at all, but a red herring. If that's the case, it means unequivocally that Cassie is working with Shriver. And I think I know why they're going to Paris. We messed up Shriver's connection with Philpot. He's desperate to find a way to unload the Cézanne and Jerome Levy, the one man who can help him out of his pickle, lives in Paris."

"That's not what it means at all. I think the Paris info is the red herring. Shriver wanted you to fall for it and take off to Paris."

"Now why would he do that?"

"Because he's going to force Cassie to help him rob the Prado. The curator, Isabella Vasquez, is a friend of Cassie's and I'm certain that's why Shriver took her hostage," she said, valiantly trying to support her own desperate theory.

Her chin was notched in the air, her hands fisted at her sides, her eyes glistening in defiance.

"I'm sorry, Maddie, but as far as I'm concerned this evidence points to Cassie's direct involvement. You're more than welcome to go to Madrid, but I'm booking the next flight to Paris."

"And while you're mucking around in Paris, Shriver will be using my sister's connections to rob the Prado."

"You're wrong."

The pulse point in her throat was beating triple time. "Now I'm beginning to understand why you've been chasing Shriver for all these years but haven't caught him."

"What's that supposed to mean?" David glared. She'd gone straight for the jugular. The woman knew how to slice a man deep.

Maddie shoved her face closer to his. He tried not to stare at her luscious lips and failed miserably. She was so incredibly sexy when she was steamed. It was all he could do not to kiss her.

"It means, Hot Shot, that if you would think things through and act more cautiously you might not waste so much time running up blind alleys."

"Not everyone needs to be as plodding and methodical as you," he retorted.

"This half-cocked loose cannon shtick is going to come back and bite you in the ass."

"This isn't the wrong move," he insisted stubbornly.

But even as he clung to his position, David knew if he made the wrong choice by traveling to Paris, not only was his FBI career in jeopardy, but his mistake could cost Cassie her life.

David Marshall was the most infuriating, arrogant man she'd ever met in her life and the fact that she was inordinately attracted to him only made things worse.

What was wrong with her? Why did she find his high-handed masculinity so exciting? Why couldn't she stop thinking about the irritating man and what had happened in the coconut grove? Why couldn't she stop wishing she'd been more awake for their kiss?

She'd given in to him. Not because she thought he was right about Paris, but because Cassie would need her protection if it turned out he was correct. She was the only thing standing between her twin and the hardheaded FBI agent determined to see her behind bars.

They chartered a plane from Grand Cayman to Miami and caught the next available flight to Paris at two A.M. Maddie took her assigned seat next to the window. She did her best to ignore David, but denying him was akin to denying the sun in the desert. Physically, he was so present. Big and prominent and . . . *there.*

Two little girls in matching dresses moved down the

aisle of the airplane. The oldest one was eight or nine, the youngest barely six. They were carrying matching tote bags and the oldest one was holding the youngest one's hand. They took the two seats in front of Maddie and David.

Watching them caused Maddie's chest to knot up. How many times had she and Cassie boarded a similar plane, shuttling from their mother and stepfather's home in Belize or Panama or South Africa bound for their father's home in San Antonio? She knew exactly how the oldest one felt.

Responsible.

The flight attendant helped the girls get situated, but she'd no more than walked away when the youngest one undid her seat belt, turned around and peered at David over the back of her seat.

"Hi " The girl grinned at him. Six years old and already an incorrigible flirt.

"Hi, yourself." He grinned back. His smile was so genuine, Maddie forgot she was mad at him.

"I'm Katy."

David winked at her and she giggled coyly. "Nice to meet you, Katy. I'm David and this is Maddie."

"Sit back down," her older sister hissed. "And leave those people alone."

"That's Rebecca," Katy said with a dismissive flip of her hand. "She's my sister. She's bor-r-ring."

Maddie felt a special kinship with Rebecca. She knew what the girl went through trying to corral her ebullient sibling.

"You know what Mom said about talking to strangers." Rebecca tugged on her sister's sleeve. "Turn around."

"They're not strange, Becca."

"We don't know them, that makes them strangers." Rebecca was trying to keep her voice low, but her perky sister was having none of the subterfuge.

"We don't know the airplane lady either and you talked to her."

"She works for the airline. It's okay if you talk to her."

"But they're very nice, Becca," Katy coaxed. "Look at 'em."

Rebecca peeked around the seat. She arrowed David and Maddie a suspicious glance. "Sorry about her," she apologized. "This is her first time traveling without our mom."

"I like how your hair sticks up," Katy said boldly to David. She tugged at her own hair, trying to make it spike like his.

"Sit down," Rebecca repeated. "Or I'm gonna tell Dad on you when we get to Paris."

Katy wrinkled her nose. "Do you think that stupid Trixie will be there?"

"Probably, she's his girlfriend now."

Katy blew a raspberry.

"Come on, sit down," Rebecca begged.

"You're not the boss of me." Katy tossed her head.

Gosh, Maddie thought, if she had a dollar for every time she'd heard that line she'd own Bill Gates.

David leaned forward and spoke softly to the little girl. "The plane's about to take off, Katy, and you don't want to get thrown out of your seat. I'd hate to see you skin your knee. Why don't you sit down and put on the seat belt until we're airborne?"

"Okay," Katy said easily, turned around and plunked down. Rebecca shot him a grateful glance.

David looked over at Maddie. He was still grinning. She realized she had never seen him looking relaxed.

"Cute kid," he said.

"You're good with her."

"She likes male attention. Sounds like she doesn't get enough of daddy's time."

"That sounds familiar," Maddie muttered and it came out harsher than she intended.

"Strike a nerve?"

She shrugged. She wasn't about to tell him about her daddy issues. It was none of his damned business.

David let it go and nodded at the back of the girls' seats. "I'm guessing their names could just have easily been Maddie and Cassie."

"They're not twins."

"You two don't act like twins anyway."

"I know. Cassie is fun and sexy and charming and I'm stodgy and anxious and overly cautious."

"I never said that."

"I'm sure, like everyone else, you prefer her company to mine." Maddie knew she sounded like she was feeling sorry for herself, and maybe she was a little. Her life had been spent not only in her sister's shadow but being there to catch Cassie when her escapades went awry. Just once, she would like to have her own limelight, her own adventures.

"No," David said. "I don't think that. I think Cassie is flighty and irresponsible and self-centered."

"Hey, no bad-mouthing my twin. She's not self-centered. She just doesn't stop and think how her actions affect others."

"Isn't that what it means to be self-centered?"

"You don't understand her."

"So help me to understand."

Maddie told him then, about Cassie's accident and how it had shaped both of their lives. She told him about her vow to God.

"Cassie was in a coma for three months and in a rehab hospital for six months after that. She had to learn how to walk all over again."

"The accident on the pond wasn't your fault," he said.

"Yes it was. My mother told me to watch her."

- "How come your mother always put you in charge? How come she wasn't the one watching Cassie?"

Maddie shrugged. "Mama is as scatterbrained as my sister. They're two peas in a pod. They're so caught up in having fun and being creative they forget about the mundane but essential things in life."

"Like?"

"For instance, Mom was famous for her odd-ball breakfasts, especially after Dad left. Cold pizza. A can of beans. Whatever was in the cupboard. If we were lucky, she would throw eggs in a plastic bowl, nuke them and call them scrambled. Of course, they exploded and guess who had to clean egg gunk off the inside of the microwave."

"Yuck."

"Could have been worse. At least she took the eggs out of the shells first."

"I can just see an industrious young Maddie scrubbing off egg plaster. I bet you wore rubber gloves and an apron."

"How did you know?"

"It fits." He smiled and she felt herself relenting toward him. Okay the guy could be a hard-ass, but sometimes he made her feel really special in a way no one else ever had.

"See. Boring even when I was ten."

"Not boring. Tough. You said your Dad left. What caused your parents to split up?"

"Cassie's illness ripped them apart. I love my Dad but he's something of a good-time Charlie. When the going got tough, Dad got going. Don't get me wrong. He stayed in our lives. We saw him every other weekend and a month in the summer but he couldn't handle serious stuff. He's still that way at fifty. I don't think he's ever going to grow up."

"You kept everyone grounded."

"Somebody had to."

"You're pretty amazing, Maddie Cooper. You know that?"

His words warmed her to the very back of her heart and she felt her throat tighten. She glanced out the window into the darkness so he couldn't see the mist of a tear in her eye. It had been a rough day and she was feeling a little emotional.

"Know what else I like about you?" he whispered.

"What?" She smiled faintly. Her cheeks tingled. God, she was actually blushing.

"You're strong and smart and thoughtful. You can be a little hardheaded at times, but so can I. You have a really sly sense of humor that slaps my funny bone. You're honest, trustworthy and dependable."

"You make me sound like a Boy Scout."

"Believe me, babe," he drawled and raked an appreciative gaze over her body. "There's nothing boyish about you."

Babe. He'd called her babe. She went all whooshy

inside. Don't smile for gosh sakes, Maddie. He'll think you like his flattery.

Trouble was, she *did* like it. A lot.

"Are you flirting with me, Agent Marshall?" She slanted him a coy glance that was pure Cassie.

Their gazes locked. Wow-o-wow-o-wow. The heat from his intelligent dark gray eyes toasted her from the inside out. She stared into him, he stared right back.

Everything faded from her mind. Cassie, Shriver, the stolen art. Her past, their future.

Nothing mattered except the breathtaking electricity of the moment. The emotion on his face was intense and knocked her off balance. She saw so many things reflected in those eyes. Desire, confusion, curiosity.

David took her hand.

She wanted to draw back. She should have drawn back, but she was so tired and his hand felt so good that she just sat there, staring at his fingers. He had very nice fingers. Long and strong and comforting.

Watch out! You know better than to trust him. He's a cop and your sister is a suspect.

He angled his head toward her. "Would you be upset if I was flirting with you?"

"I don't know."

"It's not professional of me."

"No."

He leaned closer. "I shouldn't be doing this."

"Not at all," she murmured, moving in his direction.

"We really can't depend on this attraction," he said, inching his mouth ever closer to hers.

"Absolutely not," she agreed, her gaze trained on his lips.

"The timing, the situation, it's all wrong." He was barely whispering.

"Couldn't be worse." She shifted her gaze from his lips to his eyes and her heart almost jumped right out of her chest.

"How's your headache?" he asked, reaching over to gingerly rub the spot where the coconut had struck.

What was the protocol in a situation like this? Her dating skills were rusty. Not that this was dating, but it most certainly was a sexual attraction man-woman thing.

His fingers, firm but gentle, probed the tender area. She inhaled his warm masculine scent. Using the pad of his thumb, he massaged her temple in a circular motion with light, steady pressure. It felt so good she almost moaned out loud.

"Relax," he murmured. "Just relax."

Yeah, right. How was she supposed to relax when her head was practically nestled on his shoulder and those devastating lips were oh so close?

"That's right, Maddie, let go."

And the next thing she knew, they were kissing.

She couldn't say who made the first move. Maybe it was him, maybe it was her. Bottom line? It didn't matter. They were swept away like flotsam on the sea.

Closing her eyes, she savored the warmth of his mouth, oblivious to their surroundings. Her head reeled from the intoxicating power. His kiss was a thousand times more wonderful than the fantasies she'd been spinning.

He kissed her as if he couldn't get enough, drinking her in, teasing her with his tongue. He used just the right amount of pressure. The kiss wasn't too demanding, nor was it too plain. Not too wet, but moist and hot and perfect.

Then again, what else would she have expected from a man with such raw animal magnetism. She'd bet her last dollar that sex with him would be phenomenal.

The pilot turned off the seat belt sign, the faint dinging hardly registering in the back of her mind. She didn't notice that some passengers were moving up and down the aisles, that the flight attendants were serving drinks. She wrapped her arms around his neck and he threaded his fingers through her hair.

They were welded together, singed by the kiss to beat all kisses.

And if it hadn't been for little Katy popping her head over the top of her seat to giggle at them, Maddie feared they would not have stopped kissing until they reached Paris.

Chapter
EIGHT

$\mathcal{D}$AVID NEEDED JAVA. Pronto. A double espresso would be ideal but any variety of caffeine would do the trick. Something strong to wire his system, kick his butt into high gear and buzz his brain so fast he would forget all about the taste of Maddie's lips.

Before they'd left Grand Cayman for Miami, he had contacted Henri Gault, his counterpart at Interpol and asked him to put a surveillance team on Shriver and Cassie when they arrived in Paris. He was itching to get his feet on the ground and his head back into the investigation.

Henri, a reedy man with a thick head of dark hair, an oblong face and sad-sack eyes met them at the arrival gate.

"Why don't you go on through customs?" David nodded at the checkpoint.

He wanted Maddie out of earshot so he could discuss the case privately with Henri. He also hoped to minimize the risk of her spilling his secret. He didn't want anyone else knowing he'd recruited Cassie. As far as Henri knew, Cassie was simply Shriver's doxy, not an unofficial FBI informant turned art thief accomplice.

"You're not coming through customs with me?" Maddie asked.

He pulled his badge from his pocket. "I get to circumvent."

"Can't you circumvent me?"

"Nope," he said at the same time Henri said, *"Oui."*

Henri looked at David and he shook his head.

Maddie narrowed her eyes. "This is retribution for me swiping your badge back in Dallas, isn't it?"

"Payback's a bitch." He wiggled his fingers. "Bye, bye."

She glared, shouldered her bag and headed for the long customs line.

Henri glanced from David to Maddie and smirked. David knew what the Frenchman was thinking. "She's not my mistress."

"Then she's fair game, *non?*" Henri wriggled his eyebrows suggestively.

"No. Stay away from her if you prize your neck."

"Ooh-la-la." Henri laughed. "It must be *amour.*"

"No it's not," he denied hotly. "She's Cassie Cooper's sister."

"And you let her come along with you?"

"It was either that or have her running around on her own getting into trouble. This way I can keep her under my thumb."

"As long as your thumb is the only thing you keep her under."

"Shut up."

Henri laughed and escorted him around customs. On

the other side of the barricade crowds of travelers streamed past them. They moved to one side of the walkway, waiting for Maddie to clear the inspection.

"So what's the scoop on Shriver?" David asked, resting his shoulder against the wall.

"We followed him from the airport. He's staying at the Hotel de Louvre."

"Pricey digs."

"Shriver is poetic, not subtle."

"And Cassie Cooper?"

"She's not with him."

"Huh?" David squared his posture. "What do you mean she's not with him?"

"He was alone, *mon ami*." Henri shrugged. "Cassie Cooper went to Madrid."

David ran a hand over his jaw. It was scratchy with beard stubble. He hadn't shaved in two days. "You're sure?"

"Positive."

"Do we have anyone tracking her?"

Henri nodded. "Yes, we have a man on it."

"Good work." David took a deep breath and relaxed. This was an encouraging sign. Cassie's absence in Paris meant she probably was just Shriver's girlfriend and not his partner-in-crime as David had feared.

That tidbit of information should make Maddie happy.

And then a thought occurred to him. What if he could find a way to take advantage of this identical twin stuff? He had mistaken Maddie for Cassie on the jogging path. Under the right circumstances, Shriver might easily make the same mistake. Maybe David could find a way to use Maddie to entrap the art thief. Instinctively, he knew she would never go for it. The minute Maddie found out

Cassie was in Madrid, she would hop the next plane to Spain and to hell with him.

You just can't tell her yet, the pitchfork-toting devil on his left shoulder announced.

David, chided the halo-sporting angel on his right shoulder. *You can't do that to Maddie. She's placed her trust in you.*

Trust, schmust. You wanna catch Shriver, don'tcha? Ignore goody-two-shoes and keep your trap shut, the devil urged.

Angel be damned. The devil made a lot more sense.

"Do me a favor, Henri, and don't tell Maddie her sister went to Madrid."

"Ah, I understand. You're trying to protect her."

"Uh . . . yeah . . . sure. That's it."

"Whatever you want," Henri murmured. "So we're assuming Shriver came to Paris to make amends with Jerome Levy. I've got a team on both Shriver and Levy by the way."

At the mention of Levy's name, David grit his teeth. For years he'd suspected Levy was the one who'd brokered the theft of Aunt Caroline's Rembrandt, but he'd never been able to prove it. He would love to bust Levy almost as much as he would enjoy busting Shriver.

"How else is Shriver going to unload the Cézanne if not through his old pal Levy? I cut off his connection with Philpot. There aren't too many brokers willing to fence a painting that hot."

"Shriver is taking a big chance showing up here," Henri continued. "He knows we're watching him. Why not lie low, sell the painting later?"

"I'm breathing down his neck hot and heavy, making things pretty uncomfortable. He doesn't want to get caught with the Cézanne in his possession. Circumstances are forcing him to take chances he wouldn't ordinarily take."

"Or maybe," Henri mused, "he's fallen in love with Cassie Cooper and this was his last big score before giving up a life of crime for his lady love."

"You French with the romance. Is that all you think about?" David snorted.

"One day, *mon ami*, love will hit you too," Henri predicted slyly.

"Hit who with what?" Maddie asked, arriving on the tail end of their conversation.

"Nothing," David lied, but he couldn't deny the intense awareness that smacked him in the gut whenever he looked into her eyes.

It's just lust. Nothing else, he told himself.

"I know what you're up to, Marshall," she said.

"I'm not up to anything." For one strange moment David had thought she was talking about the sexual fantasies wreaking havoc with his imagination.

"What have you been saying behind my back?" Maddie poked him in the chest with her index finger. "I know that's why you made me go through customs. You're hiding something from me about Cassie. What is it?"

The woman loved busting his chops. And the bizarre thing was, he respected her for it. Most people didn't have the courage to call him on the carpet. They bought into his bluster and let him have his way.

But that insistent index finger tapping his chest and the determined expression on her face stopped him in his tracks.

And damn if Henri wasn't snickering.

"The truth," Maddie demanded.

How in the hell did she know he was lying? Her perceptiveness knocked him off balance.

Turn the tables on her. Quick. Anything to wrestle back control and keep from feeling guilty.

"I'm offended," he said.

"Offended?"

"That you would impugn my character."

"Ha! It would be easier to offend a polecat, Agent Marshall."

Was she calling him a skunk? Man, but the woman was sharp with those zingers.

Henri guffawed. David glared at his friend.

Maddie eyed him speculatively. "You swear you're not keeping anything from me."

"Scouts honor." He raised two fingers, held her gaze and tried his best to look guileless.

"Were you ever a Boy Scout?"

"No. It's a symbolic gesture."

"You wouldn't betray my trust, would you David?" She sank her hands on her hips.

"Who me?"

That's it, the devil egged. *Lay it on thick.*

For shame. The angel clucked his tongue.

Hey, David justified himself. An FBI agent occasionally had to make a few moral judgment calls in order to score an arrest. And if catching Shriver meant delaying the truth from Maddie for a little while longer, he'd take his lumps like a man.

Because nothing, absolutely nothing, meant more to him than arresting the art thief. Bringing Shriver in meant far more than seeing justice done or evening the score for his aunt. It meant he was a winner.

At that moment, the two-way radio clamped at Henri's

belt loop squawked. Henri answered in rapid-fire French. David had trouble keeping up with the conversation.

"What is it?" Maddie asked when Henri finished speaking and turned to look at them.

"Both Shriver and Levy are on the move," Henri explained. "Shriver left his hotel carrying something large and flat and wrapped in brown paper."

"The Cézanne," David guessed.

"It looks as if they are about to make the exchange."

"What about my sister?" Maddie asked. "Is she with Shriver?"

"No," Henri answered. "He is alone."

David rubbed his hands together. "Let's hit 'em."

They crowded into Henri's Cooper Mini—Henri and David up front, Maddie crammed into the back seat—and careened through the cobblestone streets, siren blaring. Henri's chase team gave him frequent updates over the two-way radio, as they played fox and hound with Levy.

Maddie was frustrated with her inability to speak French. She was desperate to know what was happening. And where was Cassie anyway?

After the last update, David glanced at Maddie in the rearview mirror. She met his gaze. "What?"

"Levy's headed up the Eiffel Tower."

"Shriver is going to hand off a valuable Cézanne at a crowded tourist spot? Seems pretty risky to me," she said.

David shrugged. "Maybe he's thinking it's better to hide in plain sight."

"Or maybe he's afraid to meet Levy in private," Henri suggested. "He did double-cross the man."

She curled her fingers into the seat cushion and managed

to restrain herself from telling Henri to drive faster. She wanted Shriver in custody and her sister found.

"Cassie's okay," David said.

He was still studying her in the rearview mirror and that, along with the fact he'd just read her mind, unnerved Maddie.

"You don't know that. Shriver could have killed her."

"If he was going to kill her he would have done it in Grand Cayman, not paid for her ticket to Europe."

He was right, but Maddie couldn't stop imagining the worst.

Henri turned off the siren as they neared the Eiffel Tower. He made radio contact with his crew who told him Levy was headed for the top but they were holding off, waiting for Henri.

They parked, jumped out of the car and jogged toward the base of the Eiffel Tower. A swish of tires and the rumble of engines arose as vehicles passed them on the street. Henri was on the radio, contacting the team tailing Shriver.

"Where is our target now?" Henri asked. The radio crackled an answer.

Maddie moved closer to David. "What did Henri's man say?"

"Shriver's headed east on the Champs-Elysées. Coming straight toward us."

Her heart skipped. Startled she realized the irregular rhythm wasn't from fear, but from excitement. The same sort of excitement that had suffused her when she'd trained for the Olympics.

"Omigosh," she said. "We're about to catch him."

"Feels good, doesn't it?" David's eyes glowed, his excitement clearly matching her own.

The look they shared was magnetic, drawing Maddie deeper into David's world. She gulped, both invigorated and unnerved by the sensation.

Henri flashed his badge at the ticket booth and they scooted on through.

"The stairs will be quicker," Henri called over his shoulder and skirted around the huddle of tourists waiting for the elevator.

They took the stairs two at a time. The weather was a damp gray drizzle and the brisk breeze chapped Maddie's cheeks. But she didn't care. They were about to nab Shriver and this Levy person. Once Shriver was in custody, she would find out what he'd done with Cassie.

She caressed the half-a-heart necklace hanging against her chest. *Hang in there, Cassie. I'm coming to save you.*

Without meaning to give in to her fears, Maddie found herself visualizing her sister bound and gagged in a dark closet somewhere. Her heart thumped. She clenched her fists, bit on her bottom lip.

"Stop imagining the worst," David said as they topped the stairs and exited to the second floor platform. "Cassie is fine."

How in the world did he know that's what she'd been thinking? The man was uncanny.

Henri was on the radio again. "They've got Levy in sight," he repeated for Maddie's benefit. "He's waiting at the top."

"And Shriver?"

"Heading this way."

From the second floor they were forced to take the elevator to the top. Luckily, in late February, the tourist crowd was fairly sparse. Henri displayed his badge and moved them to the head of the line but Maddie couldn't help feeling frustrated as they waited for the elevator to arrive. Any other day she would love to visit the Eiffel Tower, but today all she wanted was to get this over with. By the time they reached the top of the tower she was breathless from anxiety.

"Do you see him?" she whispered to David.

"Don't look now but Levy is standing about a hundred feet to the left. He's wearing a red beret and a black leather jacket." David slipped his arm around Maddie and pressed his lips against her ears.

She tensed.

"Pretend we're honeymooning tourists taking in the sights," he whispered.

"What for?" she whispered back, disconcerted by his nearness.

"It's our cover story."

"Like someone is going to ask?"

"Let's just stand over here in the corner, with our backs to the elevator. I don't want Shriver to recognize us and blow the whole sting. I might even have to kiss you if he comes our way."

"Kiss me?" Her voice sounded as shaky as her insides felt.

"Yeah, you know. As a dodge."

"Oh yeah." Was that all?

"Look honey," he said loudly as he guided her to the corner. "You can see the Arc de Triomphe from here."

David used his tall body to shield her from the brunt of the wind blowing up the tower. "You're cold," he murmured where only she could hear.

She *was* cold but that wasn't why she was trembling.

David took off his trench coat and draped it over her shoulders. Then, he put his arm around her again and drew her close to his side, his body heat merging with hers.

She shouldn't have enjoyed the hard feel of his arm against her waist. She shouldn't have noticed how nice he smelled or how his beard stubble scratched lightly at her earlobe. She shouldn't have been stunned by the considerate loan of his coat.

But damn her, she was.

"Do you think it's safe for me to try and get a look at this Levy character?" she asked.

Maddie needed to do something, anything to get her mind off David's proximity and back on the situation at hand.

"Just don't be too obvious about it."

"Where did Henri go?"

"He and his men are taking cover on the other side of that group of Japanese tourists."

Cautiously, Maddie glanced around, pretending she was taking in the sights. To her left, she spotted Henri smoking a cigarette beside two other men. When she turned her head to look over her shoulder, she spied the man in the beret and leather jacket. He was glancing at his watch and frowning.

Where was Shriver?

The elevator door dinged open.

David took her into his arms. Her pulse quickened.

Their eyes met.

And then he was kissing her.

For one breathtaking moment she couldn't even remember what they were doing on the Eiffel Tower. All she could think about was the pressure of his mouth on hers.

Her knees went weak. Even through the layers of his

clothing, she could feel the heavy beating of his heart. In spite of the cold, he felt blisteringly hot and wonderfully solid against her body.

David pulled his lips away but crushed her in his embrace. "Watch the people getting off the elevator," he whispered, yanking her back to reality.

"Okay."

"Do you see Shriver?"

She scanned the group stepping off. All she had to identify Shriver by was the photograph they'd found in Cassie's locker. If he'd changed his look, she wouldn't recognize him. But he was supposedly carrying the Cézanne in brown paper wrapping. That should make him much easier to spot.

But no one in this crowd was carrying anything that remotely resembled a priceless work of art.

"No," she whispered back. "But there's a bald, pock-marked man of about thirty going over to talk to Levy. He's wearing a leather jacket and skull and cross bone tattoos, numerous body piercings and wearing hobnailed boots."

David inhaled audibly.

She looked into his face, saw a grim expression furrowing his forehead. What? She telegraphed him the question with her eyes.

He shook his head and then covertly, they both peeked at the dude deep in conversation with Levy.

"Shit," David hissed.

"What is it? What's happening?" Maddie asked just as Henri appeared at David's elbow. She splayed a hand against her throat, felt her pulse flutter frantically.

"That's Jocko Blanco," David muttered.

At the very same moment Henri said, "My crew tells

me Shriver went into the Louvre. He's opened the package he was carrying. It's not the Cézanne, but a sketchpad."

"Shit," David repeated himself. "Shit, shit, shit."

"What's happening?" Maddie asked, fear a rock in her throat.

"I was wrong. Shriver didn't come here to fence the Cézanne to Levy," David said grimly. "He's come to rob the Louvre!"

Chapter

NINE

"How do you know he's going to rob the Louvre?" Maddie whispered.

"It's part of Shriver's MO. He goes to a targeted museum ostensibly to sketch paintings, but what he's really doing is casing the security system," David explained. "The painting he sketches is the one he eventually steals. Then he always leaves the sketch behind at the scene."

"So he enjoys taunting you."

"Yeah." David grit his teeth. To Henri he said, "Are your men able to see what painting Shriver is sketching?"

Henri passed the question on to his team over the two-way radio and waited for the answer. He made a sour face. "You're not going to believe it."

"Let me take a wild guess. The Mona Lisa."

Henri nodded. "Surely even Shriver isn't that daring."

"Who knows what that crazy sonofabitch is capable of? All I know is that he's *not* going to get away with it this time."

After ten years of having his failure flaunted in his

face, David was past the point of no return. It was now or never. Shriver was going down. Already a plan was hatching in his head. A plan to exploit Maddie's resemblance to her absent twin.

"What about Levy and Blanco?" Henri asked, inclining his head in their direction. The two men were still absorbed in conversation, apparently unaware that just a few feet away they were being observed by Interpol and the FBI.

"Let's step back and regroup for now. But keep the surveillance team on Levy and add a man to watch Blanco."

"It's done," Henri said. "Do you suppose they are in on this heist with Shriver?"

"Either that or they're plotting revenge for the double-cross on the Cézanne. Engrossed as they are, it very well could be the latter."

"What about Cassie?" Maddie interrupted, nibbling her bottom lip and fidgeting in her handbag for some Rolaids.

"Yeah, well . . ." David scratched his beard-roughened chin. "There's something I need to discuss with you."

She folded her arms over her chest and narrowed her eyes at him. "So talk."

"Not here. Let's go grab some lunch and we'll discuss it over a beer."

"It's four-thirty in the afternoon."

"Okay, so it's an early dinner." He cupped his hand under her elbow and headed for the elevator, but she balked.

"I don't care about food. I want to find my sister."

"We'll get to that. I promise. In the meantime, you

need to keep up your strength or you won't be any good to anyone."

That convinced her.

"Nothing fancy," she said. "Let's just eat and get on with it."

"There's an English style pub that serves fish and chips a couple of blocks from here."

"Sounds perfect."

The pub was dim and smoky. The smell of nicotine had David itching for a cigarette. He asked for a table in the back. They selected the fish and chips over the steak and kidney pie and David ordered a pint of Guinness.

"Want a beer?"

Maddie shook her head. "I don't drink much."

"Well if ever there was a time to imbibe, it's now. We're tired, frustrated and road weary. A drink might just take the edge off."

"You've got a point." To the waitress she said, "Crown Royal, neat."

"Whoa." No wonder the woman ate antacids like candy.

"I figure if I'm going to drink I might as well go for the gusto," she said.

"Gusto is one thing. A coma is something else."

"One shot of whisky isn't going to put me in a coma."

What the hell? Why not join her? It had been a long time since he'd sipped whisky. "I'll have a Crown Royal too."

"Now," Maddie said, once the waitress had departed. "Where do we stand?"

David studied her across the table. In the darkly lit room her hair was a richer blonde. Her lips glistened moistly from where she'd wet them with the tip of her tongue. Watching her gave him a shiver clear to the bottom of his spine.

She tucked a strand of hair behind her right ear and he caught a glimpse of an opal earring nestled in her lobe. He wondered if she had any idea how beautiful she was.

The waitress returned with their drinks. David took a sip of whisky and grimaced as the velvety smooth burn traveled down his throat. Maddie circled the rim of her glass with her index finger.

Around and around.

Mesmerized, David watched her fingers stroke the glass and he couldn't keep himself from imagining what it would feel like to have her drawing those same luxurious circles on his bare skin.

"So what happens next?" she asked.

"Um, that's exactly what I wanted to talk to you about." How was he going to get this topic started?

"I'm listening," she said.

He held up his palms. "What I'm about to tell you is going to piss you off, but I want you to hear me out before you go ballistic. Can you do that?"

Maddie picked up her glass and in one long swallow chugged the whiskey without even blinking.

David winced, amazed. Not one to be bested by anyone, much less a woman in a drinking competition, he gulped the rest of his whisky too.

"All right. Lay it on me," she said at the same time the waitress brought their fish and chips. "Oh and could I have another Crown Royal, please."

"Yes, miss. What about you, sir?"

"Make mine a double," he said, deliberately holding Maddie's gaze.

"Me too." She did not look away.

"Two doubles. I'll just pop round to the bar and fetch it for you," the waitress said.

Maddie dug into her fish with gusto, sprinkling the fried pollock with malt vinegar. He liked watching her eat. There was something incredibly sensual in the way her pink tongue darted out to whisk away crumbs from her lips.

David got so caught up in her process he forgot what he was supposed to be doing. He felt nice and warm from the whisky and he was enjoying the buzz.

"Go ahead," she said. "I'm listening. Piss me off."

This wasn't going to be fun, but he wasn't one to beat around the bush. "Cassie's not in Paris."

She stopped with a French fry half way to her mouth. "What?"

"Cassie's not in Paris," he repeated.

"Where is she?"

He cleared his throat. "Madrid."

"What?" Maddie asked so low and controlled he knew she was way more than pissed off. If looks could kill, he would have had forty stab wounds and a gunshot hole or ten.

"Shriver came to Paris. Cassie went to Madrid."

"How long have you known this?" She put the French fry down on her plate and fisted her hand.

She wants to punch me something awful.

Why that thought should charge his sexual engines, David had no clue, but it did.

"Since we landed."

"I see." She clenched her jaw. "I promised to hear you out before losing my temper. Go ahead. Tell me why you deceived me."

"I thought we were about to nab Shriver passing off

the Cézanne to Levy and I knew you would demand to go to Madrid immediately if I told you."

"Darn straight."

He steepled his fingertips. "Here's the deal. I'm working out a plan to entrap Shriver and I need your help. In exchange, I promise to see that all charges against Cassie are dropped."

"There wouldn't be any charges in the first place if you hadn't recruited her. You're responsible for this." She was struggling to control her anger. He could see it in the jumpy pulse fluttering at her throat and the way she carefully enunciated each word.

"I didn't force her to run off with Shriver."

"She was an unwilling victim."

"If that's the case, why is she in Madrid while Shriver is here?"

He had her on that one. Maddie glared and folded her arms over her chest. "Cassie did not steal the Cézanne."

"The folks at the Kimbell don't see it that way."

"And neither do you."

"I'm offering you a chance to get your sister off the hook, scot free. Help me catch Shriver and we'll forget all about Cassie." David leaned back in his chair, watching her face and praying she would agree to his scheme.

The waitress set their drinks in front of them and Maddie polished off the double whisky as if it was Kool-Aid. She set her glass down and ordered another double.

"Don't you think you better slow down?"

She looked pointedly at his glass. "I think if you want to convince me to go along with your scheme you better keep up with me drink for drink."

"Is this a challenge?"

She shrugged.

Damn but the woman was dynamite. He didn't appreciate being goaded into drinking too much but he hated looking like a lightweight. He tossed the whisky down his throat and forced himself not to make a face at the acrid curl of heat spiraling down his throat. Or at the way his brain bobbled.

"He'll have another double, too," Maddie said to the agog waitress.

David's vision swam momentarily, but he shook it off. Maddie was watching him like the proverbial canary-eating cat. She thought he was a wuss. Well, he was beginning to think she was the queen of boozers. Who'd have thought a cautious, worrywart possessed such a high tolerance for hooch?

Never mind. He could handle this. Focus, concentrate. He blinked at her and smiled.

She smiled back and coyly lowered her eyelids. Was she feeling as sexy as he was? His heart thumped. He couldn't help but notice how well she filled out that print shirt. He chided himself for noticing but he couldn't stop sneaking covert peeks.

"Okay," he said, struggling to get his tongue in gear without slurring his words. "Here's the plan. I want you to impersonate Cassie. That shouldn't be too hard for you. We'll just get you sexier clothes."

At the thought of Maddie prancing around in the skimpy outfits Cassie preferred, David's temperature soared. But if his plot was going to work, Shriver had to believe Maddie was her twin sister. And Cassie wore tight skirts, super high heels and belly baring blouses.

"What else?" She cocked her head and eyed him speculatively.

Funny, she didn't seem the least bit impaired from

downing three double shots of whisky in less than fifteen minutes.

"Shriver is staying at the Hotel de Louvre. Henri's team still has him under strict surveillance. We want you to go to his hotel room, pretending to be Cassie and tell him you found out the digital signature code that will shut down the alarm system at the Louvre from your friend who works at the Prado. The Prado and the Louvre now have the same security system so he'll believe you."

"Then what?"

"You and Shriver will break into the Louvre and steal the Mona Lisa together."

"You're asking me to commit a crime?"

"Under the auspices of Interpol and the FBI. We'll let you get away and then swoop down when Shriver passes the art off to Levy."

"How do you know he'll pass the art off to Levy?"

"Because," David said, "before you go see Shriver, you'll call Levy, pretending to be this fabulously wealthy countess referred to him by a mutual collector who wants a bargain for a very special work of art for her daughter's birthday. Levy knows exactly where to go for such a unique gift."

"Shriver."

"You got it."

"Don't you think Levy will be suspicious after we tailed him to the Eiffel Tower? He's got to know he's under surveillance."

"Levy's always under surveillance. He's the biggest art fence in Europe. He expects it. All part of his usual routine."

"I dunno." She shook her head.

"About what?"

"I can't trust you. You turned against my sister, how do I know you won't do it again?"

"Your sister was the one who turned, not me."

"Who knows, maybe I'll fall madly in love with Shriver too."

She enjoyed yanking his chain. If he hadn't been on the verge of drunkenness, he would have realized it sooner. He decided to ignore that last remark.

"Here's the bottom line. Help us catch Shriver and your sister goes free. Don't help and she's right back to being an accomplice."

"There's one other option," Maddie said as the waitress set down the fresh round of drinks. She lifted her glass to his. "Bottoms up."

If it took getting plastered to seal this deal with her, then he would do it. David raised his whisky. "Cheers."

They toasted and swallowed their drinks in unison.

He had trouble getting it down. His gut was asking him what in hell he was doing as his brain went wee-hee! He was dizzy and hot. He needed to go to the bathroom but he was afraid to stand up.

Maddie sat across from him, a calm smile on her face. His vision blurred. He wanted to tell her how pretty she was but it came out like, "Youm a berry bootipul wooman."

"One more." She leaned forward and pressed her lips against his ear and whispered. "You drink one more double shot with me and I'll go along with your plan to impersonate Cassie and rob the Louvre with Shriver."

"Okey-dokey." He felt sloppy happy. Maybe she was planning on taking him back to their hotel and having her way with him. He certainly wasn't opposed.

Maddie motioned for the waitress to bring them another set of drinks and a few minutes later, she brought over the double shots.

"Down the hatch," Maddie murmured.

Hell, he didn't know if he could even get the glass to his lips. Where were his lips by the way? They were tingly numb.

He watched the column of Maddie's throat move as she dispatched the final shot.

Are you a man or a mouse? That irritating devil voice that got him in so much trouble whispered.

With considerable effort, David raised the glass to his lips, closed his eyes and knocked the whisky back. "Ahh."

Maddie's mouth twitched and he realized she was trying not to laugh.

"Whassso funny?" he slurred.

"Remember I said there was one more option?"

He nodded. Or at least he thought he nodded. "Whaz-zat?"

"Drink you under the table, go to Madrid, retrieve my sister and head home to the States."

"You can't drink me unner the table." He wobbled in his chair.

"I think I already have."

"Uh-huh." He pushed back his chair and staggered to his feet. "See. I perrrfetly fine."

"Yeah, you're fine." She got up and picked up her shoulder bag.

"Hey," he said, trying to point a finger at her but his frickin' finger wouldn't hold still. "Where ya goin'?"

She waved and headed for the door.

"Wait." He charged after her, only to have the floor rise up to meet his face.

He hit the wood with a resounding thunk. If he hadn't stuck out a hand to break his fall he probably would have fractured his skull. He ended up staring at a French fry squashed on the floor next to his nose.

Maddie squatted down beside him.

"Oh," she said. "Maybe I forgot to tell you. The reason I don't often drink alcohol is because I have a mutant metabolic disorder of the liver enzymes. I can drink all the liquor I want and I never even get buzzed, so what's the point? Well, unless you're trying to drink some smart-assed guy under the table."

He groaned.

"And remember what you told me at the airport? Payback really *is* a bitch."

She rose to her feet and swished away before David could reach out and grab her ankle.

And just before he passed out he heard her tell the waitress, "He'll be paying the bill."

If David hadn't lied to her, Maddie would have felt bad about drinking him under the table. He wasn't the first man she'd bested in a tippling contest, but he was the only one she hadn't told about her metabolic condition beforehand.

Of course, if he hadn't lied to her, she would have had no reason to drink him under the table.

She'd discovered her dubious gift quite by accident. In college, Cassie got buzzed on one shot of tequila, but Maddie could down the whole bottle, including the worm and not get the least bit soused. The handy talent had earned her a few dare bucks when she was twenty-one, but since then, she'd never exploited her talent.

Until now.

Maddie marched to their hotel, head held high. Once in her room, she checked the transportation schedule and ended up booking the next supersonic train to Madrid. She had a little less than an hour to pack and get to the station. By the time David roused himself from his Crown Royal stupor, Maddie would already be in Spain.

For the sake of time, she eschewed the elevator and hurried down the stairs. She had a map of Paris in one hand, her carry-on in the other.

Imagine! David Marshall actually thinking she'd go along with his crazy scheme to nail Shriver by pretending to be her sister.

At least he has a lot of confidence in you.

Bullshit. The man had just been desperate.

She hurried through the cobblestone square, past a gorgeous fountain. It was already dark and the lights had come on, bathing the city in a festive glow.

On the steps of the Louvre, a group of sightseers in mittens and parkas stood in a semicircle, observing something. Maddie cut around them and discovered they were watching a mime.

She shuddered. She hated mimes. She found their silent gesturing menacing.

This mime wore a top hat with red wig springing out from underneath. His face was made-up with the traditional white grease paint and he wore black trousers with wide suspenders. His black shirt was slashed with white horizontal stripes. A CD player spinning Parisian cabaret torch songs sat at his feet. He had a blanket spread out to collect the coins people tossed.

Pathetic way to make a living. To avoid walking in front of him, Maddie veered to the left.

And the mime shuffled in front of her, blocking her path.

Maddie gave him a quick, tolerant smile that said, *Hey, dude. Even though I have no respect for what you do, that doesn't mean we can't both coexist. Now get the hell out of my way.*

She sidestepped.

He followed. The serious expression on his face never changed.

Maddie ducked her head, feinted left but zipped right.

He wasn't faked out.

She cleared her throat and spoke one of the few phrases in French that she knew. *"Excusez moi."*

He didn't budge. In fact, he cocked his head as if she was from another planet and he was an anthropologist studying her alien behavior.

She stepped to the left again.

And damn if he didn't match her movements exactly.

Why was the freak mocking her? Maddie planted a hand against his sternum and shoved.

He pushed back with his chest.

The stupid crowd loved it. They were clapping and cheering him on.

"Get out of my way," she insisted.

Silently, he aped her words, all the while creating dramatic sweeping gestures with his arms.

She jumped right and darted forward but he ran backward, staying directly in front of her. Somewhere, a clock chimed the hour. Six elongated chimes. The train left at six-twenty and the station was over a mile away. She'd have to hail a taxi in order to make it.

Hurry, hurry, you don't have time for this.

The mime sank his hands on his hips and flounced

prissily, wagging his head back and forth and shaking his behind.

Angered, she dropped her suitcase and took a kick-boxing stance. "Come on dude, I've taken down one arrogant man today, I have no trouble making it two."

He mimed her. Fisting his hands and raising them in mirror image of hers. He gave a taunting smile.

The crowd roared with laughter.

Maddie's cheeks flamed with shame. Oh this was too much. Being humiliated by an annoying mime.

Maybe there was a policeman nearby. She glanced around but didn't see one. Typical.

The mime stared at her chest and narrowed his eyes. Pervert.

And then he made the grandest *faux pas* of all. He reached out, ran his hand over Maddie's half-a-heart necklace and tugged on it.

The delicate chain snapped.

Now his behavior made sense. It was just a ploy to steal her necklace.

Rage suffused her. Nobody messed with her necklace. Growling, hands in attack position, Maddie launched herself at the mime.

She tackled him like a defensive end sacking a quarterback. They fell to the ground together. She sat on his chest and wrapped her hands around his neck. With each word, she pounded his head against the stone steps.

"Give." Pound.

"Me." Pound.

"Back." Pound.

"My." Pound.

"Necklace." Pound.

The crowd gasped.

Maddie felt a fist at the nape of her neck. Someone grasped her by her collar and yanked her off the dazed mime. "Stop it right now, before you murder Marcel Marceau."

"He stole my necklace," she howled, arms flailing. She was prepared to fight anyone and everyone for that necklace.

"Maddie," David's voice broke through her bloodlust and she realized he was the someone who'd pulled her off the mime. "Is this what you're battling for?"

She spun around to look at him. His knees were wobbling like a top, his eyes were bloodshot and he reeked of whisky, but in his hand he was clutching her necklace.

"Yeah. He ripped it off my neck," she said breathlessly and turned back to point an accusing finger at the mime.

But the guy was already gone. All they could see was the top hat and red wig dashing away through street traffic.

Chapter

TEN

Something about the mime niggled at him, but David was too drunk to recognize what it was and too late to confront the guy head on. He was long gone.

But Maddie was right here. In his grasp. He wasn't about to let her escape again.

David pulled handcuffs from his pocket. Before his intent had time to register, he quickly clamped one end around Maddie's right wrist and the other end around his left. He had to manacle her to him. If she decided to bolt and run, he was in no condition to pursue her.

"Hey!" Maddie protested, alarm in her eyes. "Hey!"

The crowd applauded.

She stuck out her tongue at them.

They jeered.

"Come on." David jerked her in the direction of the hotel where Henri had reserved rooms for them. "Before you start an international incident."

She dug her heels in.

"Don't give me a hard time," he growled, "or I'll let

the crowd at you. You'd be mincemeat in a matter of minutes. The French take their mimes very seriously."

"I'm not going with you."

"Yes you are." It required every bit of strength he could muster to bend down, scoop up her carry-on and drag her in the direction he wanted her to go.

"Nazi."

"Let's not get into the name calling." He was slurring his words, his gut roiled precariously and his head was pounding like a bass drum, but he wasn't about to let her know that. He still couldn't get over the way she'd outsmarted him.

Again.

"Where are you taking me?"

He grit his teeth. "Thanks to your ruthless cunning, I'm not in any shape to plot a *coup* against Shriver tonight. We're going to the hotel so I can sleep off the whisky. But here's how it's gonna go down. In the morning, you're going to Shriver's room, impersonating Cassie, and convincing him to let you help him rob the Louvre. Got it?"

"You think I'm cunning?" She cast him a sideways glance.

"Yes I do," he said and damned if she didn't look inordinately pleased.

He noticed she was no longer resisting him as they walked wrist in wrist up the Champs-Elysées. People were staring at them curiously. He paused a moment to slip his raincoat off his shoulders and slide it down his left arm to hide the handcuffs.

"But," he reminded her, "I also said you were ruthless."

"I'm not ruthless."

"Oh, yeah? What do you call taking advantage of your peculiar metabolism in order to drink a man under the table and then leaving him passed out in a bar? That's not a particularly nice thing to do."

"Neither is lying." She glared.

He might have enjoyed their verbal sparring if he hadn't felt so utterly wretched. As it was, with each word he spoke it seemed as if someone was driving a pickaxe clean through the base of his skull. Each step was a slog through half-set cement. And when he tried to think, his brain shrieked.

All he wanted was to get to the hotel, flop down on the bed and sink into oblivion. He'd worry about Shriver when his drunken toot subsided.

Maddie, however, had totally opposite goals.

"I think we should go to Madrid and get Cassie," she wheedled.

"No."

"Why not?"

"Because you're damned lucky I'm even standing and it's all your fault. You owe me. Big time."

By the grace of God, they arrived at the hotel. David hurried for the door and stumbled over the curb. He would have taken a header for the second time that day if Maddie hadn't tugged him back with the handcuff.

"I see your point," she said.

The trip upstairs was a blur. They reached his room and David set her bag down in the corridor and weaved as he tried to insert the card key.

"What are you doing?" she asked.

"Trying to get into my damned room."

"Aren't you going to uncuff me so I can go to my own room?"

"Hell no." His knees buckled and he fell against the door. He was sinking fast. Only sheer effort of will had carried him this far from the floor of the pub. "You're spending the night with me."

"Alone? In your bed?"

"Don't sound so panicky. Even if I was inclined to molest you, which I'm not, Herman is in a whisky induced coma."

"Herman?"

He glanced at his crotch, then looked at her and arched an eyebrow. Or at least he thought he arched an eyebrow. He really didn't know for sure. He couldn't feel his facial muscles.

"Oh. You named your penis Herman? Wait, don't confirm that, I really don't want to know."

He grinned. "Are you charmed?"

"Hardly."

Again, he reached out to swipe it through the sensor pad but damned if there weren't two of them blending and blurring together. He closed one eye.

Ah, that was better. He leaned forward and almost toppled over again.

"Jeez, you're a menace to society, Marshall. Give me that." Maddie snatched the key card from him and easily opened the door.

He still couldn't believe she was unaffected by the alcohol she'd consumed. The woman was amazing.

Charging over the threshold with Maddie in tow, he made a beeline for the bed and collapsed face down. He was asleep before his head hit the pillow.

Maddie stood at the side of the bed staring down at her heavy tether. David was snoring softly, his face plowed into the bedspread, his left arm raised in the air. His rain-coat stretched across the handcuffs linking them.

Great. She was chained to the sexiest man to ever irritate the bejeezus out of her.

She supposed she deserved this. Her plan had back-fired. Thanks to that stupid mime.

But at least she had the necklace back. Maddie stuck her free hand into her pocket and fisted her fingers around the gold half-heart. The cool feel of it reassured her.

Cassie was okay. At least that's what she kept telling herself.

In the meantime what was she going to do about David?

She couldn't stand here all night, and from the amount of whisky singing through his system, he wasn't likely to move for hours. Then again, he had managed to rouse himself off the floor of the bar and show up just in the nick of time to prevent her from committing first-degree mime-a-cide.

The man had an indomitable will. She'd grant him that.

And he was very cute in a brute force sort of way.

Cocking her head, Maddie studied the logistics of po-sitioning herself on the bed beside him. Why couldn't he have passed out on his back instead of his stomach?

Gingerly, she crawled onto the bed and stretched out on her belly. Cheek pressed into the bedspread, she forced herself to forget those unsavory stories she'd read about hotel bedspreads.

Don't be so persnickety for once, Maddie. Just go with the flow. Cassie's voice popped into her head. *You can't regulate everything in life.*

Ah, but going with the flow was Cassie's forte, not hers. To distract herself, she studied the back of David's head.

He had a nice hairline and she loved the spiky cut. His neck was strong, but not too thick. And he had free-hanging earlobes. She preferred unattached earlobes. They were much nicer for nibbling on than the attached kind.

In that moment, it was all she could do not to prop herself up on her elbow, lean over and take that delectable lobe between her teeth and lightly bite him.

A treacherous heat started in the pit of her stomach and spread outward.

Good grief!

What was the matter with her? She was better off thinking about bedspread stains instead of this push-pull of attraction that made her want to kick him off the bed at the same time she yearned to cuddle him.

This was whacky. She was going to stop thinking all together. She was just going to close her eyes and go to sleep.

Yeah. Right.

How come her eyes were still open?

She toed off her Nikes and they fell, plop, plop, to the floor, all the while her gaze tracked from David's neck to his broad shoulders to the slope of his ribcage.

Even through the material of his shirt, she could detect the honed ridges of his muscles.

Ach! Go to sleep.

She eased his coat up the handcuff and used it to drape her shoulder, as much to put a barrier between them as to keep warm. She wasn't afraid he was going to try and jump her bones in the night. He was out. No, what she really feared was that her own fingers would betray her and go exploring in places they had no business exploring.

The scent of him teased her nostrils and stormed her imagination. His smell resurrected the memory of last night on the plane and the unexpected kisses they'd shared. No kisses had ever moved her the way his did.

Or left her wanting so much more.

Why was she so turned on by him? Why now? This was the totally wrong time in her life. Plus, he was arrogant and high-handed and overly competitive.

And brave and protective and generous.

Face it. You're enjoying this.

Damn her hide, she was. But David must never know.

It had been a very long time since she'd shared a bed with a man and she had forgotten how nice it felt. That's all this sensation was about. David wasn't any more special than any other guy.

Ummm-huh. Sure. Go ahead. Lie to yourself.

Suddenly, the cell phone in David's jacket pocket played the *Dragnet* tune.

"Pssttt, David," she said.

He didn't move.

"Joe Friday's callin'." She raked her fingers lightly over his ribs. "Wake up. It might be Henri with news about Shriver."

He didn't so much as groan.

She bumped his butt with her knees. "Hey, wake up."

What if the phone call was from Cassie?

The second the thought occurred to her, Maddie was fumbling for the phone with her free hand, desperately searching for the pocket.

Don't hang up, don't hang up, don't hang up, she prayed.

At last she found the phone and managed to flip it open one-handedly. "Hello."

"*Bonsoir*, Mademoiselle Cooper," Henri's voice greeted her and Maddie's hopes fell.

"Hello, Henri."

"May I speak to David, please?"

Maddie propped herself on her elbow and stared down at David. Dead to the world. "I'm afraid he's . . . um . . ." She didn't want to rat him out and tell Henri he was drunk. "Indisposed."

"I see."

It sounded as if Henri was struggling not to laugh. What was so funny?

"May I take a message?"

"I just wanted to see if David had convinced you to go along with his plan to entrap Monsieurs Shriver and Levy. Since you're answering his phone, I assume you have agreed. *Mais non?*"

Maddie sighed. It seemed she really didn't have much of a choice. "I haven't decided."

"I understand. Pulling off this deception would take a great deal of courage. Even if David is too stubborn to tell you so himself, I know he would appreciate your assistance. He's been chasing Shriver a very long time but David never gives up. He refuses to accept defeat."

"He's got a lot invested in the outcome of this case, doesn't he?"

"He didn't tell you about his Aunt Caroline?" Henri asked and Maddie realized he was trying to determine the exact nature of her relationship with David.

"No," she admitted.

Henri hesitated. "I'm not sure I should tell you. Most

of it I know only through office gossip. David doesn't talk about himself much."

"If I'm going to do this thing, then I need to know why."

"Good enough," Henri said after a long moment. "Just don't tell David I told you."

"Done."

"David was in college when it happened. He was about to start his junior year as an art history major."

"David majored in art history?"

"Initially, *oui*. But what happened with his Aunt Caroline caused him to go into law enforcement instead."

Maddie had to strain to hear what he was saying. Between Henri's soft French accent and the crackly cell phone static, she didn't want to miss any of the conversation. It sounded as if Henri was about to give her the key to David's vulnerability. And when it came to dealing with the uncompromising David Marshall, the more she understood him, the better.

"That was a big leap," she said, ears pricked, body tensed. "From art history to police work."

"Not really. David was always pulled in two directions. His mother and his aunt came from high society, but over the years the family fortune dwindled to the value of one Rembrandt. David's father was an army intelligence officer. He wanted David to become a soldier, but his mother was dead set against it. His parents were killed when he was twelve or thirteen and he went to live with his Aunt Caroline. She urged him to follow his mother's wishes and become an art dealer."

"I don't see that refined side of him at all," Maddie murmured, her gaze roving over David's sleeping form.

"He looks like a bloodthirsty soldier through and through."

"Ah, don't let his toughness fool you. It takes a long time for him to let down his guard, but he's got a very soft heart."

Henri's words caused Maddie's own heart to go all mushy. The idea that David wasn't all brute strength and arrogant bluster stirred her in a weird way.

"While David was away at college, his aunt met a much younger man through her volunteer association with the Metropolitan Museum of Art. The man romanced her and then stole the Rembrandt right out from under her nose. The painting was meant to fund her retirement and David's inheritance."

"I think I understand. The much younger man was Peyton Shriver."

"*Oui.* Jerome Levy was the broker who commissioned the theft and we're convinced Levy still has the Rembrandt in his vaulted collection."

"All this time David's been trying to catch those two."

No wonder he'd been desperate enough to recruit Cassie as an informant. Maddie already knew David hated to lose and Shriver had given him the slip for almost a decade. That had to burn.

"While Shriver went underground for several years, living off the spoils of the Rembrandt, David became an FBI agent and specialized in art theft detection."

"He wants revenge," Maddie said.

"Justice would be a fairer word. His loyalty to his aunt runs deep. She took him in when he had no one. The poor woman would be penniless if it weren't for the money David sends her every month."

Maddie's heart did another smooshy, whooshy dive.

She wondered how David would react if he knew Henri had spilled his most tender secret.

"Thank you for telling me all this," she said. "It makes a difference."

"No matter how gruff he might seem at times, he is a good man," Henri said.

"I'm beginning to see that."

"So tomorrow you will help us trap Shriver?"

Maddie swallowed hard and moistened her lips. She felt a jolt of adrenaline—part fear and part excitement—surge through her. Could she do it? Could she convince Shriver that she was Cassie and then rob the Louvre with him?

The thought grated against every cautious bone in her body, and yet, she wanted to do this. For her twin sister.

And for David?

"Yes," she told Henri, committing herself to something that scared the wits out of her. "I'll do it."

In the middle of the night, David's brain flung off the Crown Royal-induced fog and started poking at him with a vengeance.

Wake up, screamed his conscience. *You've missed something important.*

Haltingly, his synapses backfired as he tried to recollect what he couldn't quite recall.

He remembered the third double whisky he'd downed at the pub—but just barely. He remembered Maddie stepping over his prostrate body and waltzing out of the pub. He vaguely remembered staggering through the streets of Paris looking for her and finding her attacking a mime.

The mime.

His brain niggled and his gut clenched. Yes. There was something about the mime.

Wake up. Sit up. Get up. This is urgent.

What was it about the damned mime?

The mime had tried to steal Maddie's necklace. The necklace that was the mate to the one Cassie always wore.

No, no, that wasn't it. David struggled to force his eyelids open.

Something about the mime had seemed very familiar but he'd been too busy with Maddie and too drunk to notice it at the time.

David tried to turn over in bed. Maddie groaned beside him.

He froze. What was she doing in his bed?

Had he . . . had they . . . um, done it? He had wanted to make love to Maddie, that was for sure. But he didn't remember doing the deed. If he'd made love to the woman of his dreams, surely he would have remembered that, no matter how much whisky he'd consumed.

He raised his left hand and discovered Maddie's slender wrist was handcuffed to his thick one.

Holy shit, what *had* happened?

Oh yeah.

He'd forgotten he'd handcuffed himself to her to keep her from running off to Madrid without him while he slept off his accidental bender.

They hadn't had wild, kinky, handcuff sex after all. Bummer.

But that was a good thing.

Right?

Forget about sex. Get your mind back on the mime.

Yeah, yeah. What was it about the mime that had

dragged him out of his slumber with a bastard of a headache and a mouth so dry he feared two gallons of water wouldn't quench his thirst?

Think. Think.

He blinked.

Maddie mumbled and moved against him. The touch of her against him sent a thrust of blood to his groin.

"What is it? What's wrong?" she asked. Her hair was tousled, making her look impossibly sexy.

"Where were you standing when you run afoul of that mime?"

"On the steps outside the Louvre. Why?"

"Sonofabitch," he cursed as his mind exploded with the answer he'd been scrambling for. "I had it all wrong."

"Had what all wrong?"

"He didn't come here to rob the Louvre but to case the security system so he could rob the Prado."

"What are you talking about?" Maddie frowned. "I'm not following."

"Don't you see? That was no ordinary mime. That was Peyton Shriver!"

Chapter
❤
ELEVEN

MADDIE FIDGETED IN the dining car of the high-speed train at seven A.M. on Thursday morning while the Spanish countryside zipped past the window. They'd taken the train because the airport was in chaos with delayed flights following a bomb threat. She wore a practical traveling ensemble of loose fitting blue jeans, a long-sleeved red V-neck pullover sweater, her denim jacket and her favorite sneakers. She always felt more in control when she had her Nikes on.

David sat across from her, glowering intently. Between massaging his temple repeatedly and snarling at her over his coffee, she'd figured out his hangover must be pretty damned intense.

Following his three A.M. revelation that had whipped Maddie from a dead sleep, he had called Henri and the three of them had rushed to Shriver's hotel.

Henri's surveillance team had sworn it was impossible for Shriver to have left his hotel room, but when the manager opened the door, they had found a forlorn room service waiter trussed up on the floor in his underwear. Shriver had ordered a Monte Cristo and tea around five o'clock the previous afternoon. When the waiter had arrived with his order, Shriver had bonked the guy on the head with a lamp, stolen his clothes and taken off.

Henri's men checked all out-of-town transportation and discovered Shriver had bought a ticket for the ten P.M. superspeed train to Madrid the night before. David immediately booked seats for himself and Maddie on the next train out.

And now here they were, barreling toward their destiny.

Maddie crossed her legs and then uncrossed them again. She rolled her linen napkin up and then unrolled it. She tapped her foot and drummed her fingers and cleared her throat several times but never said anything. She squeezed and released her abdominal muscles in a series of isometric exercises. She fingered the necklace she'd repaired just before the trip, checking to make sure the clasp Shriver had broken would hold. She mentally prepared herself for any eventuality, but nothing alleviated her escalating trepidation.

A cheese omelet and buttered toast sat in front of her but she was so wound up she couldn't force food into her mouth.

"Eat," David growled and pointed at her plate with his fork. The expression in his eyes was dangerous, edgy, as if he knew what she looked like without her clothes on.

Heat rose to her cheeks and she hopped up from the table, her legs restless to pace the miles ticking down the track and release the nervous sexual energy clogging her brain. "I've got to walk. Clear my head."

"I'll come with you."

"I'll be all right on my own," she said firmly.

"My legs need stretching too."

She wished he would leave her alone. She felt irritable, out of sorts, short-tempered.

Maddie was accustomed to being in control but whenever she got around David, he tried to take the reins. She didn't like his high-handedness. Nor did she care for her occasional odd longing to simply allow him to take over so she didn't have to worry anymore.

"So," David said after they'd traversed the train twice, weaving in and out of the cars packed with people speaking French and Spanish, Portuguese and Italian. "What was your event in the Olympics?"

"You knew I was an Olympian?"

"I ran a background check on you before we left the States," he said.

"Then don't play coy, if you ran a check on me you already know the answer to your question."

"Hundred meter dash. You were very fast."

She raised her chin. "I still am."

"What happened in Atlanta? Why didn't you take home a medal? You were favored to win. How come you never raced again?"

They had come to a stop in the last car. Maddie ducked her head, ostensibly to look at the scenery whizzing by, but she was actually struggling to put on a cool impassive face. She could tell him it was none of his business, but then he would know her failure still bothered her.

He was leaning against the only empty seat at the back of the car, trying to get a peek at her face. They were sandwiched between the lavatory and the exit door and he was scrutinizing her like a quality control examiner giving a pair of panties the thrice-over before tagging an 'inspected by #32' sticker in the waistband.

That irreverent thought stirred a complicated visual of David slipping his rough, masculine fingers inside the waistband of her red cotton bikini briefs.

"Pardon," apologized an elderly Spanish woman with a very generous caboose. The woman tried to squeeze past them on her way to the lavatory. Maddie stepped to one side, David to the other, but the woman's ample bottom got wedged between them.

Maddie inched back, but she ended up stepping on a little boy's foot. He screamed and his mother scolded her in Spanish. Maddie apologized profusely in the same language.

David plunked down in the empty seat. The elderly woman popped free. He reached out, grabbed Maddie by the wrist and pulled her into his lap. He offered the disgruntled mother a disarming smile, then pulled a package of airplane pretzels from his pocket and gave them to the little boy.

"There," he said. "Now everyone's happy."

"Such a little problem solver," Maddie said from her perch on his lap.

"Sarcasm becomes you."

"Just my luck."

"Are you trying to get my goat?"

"Who me?" She wanted to get up, but there was nowhere else to go and continuing to block the aisle seemed perilous.

On the seat beside them sat a blade thin young man in his late teens. He kept eyeing Maddie. David bared his teeth at the kid and wrapped a possessive arm around her waist.

"What are you doing?" she asked.

"Staking my claim."

"What?"

"Relax. It's just for appearances. To keep the locals from getting any funny ideas about feeling you up."

"Thanks for watching after my virtue," she said. "But I'm perfectly capable of slapping grabby hands. I lived in Madrid for a year, remember?"

"Yep, the year you flubbed up in the Olympics," he said. "Speaking of the Olympics, you never did tell me why you quit running."

"I didn't quit running. You met me on the jogging trail, remember?"

"I meant how come you stopped competing?"

She could ignore him, she could tell him to shut up, or she could just tell him the truth and get the man off her back.

The elderly woman meandered back up the aisle. She looked at Maddie sitting on David's lap, winked and murmured the Spanish word for kismet before moving on her way.

Europeans. What a romantic bunch. Good thing Maddie didn't believe in any of that soulmate rot.

"Why not?" David repeated. God, but this guy had a one-track mind.

"I blew it, okay? I choked. I collapsed under pressure. I hesitated and I was lost."

"Funny," he said.

"Funny ha-ha or funny odd?"

"Funny, in I never figured you for a quitter."

"My coach dumped me. He said I didn't have star quality. How do you deal with something like that?"

"You prove him wrong."

Maddie shook her head. "Water under the bridge. I'm too old to compete now. My gym is very successful, I don't need to prove myself to anyone."

"Is that all there is to it?"

"Yes."

"Bullshit. You're kidding yourself."

"How do you mean?" His breath was tickling the back of her neck. She squirmed and tilted her head away from him.

"What about Cassie?"

"What about her?"

"Subconsciously I think you lost the race on purpose. I think you were afraid to win."

"Excuse me, that doesn't make any sense. What does me winning a race have to do with Cassie?" But as non-sensical as his theory was, her pulse quickened.

"Because if you won the gold, you would grow as an athlete and as a person. And if your world expanded and you changed then you might outgrow your role as Cassie's protector." David hooked a finger under her chin and forced her to look him in the eyes. "And you can't handle the thought of losing the role you've clung to since childhood. You've filtered your life through Cassie's experiences. That way, you don't have to get out there and mix it up on your own."

"You are so full of it."

She felt hot and slightly sick to her stomach. She didn't have to sit here and listen to his amateur psycho-analysis. But something inside her resonated with the truth.

Maybe? Yes? Could he be right?

Had she intentionally bungled the race? Did she live vicariously through Cassie while keeping her own life steady and low-key to accommodate her twin? It was a stunning and uncomfortable prospect.

Without any warning, without rhyme or reason, the stress of the past three days took control. She hated the tears welling up behind her eyelids. She was tough and in control and she would not cry in front of him.

It was PMS. That's why she was so emotional. Not because David had just seen straight into her soul.

Leaping from his lap, she turned and barreled into the lavatory behind them.

She should have known he would follow. Before she could get the door slammed, he'd jammed his foot in the opening fast as a smarmy door-to-door salesman.

"Talk to me, Maddie. I want to help."

"Get your foot out of the door, please. I gotta pee," she said.

"You're lying."

"Leave me alone. I'm fine." She sniffled. She caught a glimpse of her face in the mirror mounted over the sink.

The tears had already started to fall. She wiped at her cheeks, desperate to get rid of him and collect herself, but the man was a friggin' bulldozer.

"Nope. I'm staying right here until I know you're all right."

"I don't want or need your sympathy. Don't you get it?"

"I'm thickheaded, so sue me." He shouldered his way into the tiny lavatory with her and slammed the door locked behind him.

They glared, both breathing hard. The train jostled and they careened into each other.

Maddie gulped. She was trapped. There was no room to turn around, nowhere to run.

"Talk to me," he demanded.

She shook her head.

"Okay then, don't talk." He wrapped his arms around her waist and pulled her against him. "Go ahead and cry. Just let it out."

"No," she said stubbornly. "I'm not crying. I don't cry. I'm not a crier."

"Of course you're not."

He gently stroked her hair. She could feel the steady strumming of his heart. In spite of her best intentions, Maddie found herself weeping helplessly on his shoulder.

Dammit!

Why was she so susceptible to this man? How did he seem to know exactly when she was at her most vulnerable? What was it about him that pried her from her defenses in a way no one else ever had?

Pull back. Get away. For heaven's sake, Maddie, stop with the waterworks.

But she did none of those things.

"Look at me."

Reluctantly, she met his gaze.

His eyes locked onto hers and she couldn't look away. No, that wasn't right, she didn't *want* to look away.

She wanted to contradict their reality. She wanted to forget that he was a determined FBI agent and her sister was a robbery suspect. She wanted to ignore the fact they were in a cramped lavatory on a speeding train in a foreign country with every passing mile thrusting them closer to an uncertain and unpleasant destination.

What she wanted was to pretend they were a normal couple in a normal place under normal circumstances, quietly, sweetly, tenderly seducing each other.

But when his mouth came down to capture hers, his kiss was anything but quiet or sweet or tender.

"What are you doing?" she whispered.

"What does it feel like to you?"

"Like you're taking your frustrations out on me."

"You might have something there," he concurred. The hum of his words caused her lips to vibrate in a tingly, pleasant way.

"Since your motives are suspect you should probably stop kissing me."

"And you should probably stop talking."

Her lips were cool, but his were fiery hot. They came together like fresh-from-the-oven apple pie and two scoops of premium vanilla ice cream.

Tangy. Melting. Sinfully delicious.

She kissed him back, her tongue tentatively exploring his mouth.

He nibbled and sucked.

She followed his dance, not fighting him. In fact, she was kissing him back with an uncontrollable urgency that stole her breath.

He threaded his fingers through her hair, tugging out the hairclip that held her ponytail. He bathed his hand in the silky cascade.

"David," she moaned softly and then reached up to undo the top button on his shirt. She meant to scare some sense into him. To get him to stop kissing her. Or at least that's what she told herself.

"Yes?"

"You're right. I have been living my life through Cassie, not branching out on my own. Never doing anything impulsive. I want to do something crazy and impulsive right now."

"Oh yeah?"

Her heart thumped. Was this really part of a plan to chase him off or did she actually want him to make love to her? She did not know her own motives. How unsettling.

"Make love to me," she blurted. "Right here, right now, right this very minute."

"Huh?" He looked nervous.

"They have the mile high club for people who do it on a plane. What do they call it when you hook up on a train? The all aboard club?"

"Whoa!" He took one step back but there was nowhere else to go. "Maddie, let's not rush into something we'll both regret."

"I spent too much time worrying about tomorrow and not enough time living in the moment," she bluffed. "I want to live, David. I want to experience everything life has to offer."

She undid another button on his shirt and wriggled her pelvis against his hip. "Come on, kiss me again."

His erection burgeoned. He blushed. "I'm sorry about that."

"No reason to apologize. I'm flattered." She smiled and cupped him through his trousers. What in the hell was she going to do if he didn't retreat?

At that moment she knew she didn't want him to retreat. She wanted to make love to him. This wasn't a bid to chase him off. This was what she really needed. His hard masculine body shattering to completion inside hers.

"I think we should forget about the all aboard club," he whispered shakily. She loved that she'd reduced him to quivering jelly.

"Why?" she asked and nibbled at his chin.

"It's . . . um . . . I have a headache."

"And I've got just the cure for what ails you, big man."

Hungrily, she jerked his shirt from his waistband and shoved her palms up the bare planes of his abdomen. She shivered with delight as her hands skimmed his heated flesh.

He groaned. "Please Maddie, don't do this unless you mean it. Do you have any idea what you're doing to me?"

"I think I can guess."

"Vixen."

"Stud."

"I want nothing more than to nail you against this wall with your legs wrapped around my waist."

"Do it then." She met his gaze, challenging him to make good on his threat.

His eyes glistened with passion. He was hot for her and his desire stoked her higher, egging her on.

She'd never behaved so imprudently. Had never done anything so daring. But she was tired of Cassie having all the fun. It was her turn to do something crazy and down-right stupid for once.

David's fingers were at her jeans, working the snaps. For the first time in her life she wished she was wearing a short, flirty accessible skirt instead of comfortable jeans.

Egad! What was happening to her? She was turning into her twin.

But it was too late for regrets or second thoughts. David had her zipper down and his hand inside her panties.

Maddie groaned and his fingers went exploring. He found her sweet spot. She clutched the muscles of his upper arms to hold herself steady but the rock hard feel of him only served to further unbalance her precarious equilibrium.

Her heart churned and her head spun. His thumb moved over her feminine button of arousal with the sure, gentle strokes of a man who'd done this many times before. Her eyes rolled back in her head. It felt that exquisite and she exhaled his name on a sigh.

David.

His name seemed to echo in the small confines but maybe the sound was only reverberating in her head.

David, David, David.

"Don't stop, don't stop, don't stop," she begged as his hand rhythmically worked magic.

"Never, babe, never." His head was bent to her ear and he ran his hot, wet tongue over the outer edge.

Such bliss!

She was so very close to coming.

Then the train jerked to a stop sending them tumbling atop the closed toilet lid together in a tangle of arms and legs.

Well hell.

David scrambled off her. "Are you okay?" he asked tenderly.

No! Of course she wasn't okay. She'd just been robbed of an orgasm.

What was wrong with her? She should be thanking her lucky stars he hadn't tripped her trigger. The fact no man had ever given her an orgasm would place him in a class all by himself.

And that would make him special.

And if he was special that meant she was starting to care about him.

And if she was starting to care about him that would mean . . . well, what *did* it mean?

"Maddie?"

"I'm fine." She reached down and hastily did up her pants.

She stared at the lavatory floor unable to look him in the eyes. Her gaze landed on his black leather shoes. Oh Jeez, she was in trouble here.

Don't overanalyze. Just breathe.

But she couldn't seem to draw in air through her constricted lungs.

Calm down. You didn't completely lose your head and almost practically rape an FBI agent. You really didn't.

No?

No.

Yeah? Then who was that ripping the shirt off his back and sticking her tongue down his throat? You trying to tell me that wasn't you?

But he had started it.

And she had taken things to a whole new level. Maddie wrung her hands. She was going to be sick.

Breathe. Just breathe.

How did Cassie manage being so impulsive? It felt terrible and out of control and . . . very exciting.

She clamped her lips together to keep from moaning out loud. Her mouth still sizzled from the imprint of his.

He reached out to her.

Don't touch me. Please don't touch me.

He touched her.

And she melted as his fingers lightly skimmed over her forearm.

"It's okay. Don't be embarrassed. I'm honored. Flattered."

Ah damn. He was still trying to comfort her. How sweet. How obnoxious.

"I'm not embarrassed."

He must think she was Looney Toons. One minute crying on his shoulder, the next minute begging him for sex. She closed her eyes and swallowed back the lump of shame lodged in her throat.

Maybe she could blame it on hormones. Was it hormones? God, she was Looney Toons. She needed to get away from him. She needed to pace.

Before she ended up throwing herself at him again.

She wasn't accustomed to these wild, crazy emotions, didn't understand how to exorcise them. She'd never made out with a near stranger in a lavatory before. She had no idea why she'd done so now.

Looney Toons. It was the only explanation.

Someone knocked on the door. A masculine voice asked in Spanish if they were through with the lavatory.

"I think we're in Madrid," David murmured.

"Yeah."

"You wanna . . ." He made a circular gesture at her eyes. "Wash your face?"

The man outside knocked again.

"Un momento," Maddie called.

"I'll just wait outside," David said.

"Good idea."

But he didn't leave. He just kept standing there. Looking at her.

"And you uh . . ." She waved a hand. "You better button up your shirt and wash your hands. I'm sure you smell of me."

"I do." He grinned wickedly. "And your scent is intoxicating."

Oh God. This was more awkward than the morning after drunken-one-night-stand-sex. Not that she knew what that felt like from personal experience, but she could imagine it would go something like this.

Great, she had all the guilt of a one-night stand and none of the fun. Wasn't that just her luck?

David's cell phone picked that moment to do the *Dragnet* thing. He listened for a moment, the expression on his face impassive, but the muscle at his jaw twitched and she knew immediately something bad had happened.

"What is it?" she asked after he rang off.

His eyes looked both solemn and sorrowful. The way you looked at someone when the news was very bad indeed.

She raised a hand to her throat. "Tell me."

"That was Henri."

She swallowed and braced herself against the sink. "Yes?"

"Early this morning, about the same time we were boarding the train in Paris, a blonde woman matching Cassie's description and a masked man robbed the Prado at gunpoint."

Chapter

♥

TWELVE

THE STEPS OF the Prado were thick with uniformed officers. Curious tourists ringed the area cordoned off by the *policia*. A flash of his badge got David and Maddie escorted to the front office. David introduced himself to the officer in charge.

"*Buenos dias,* Señor Marshall. I am Antonio Banderas," the man said in heavily accented English.

"Antonio Banderas?" David repeated.

"*Si,* like the actor. We are distant cousins." Antonio presented them with his profile. "You can see the family resemblance."

David pressed his lips together to keep from chuckling. *This* Antonio Banderas looked nothing like the actor. He was short and bald with a paunch, thin lips and a nose shaped like a button mushroom.

He caught Maddie's gaze. Her eyes twinkled and she had slapped a hand over her mouth. Her sides shook with suppressed mirth. The harder she tried to stop, the more noises she made. If she didn't knock it off, he was going to start laughing too.

Antonio stared intently at Maddie, his brows pulled down in a frown.

At first David thought Antonio was mad at her for mocking his name. But when the stocky policeman wouldn't quit ogling her even after David spoke to him, he got offended.

"Señor Banderas," he said sharply.

Europeans might have a different outlook on the whole sexual thing but it was just damned rude to undress another man's woman with your eyes when he was standing right beside you.

There you go. Letting your feelings for Maddie get in the way of business. You gotta stop wanting to punch his lights out.

"You!" Antonio pointed an accusing finger at Maddie. "You are the one who stole the El Greco."

Oops. His mistake. Antonio hadn't been staring at Maddie because he was mad or because he thought she was sexy, but because he'd mistaken her for Cassie.

"No." Maddie shook her head and raised her hand.

"Arrest her!" Antonio commanded his armed men.

"Wait, wait, wait." David stepped between Maddie and the approaching officers. "This is Maddie Cooper, the suspect's identical twin sister."

Antonio looked suspicious. "Twins?"

"Yes, Señor Banderas." A tall, lithe Castilian woman spoke from the doorway in flawless English. She was dressed impeccably in a cream colored pantsuit and her thick black hair hung in a single braid down her back. "That's her twin. You must be quite concerned, Maddie."

"Hello, Izzy," Maddie greeted the woman.

"Izzy?" David asked.

The woman clasped his palm in a firm handshake. "Isabella Vasquez. The curator."

"Special agent David Marshall, FBI, art theft division."

"I know who you are, Mr. Marshall. Your reputation precedes you."

"I'm so sorry about the mixup," Maddie apologized. "I don't know why they think Cassie was involved in the robbery."

"Mixup?" Isabella laughed humorlessly. "I'm afraid there is no mixup. Your sister used our friendship to lure me to the delivery entrance before the museum opened. That's when she and her lover, dressed like delivery personnel, attacked me at gunpoint and held me hostage while they stole El Greco's *Knight with His Hand on Chest*."

"But how did they just waltz out of here? Why didn't someone try to stop them?" David asked.

"They used a dolly to smuggle the painting out of the museum in a shipping crate. Because I had let them in and they had arrived in a delivery truck, the security officer thought they were just picking up a special package for me."

"That was always Cassie's favorite El Greco," Maddie murmured.

"I know," Isabella said. "I'm very angry with her. I feel betrayed."

"There must be some mistake. Cassie, wielding a gun and holding you hostage?" Maddie shook her head, denying reality.

"There is no mistake." Isabella narrowed her dark eyes.

David hated the desperate tone in Maddie's voice. He felt her pain low in his gut. It was the same, helpless sensation he'd felt when Aunt Caroline had told him that Shriver had swindled her out of the Rembrandt.

"We have proof," Antonio Banderas interjected. "Would you like to see the security tape?"

"Absolutely," David said.

"This way."

Antonio led them into a room filled with television monitors and spy cameras. Isabella Vasquez followed at their heels. In Spanish, Antonio instructed the technician to play the tape of the robbery, while Isabella remained standing in the doorway, arms crossed.

"I can't bear to watch," Isabella shuddered. "I'll wait in my office."

The screen filled with Isabella's image. They watched while she walked down an empty corridor toward a heavy metal door. Isabella punched a series of numbers into the electronic keypad on the wall and the door opened.

Cassie appeared first. She wore the uniform of an international delivery service. She was smiling and although there was no audio, you could tell she had greeted Isabella with a friendly, *"Buenos dias,* Izzy."

David slid a side glance over at Maddie, saw her hands were fisted in her lap and her breathing had grown both rapid and shallow. He leaned close to her ear and whispered, "Breathe deeply. Don't hyperventilate."

She glared at him. He knew she hated being told what to do, but she did obey, forcing in a deep but jerky breath.

On the screen Cassie stepped over the threshold and into the museum. Immediately a man wearing a uniform that matched Cassie's but with a ski mask pulled down over his face and a deadly .45 magnum clutched in his left hand, barged in behind her.

The man clamped his fingers around Cassie's upper arm and pointed the gun at Isabella's heart.

"Freeze it there a moment," David said.

Antonio repeated David's instruction to the technician who stopped the tape. David narrowed his eyes and studied the frame.

Cassie looked almost as panicked as Isabella. Her eyes were wide, her face pale and she was gnawing her bottom lip. He leaned in closer to the monitor. The gunman's fingers dug so deeply into Cassie's arm that her sleeve bunched around his sausage-sized digits.

David shifted his attention to the man's left hand. The hand that clutched the .45.

What he saw sent a river of chills coursing down his spine.

A skull and crossbones tattoo.

Deep in his heart he instantly knew two things. One, Cassie Cooper had not willingly robbed the Prado; she was as much a victim as Isabella Vasquez.

And two, the gunman was not Peyton Shriver.

The thug in the ski mask was none other than Jocko Blanco.

Maddie couldn't believe what she was seeing. She rubbed her eyes, blinked twice and looked again.

No denying it. The woman caught on camera was her sister.

David had been right all along. Her twin had gone renegade. How could she tell her mother that Cassie was headed for prison?

Nausea ambushed her, slick and hot.

"I'm going to be sick," she moaned, and clamped a hand over her mouth.

David grabbed a nearby trashcan and shoved it under her face. It smelled of pencil shavings, coffee grounds and orange peel.

Maddie gagged.

A lock of her hair broke free from her ponytail clip and David gently swept back the errant strand while at the same time, pressed a cool palm to her heated forehead.

He rubbed her back and murmured sweet nothings the way her mother had when she was ill. Her father had never been there when she got sick. She remembered one time, before the divorce and after a trip to Six Flags where she'd wolfed down too much junk food, and she told her dad she was going to throw up, he'd thrust her toward her mother, said "You deal with her." Then he'd taken off to the local bar.

"It's okay," David murmured. "It's perfectly all right. Throw up if you need to."

She closed her eyes, took a deep breath and managed to hold onto what little breakfast she'd eaten on the train. "I think I'm okay now."

She lifted her head. David passed her the glass of water Antonio had fetched.

"I still can't believe, Cassie would . . ." Overcome with emotion, Maddie broke off and closed her eyes against the image frozen on the monitor.

"Is there some place where Maddie can lie down?" he asked Antonio.

"In Isabella's office," Antonio replied.

"I'm okay," Maddie insisted. "I want to keep watching the tape."

"I don't think that's such a good idea," David said.

"I'm not moving until I know exactly what we're up against."

"All right," he conceded and nodded at the technician. "Roll it."

They watched as Cassie and the gunman forced Isabella down the corridor and into the main gallery. Walking stiffly but with her head held high, Isabella led them to the room housing the El Greco.

The masked man kept the gun trained on Isabella while Cassie tied her up and left her on the floor. Then together, Cassie and the man boxed up the El Greco in the crate they'd brought with them and left the room. They disappeared off camera for several minutes.

"Where did they go?" David asked Antonio.

The policeman shrugged. "There are a few areas of the museum out of camera range."

Cassie and the gunman reappeared on the hallway camera wheeling the crate on the dolly.

David blew air through his teeth with a prolonged hissing sound but Maddie didn't dare glance over at him. She couldn't stand to see the pity on his face. Nausea swept over her again and she felt dizzy.

"I think I'll lie down now," she said.

"Good choice," David said. "Come on."

Antonio led the way to Isabella's office. David kept his hand braced against the small of Maddie's back, guiding her along, offering support. They passed the ladies room on the way and Maddie made note of it in case she felt the urge to puke again.

"Hang in there," he whispered.

God, he was being too nice to her. She wished he would stop being so nice so she could hate him for being right about Cassie.

She was still having trouble absorbing everything she'd just seen. Disoriented, she eased down on the black leather couch in Isabella's office and didn't resist when David told her to tuck her head between her knees.

This wasn't like her. She didn't come unglued. She was the strong one. If she wasn't cool and calm and thoroughly in control, then who in the hell was she? She'd always been so certain of herself. She was Cassie's twin sister. Her loyal protector, her staunchest defender.

Isabella voiced her internal fears. "You must be very shocked, Maddie. I've never seen you fall apart. It is frightening, though, to think that Cassie has become a common criminal. I can hardly believe it myself."

"Could you give us a moment in private, Señora Vasquez?" David asked.

Isabella nodded and departed, pulling the door closed behind her.

David threaded a hand through his hair and plunked down on the couch beside Maddie. "It looks bad for Cassie," he said and she had a feeling he was choosing his words very carefully.

"I can't believe she did it." Maddie shook her head repeatedly. "But it's right there, caught on tape. My twin sister is a thief."

David said nothing.

"Why?" Maddie asked. "Why would she do this?"

"Maybe it's a case of Stockholm Syndrome. Where the kidnapped victim identifies with her captor. Like Patty Hearst."

"Patty Hearst went to jail," Maddie said gloomily, but she clung to his explanation.

"Yes, but she got a light sentence."

"That's supposed to comfort me?"

He shrugged. "I'm trying my best."

"I thought you didn't believe Cassie had been kidnapped."

"Maybe I was wrong."

She looked at him. "I know you're just trying to make me feel better, but it's not working."

"Then how about this?" David slipped an arm around her.

"How about what?"

"This."

He kissed her. Lightly, slowly, tenderly. The exact opposite of the way he'd kissed her on the train.

His lips tasted like cool peppermint and total calamity, but she didn't even care. His arms were strong around her waist and his tongue was welcoming against hers. She accepted what he offered and heaven help her, she kissed him back.

In past relationships, she'd had trouble letting go. Kissing was often awkward and fraught with expectation. She usually thought about her performance too much, worried what the guy was thinking about.

But with David, she just melted.

His thumb slid along her jaw, stopped at the pulse point in her neck. Her heartbeat jumped against the pad of his thumb and something primordial in her throbbed in response.

David picked up on her mood and deepened the kiss while his hands got busy elsewhere. He spread his fingers against the base of her skull, threading through her hair while his other hand inched up inside her sweater.

She could feel the urgent need in the eager yet hesitant way his hand skimmed over her bra, touching her breasts with an excited caress. His eagerness told her he hadn't been with a woman in a long time.

She tasted his yearning, smelled his impatience.

It matched her own.

She sank into him. Instinct, nature and her body crowding out the protests telling her this was the wrong time, the wrong place, the wrong man.

But she could think of nothing except how good his tongue tasted in her mouth, how sweetly her breasts tingled against the brush of his knuckles, how wonderfully numb her mind was.

He swept her away and she allowed herself to be tossed by uncertain waters, clinging with her arms around his neck, her eyes closed, her body immersed in sensation.

His breath was warm. The room was warm. Her feminine core warmer still.

Warm and moist and willing.

Dear God, what was she doing?

Her body's wet reaction to his kisses yanked her back to reality. How could she have let herself go so irresponsibly?

For two breathtaking minutes she had been absorbed in her own selfish needs and had completely forgotten about Cassie's predicament.

What kind of sister was she?

To assuage her guilt and remind herself of her mission, she reached up to touch the half-a-heart necklace. But it was gone.

Vanished.

And she had no idea when or where she'd lost it.

"Oh no," Maddie moaned. "I really am going to throw up."

Bewildered, David watched Maddie dash into the hallway in hot pursuit of the ladies room. Well, that was a first. His kisses had never made a woman toss her cookies before.

Yeah, Marshall, you're a real lady-killer.

Problem was, he felt woozy himself and it had nothing to do with the kiss and everything to do with the fact he'd just violated every one of his ethical standards.

What was it about Maddie that shattered his best intentions? How come his instincts to comfort and protect her always seemed to end up with him getting touchy-feely?

Because this attraction wasn't purely physical.

And that's what scared the living hell out of him. This stupid, inexplicable need to be her knight in shining armor.

He'd crossed some bizarre threshold into a funhouse mirror of distorted emotions that he could not trust. Hadn't he learned the hard way you couldn't depend on love to be there when you needed it?

He couldn't be in love with her. He wasn't in love with her.

And yet, why did it feel like magic every time he kissed her?

David shook off his mental confusion. Forget the kiss. Forget your feelings. Forget trying to make sense of your relationship with Maddie. You've got bigger troubles.

Like, where was Cassie? And how had Jocko Blanco

gotten his hands on her? And what had happened to Shriver?

He hadn't been able to bring himself to tell Maddie his suspicions that Blanco had kidnapped Cassie, used her to break into the Prado and then spirited her away along with the El Greco. He would need to study the tape again, but every bone in his body was telling him Cassie had not been a willing participant in the crime.

When he thought about Blanco's ruthless reputation, his own stomach churned.

So what to do? Tell Maddie about his fears concerning Blanco or let her go on believing it was Cassie and Shriver on the tape?

He didn't like either alternative, but he knew one thing for sure, the longer Cassie was with Blanco, the more dire her situation. He had to take action and the sooner the better.

Before he could make a decision, Maddie came staggering back into the room.

"David," she cried. "Come quick. I know where Cassie's gone and I have proof Shriver forced her to help him steal the El Greco!"

When they heard Maddie shout, Antonio and Isabella came running from the security office and spilled into the corridor to join David and Maddie on their mad trot into the ladies room.

Maddie had David by the hand and she was dragging him through the door.

"What is it?" he said. "What did you find?"

She screeched to a halt in front of the bathroom mirror so suddenly he almost smacked into her.

"Look, look!" she cried triumphantly and gestured at

what was written in flaming scarlet lipstick across the mirror.

Midnight Rendezvous.

"What in the hell is that supposed to mean?" David asked, not getting what she was babbling about.

"When we lived in Madrid Cassie had a hush-hush affair with a notorious playboy from Monaco. He would send his private plane—*Midnight Rendezvous*—to pick her up."

"You've got to be kidding."

"I'm afraid not. My sister is very flamboyant. She even partied with members of the royal family. Of course, I was a nervous wreck during the fling. Those small planes go down all the time and who knew if the pilot shared the playboy's party-hearty philosophy."

"So what's that got to do with anything?"

Maddie clutched his sleeve and tugged like an impatient child trying to capture her father's attention. "This proves Cassie's not guilty. This is her favorite lipstick. She had to write the message in code in case Shriver came into the restroom and caught her. She's sending me a clue, David. This clue says she's been forced to help steal the painting and Shriver's taken her to Monaco."

Chapter ♥ THIRTEEN

CASSIE HUDDLED IN the passenger seat of the rented Peugeot with Jocko Blanco behind the wheel. They'd flown from Madrid to Nice, rented a car there and were driving to Monaco where Jocko had a buyer for the El Greco—which was now locked in the trunk—all lined up.

He was taking the curves like Lucifer, snarling and honking at slower moving vehicles. Whenever Cassie so much as gasped, Blanco would fling her a threatening glance and fondle the ugly looking gun in his lap.

Oh God, where was Maddie when you needed her?

Cassie clutched the dashboard until her knuckles were white and prayed for a miraculous deliverance.

Jocko Blanco had entered her bedroom through the open balcony window the night before and taken her hostage. The Interpol guy who'd been tailing her ever since she'd arrived in Madrid had attempted to come to her rescue when Blanco dragged her out the side entrance of the hotel, but Blanco had shot him in the shoulder and left him for dead in the alley.

Blanco had then stolen a delivery service van. Just before dawn, he'd forced her to call Isabella Vasquez and ask the curator to meet her at the delivery entrance.

He'd spoiled all her intricate plans.

Cassie had tried to resist, but he'd twisted her arm so it brought tears to her eyes. She wasn't physically tough like Maddie. Between the threat of more pain and the cold handgun shoved hard against her side, she'd had little choice but to play along. She kept hoping she would think of a way out of this.

She wondered where Peyton was and what he would do when he showed up in Madrid and found her gone. Would he assume the worst and think she'd thrown in her lot with Jocko?

And what about Isabella? Was her friend still trussed in the museum? Cassie chewed the inside of her cheek. Had anyone found her yet? She prayed that Izzy was okay. She'd made sure to tie the ropes as loosely as she dared and she'd apologized for having to gag her.

How badly she had wanted to give her friend some clue that Blanco was holding her hostage. But she'd been terrified that if Blanco knew what she was up to, he would simply shoot Izzy, the way he'd shot the Interpol guy. She refused to risk Izzy's life in order to save her own skin, so she'd kept quiet.

Cassie knew the heist had been recorded on security cameras. She knew the authorities would assume that the masked, gloved Blanco was Peyton. She had realized she would have to do something to prove her innocence while keeping Izzy safe. She had to let Maddie know she'd been taken prisoner to Monaco.

Seized with inspiration, she had begged Blanco to let her go to the bathroom before they left the museum. At first, she thought he was going to say no. She hopped around like a four year old on the playground until he finally relinquished and told her to make it snappy.

She dashed into the bathroom and scrawled *Midnight Rendezvous* in the only thing she had handy—her favorite tube of Lancôme. Never mind that the lipstick cost twenty-eight dollars a pop, once on, the stuff did not come off without a high quality make-up remover.

She was certain her sister would know what *Midnight Rendezvous* meant. Maddie had certainly been pissed off enough about her madcap affair with the flashy playboy.

What if Maddie doesn't come after you?

When has she *not* come after you? No need to worry on that score. Her sister was as predictable as Big Ben.

Blanco whipped the car around a puttering truck loaded with crates of live chickens and snarled a fresh batch of expletives. Feathers flew across the windshield as the startled driver swerved onto the narrow shoulder.

Cassie caught her breath. Okay, okay, okay. Calm down. What would Maddie do in this particular situation?

Um, well, Maddie probably would never be in this situation.

Of course that was a given, never mind that part. Think rational. Think reasonable. Think common sense.

She could grab the steering wheel. Hmm, yeah, right. Blanco weighed a good two fifty. She was a hundred pounds lighter. He'd probably just elbow her in the mouth and bye-bye dental work.

Think, think.

Gosh, this thinking before you acted stuff was really hard work. No wonder Maddie was perpetually crabby.

If she was quick, she could just lean over and bite the blazing thunder out of his hand.

And then he would probably just knock her head into his lap.

Yikes! She didn't want to go there.

So what? You're just going to sit here like a helpless ninny? This is not going to help you prove you're as smart as Maddie.

Yeah, well, maybe she was over that.

Cassie sneaked a glance at Blanco. Maybe she could stab him in the neck with her stiletto?

Now there was an idea whose time had come.

Slowly, she leaned forward and reached down to slip off her sharp-heeled sling back.

Blanco glowered and stroked his gun. "Don't even think about it."

"What?" She rounded her eyes and tried to look totally ingenuous.

"Sonofabitch, motherf—" he exploded.

Cassie jammed her fingers in her ears so she wouldn't have to hear the rest of Blanco's cursing. He was glaring intently into the rearview mirror and swerving like a drunk on New Year's Eve.

Tremulously, Cassie peeked into the side mirror and her heart lurched into her throat. There was a boxy ice cream truck behind them, coming up fast.

Too fast.

Sweet tea and almond cookies! Blanco was already doing eighty, how fast was this other driver going?

Then her heart leaped with hope. Maybe it was Maddie or David or both. Maybe they'd already found her message, pieced together what had happened and were on their way to save her.

In an ice cream truck?

Sure, why not?

Blanco goosed the car faster just as they rounded the side of an imposing hill.

The ice cream truck dogged them, gaining ground. Over the loudspeaker attached on the roof, the truck was playing what sounded like *Pop Goes the Weasel*.

Blanco cornered the next curve, the car almost tipping on two wheels.

All around the cobbler's bench.

Cassie yelped.

"Shuddup."

She gulped and hung on tight.

The monkey chased the weasel.

The ice cream truck was getting closer. Blanco had his foot jammed to the floor. Their car had reached its top speed.

And then the ice cream truck smashed into their bumper.

Hard.

This time Cassie did more than yelp, she shrieked. Omigod, who was ramming them and why?

She tried to see who was behind the wheel of the ice cream truck, but the windshield was tinted, obstructing her view and things were moving way too fast.

Blanco lost control of both the car and his gun. The handgun slid across the seat and landed on the floor at Cassie's feet.

"Leave it," Blanco shouted as if to an obedient dog and trod the brakes.

Cassie's head jerked at the unexpected change in tempo, but she didn't take her eyes off that gun. She unbuckled her seatbelt and dived for the .45 at the same time the ice cream truck rammed them again.

The passenger door flew open and Cassie tumbled out—along with the .45—onto the graveled shoulder of the road. She landed on her butt and bounced a couple of times. The impact hurt like hell. Forget about that. You're free, you're free.

Pebbles bit into her palms and her knees were skinned but she was okay.

Which was more than she could say for Blanco. Dumbfounded, she watched open-mouthed as the car went smashing down over the side of the cliff.

Pop goes the weasel.

The ice cream truck stopped just short of the edge. Terrified, Cassie shifted her gaze to the driver.

The door swung open.

And Peyton Shriver got out, concern knitting his brow. "Cassie, luv, are you all right?"

My antihero!

Cassie dusted herself off and ran into his open arms.

"What aren't you telling me?" David grilled Isabella Vasquez. He'd managed to talk Maddie into staying with Antonio Banderas while he questioned Isabella alone. He'd had a sneaking suspicion the woman wasn't telling everything she knew about the robbery.

Isabella nervously clasped and unclasped her hands. "I don't know what you're talking about, Señor Marshall."

"Oh, I think you do. Why did you so willingly let Cassie Cooper in the private entrance? How come the robbery went off so smoothly?"

"Are you accusing me of something?"

"Are you guilty of something?"

She kneaded her brow and began to pace. "It's not what you think. Or at least it wasn't."

"So why don't you tell me what happened?"

"If this gets out to the press, I'll lose my job."

"Or perhaps go to jail?"

"It wasn't supposed to happen this way. Cassie lied to me. She betrayed me."

"Talk to me Isabella. I'm on your side."

She stared at him long and hard.

"All right," she relented at last. "Two days ago Cassie came to see me. She told me about this plan she had to catch Peyton Shriver. She told me she was working with the FBI and she needed my help."

"You agreed, just like that?"

"Cassie is very persuasive, but the reason I agreed to help her is because of the political infighting; my job at the Prado is in jeopardy. If I could be instrumental in helping catch one of the world's most infamous art thieves my position here would be solidified."

"So exactly what were you supposed to do for Cassie?"

"She wanted to copy the El Greco. She's very talented at re-creations."

"You mean forgeries."

"It's only forgery if you try to pass it off as the real thing."

"Go on."

"I was supposed to place the real El Greco in the vault and replace it with the copy so she and her art thief ac-complice could steal it. Her accomplice of course wouldn't know it was a copy. I was to let them in the side entrance, give them the digital signature code and let them rob the Prado. They would be taking a fake. I didn't see how the plan could go wrong. But instead of showing up on Friday night as we'd planned, she and the masked gunman held me up at daybreak this morning. Cassie never brought me the reproduction, so it was the real El Greco that they stole."

David stared at Isabella, stunned, his mind whirling with what she had just told him. He and Maddie had both been wrong. Cassie had not fallen for Shriver. Nor had she been kidnapped. She had gone willingly with him, yes. But not because she'd become enamored with Shriver and his lifestyle as David had initially suspected but because she'd gotten off on playing spy girl and was trying to trap Shriver on her own.

Holy shit, what an airhead plan.

The thing was, Cassie's scheme just might have worked. Except for the unexpected interference of Jocko Blanco.

Dammit. Recruiting Cassie Cooper was turning out to be the stupidest thing he'd ever done in his entire life.

Maddie paced the terrazzo floor of Antonio Banderas's office, tensing and relaxing her abdominal muscles. The isometric exercises were designed to help her deal constructively with tension.

The security officer watched her from behind his desk with somnolent eyes. He was smoking a stogie and the pungent scent of cigar tobacco filled the room.

She glanced at her watch. It was almost lunchtime. Which explained Antonio's laziness, but didn't tell her why David was taking his sweet time wrapping things up with Isabella. They needed to get on the road to Monaco ASAP. Each passing moment put them farther away from her sister.

After seeing Cassie's message scrawled on the bathroom mirror, David had asked her to hang out with Antonio for a few minutes while he took Isabella aside for more detailed questioning. She hadn't wanted to let him question Isabella on his own, but David told her that he thought she might be more forthcoming if Maddie wasn't in the room.

But that was over an hour ago.

"I think I'm just going to go check on David." Maddie motioned with her thumb toward the corridor. "See if there's some kind of problem."

Antonio waved a hand at the sofa. "Please Señorita Cooper, sit down, relax. Have a snooze."

"A snooze?"

"Did I say it wrong?" He seemed concerned that he might have made a language *faux pas*.

"No. I just don't understand how you can expect me to snooze when my sister is in such trouble. I need to be out there looking for her, doing something."

"You Americans." Antonio took a puff of his cigar. "Always with the hurry."

It had been five years since she had lived in Spain and she'd forgotten how irritatingly leisurely the natives could be. What they perceived as relaxed, spontaneous and flexible Maddie saw as indolent, disorganized and unreliable. Cassie, of course, had fit right in, while Maddie, with her need for order, structure and discipline had stood out like a prison warden in kindergarten.

"You are very stressed," Antonio said.

"No kidding."

"Would you like some coffee?"

"Like caffeine is going to help me relax?"

"You're right, bad idea. Please sit." He gestured at the sofa again.

"No thanks. I really do have to find Agent Marshall." She made a move for the door.

And a policeman stepped forward from the corridor to block her way.

"Excuse me." She moved to the left.

He waltzed with her.

Alarm knotted her chest. She turned and looked back at Antonio. "Am I being detained?"

Antonio gestured at the sofa a third time. "Please, no trouble."

"Are you arresting me?"

He shook his head. "Not arresting. No."

"But I'm not allowed to leave."

"Not until Agent Marshall gets back."

"And where has he gone?" Maddie's voice went up an octave and she realized she was within inches of losing her composure.

"I'm not sure." His smile was apologetic but unwavering.

"When will he be back?"

Antonio shrugged.

"What's going on here?" she asked in a careful, modulated tone, when she wanted to yell at the top of her lungs.

"Señor Marshall said you were getting in his way. He asked me to keep you here until he returns."

What? What! David had ditched her?

Bastard. She couldn't believe she'd trusted him. Why had she trusted him? She'd known better.

Maddie started pacing again. Wasn't that just like a man? When the going gets tough, the men take off.

Bastards. The lot of them.

"Señorita Cooper?" Antonio got up from his desk and tentatively approached her.

"What?" she snapped.

Quickly, he backpedaled, raising his palms in a defensive gesture. "Calm down."

"I'm calm. I'm completely calm." She glared and gnawed her thumbnail. "Why would you think I'm not calm? I'm always calm. It's what I do. I'm the calm one. Ask anybody."

"Calm as a time bomb," Antonio muttered under his breath.

"What? What did you say?"

Antonio looked terror stricken. "If you will just calm . . . er . . . sit down, I can phone Agent Marshall and discover when he intends to return. Is that acceptable?"

"How about this? How about I call him instead?" Maddie reached for the phone and then realized she didn't know David's cell phone number. "What's his number?"

"I'm afraid I cannot give you that information."

"Why not?"

"Please." With the cautious movements of a man trying to soothe a wild tiger with a toothache, Antonio eased around his desk.

"You wait with Paulo." He nodded toward his man blocking the doorway. "And soon I will return with news from Agent Marshall."

Yeah, right, okay, bucko.

Maddie faked a smile and forced herself to sit. "See? I'm sitting like a good girl. Now go call Marshall."

Antonio slipped past her as if he thought she might spontaneously combust at any moment. She savored her anger while her mind churned. She didn't know where David had gone or what he was up to but she knew what she had to do. Get the hell out of here and find a ride to Monaco.

David probably didn't believe her about Cassie. In fact, that whole time he was being nice to her, telling her he thought maybe her sister had a case of Stockholm Syndrome was nothing but a big fat lie.

And, she recognized the kiss he'd given for what it undoubtedly was, a ruse to get her to let her guard down with him so he could ditch her.

Grrr.

David Marshall, you are so going to pay for this stunt when I catch up with you.

She had to get out of here. Now.

Maddie glanced at the guard in the doorway. "Paulo," she said in Spanish. "I'm feeling overheated." She fanned herself. "Could you get me a drink of water, please?"

"When Officer Banderas returns."

"I think I might faint. Please."

Taking a cue from her sister, she fluttered her eyelashes, undid a button on her blouse and slowly ran her tongue over her lips.

Paulo shook his head.

Terrific, first time she ever tried to flirt her way out of a bad situation and the guy turns out to be gay. Just her luck.

She sat a moment, scanning the room and thinking.

Her gaze fell on Antonio's desk. His still lit cigar smoldered in the ashtray. Beside the desk sat a trashcan full of discarded paper.

Hmm.

"You don't mind if I pace, do you?" she asked Paulo. "I pace when I get nervous."

He shrugged.

"Thank you." Maddie rose to her feet.

Nonchalantly, she paced. La-di-dah.

She cast a sidelong glance at Paulo, he was leaning one shoulder against the doorjamb, not paying her too much attention.

Good.

She paced closer to Antonio's desk. She spied a picture of an attractive woman and two smiling girls by the window.

Eureka.

"Oh," she squealed in Spanish. "Is this Antonio's family?" She made a beeline for the photograph and held it up for Paulo to see.

Paulo nodded. "*Si,* it's his family. But he doesn't like anyone touching his stuff. Put it down and come back over here." He waved at the sofa.

"Oh, okay."

Then oh so casually, she leaned over to set the picture frame back on the window ledge. Wiggling her fanny to hide what she was doing, Maddie bumped the cigar into the trashcan.

Paulo never saw it and Maddie sauntered back to the sofa.

One minute passed. Then two.

Crap. Had the cigar gone out?

Three minutes. Four.

Just when she was about to despair over her foiled attempt to start a fire, the acrid smell of smoldering paper filled the air.

Paulo sniffed. "Do you smell something burning?"

Maddie shook her head. "I think it's just Antonio's cigar."

Paulo nodded, her explanation appeasing him. Until bright orange flames began licking above the trashcan.

"Oooh, oooh," Maddie gasped, playing her part to the hilt. "Fire! Fire! *Fuego! Fuego!*"

The minute Paulo ran for the fire extinguisher, Maddie darted out the door.

Chapter
FOURTEEN

THE ROAD FROM Nice to Monaco was breathtakingly picturesque, but David barely noticed. His focus was on Cassie and the disturbing realization that she had some-how fallen into Blanco's clutches.

Was she even still with Blanco? The man was ruthless. Once she'd served her purpose, he was just as likely to kill her as he was to keep her. Unless he had an even uglier, more nefarious plan in store.

That thought shoved ice cubes up his spine.

What was Blanco up to? Was Levy behind Cassie's kidnapping? Were they going to ransom her to Shriver in exchange for the Cézanne? Or was Blanco still in cahoots with Shriver and they were making some kind of an end-run around Levy?

Remorse gigged him unmercifully. Guilt over ditching Maddie at the Prado joined the party. He shouldn't have left her, but he'd had no real choice. He'd already gotten one sister mixed up with Jocko Blanco; he certainly wasn't placing both of them in danger. He had grabbed the next flight from Madrid to Nice, and then rented a car to drive the rest of the way into Monaco.

By now, Maddie had probably realized he wasn't coming back. Which might explain the inexplicable burning sensation around his ears. No doubt, at this very moment, she was cussing him up a blue streak.

Oh well, he would live.

But would Antonio? David had left the poor policeman to deal with the fallout of Maddie's obsessive devotion to her sister. He definitely owed the guy for keeping Maddie safe and off his hands.

The sky darkened the closer he drew to Monaco. It was early afternoon and a wicked rainstorm was on the way. He rounded a sharp curve and noticed the roadside barrier at the edge of the cliff looked as if it had recently been broken through.

He followed the curve, casually glancing in his rearview mirror and saw the glint of metal in a swatch of sun that managed to break free from the cloud covering.

Squinting, he took a second look. Could that be an automobile bumper?

Yes. It was definitely a car bumper.

Shades of Princess Grace. Had someone taken a header off the bluff?

Dammit.

He was already too far behind Blanco. He really couldn't spare another moment, but how could he not stop and render aid if there had been a car accident?

Tick-tock. Cassie was in trouble.

But the people in the car might be seriously injured and he was the only one in sight.

He who hesitates is lost, the phrase his father had

drilled into his head from the time he was a tiny tot, sprang into his brain. *You must win at all costs.*

Yet how could he ignore someone in need? And how could he overlook the lesson he'd just learned? His hunger to win at all costs had unnecessarily put Cassie in danger. Stopping to help would be a form of making amends.

David's gut tightened, telling him what he must do. No matter how much stopping might go against his instincts to plunge after Blanco. He simply had to detour.

He braked and did a U-turn. He slowed and pulled over at the smashed barrier. He killed the engine, got out and walked to the edge of the cliff, gravel crunching beneath his shoes.

Cautiously, he peered over and caught his breath at what he saw.

It was a car wreck all right.

The reflective taillight of a nondescript tan rental car winked at him. The trunk flapped open. The hood was solidly embedded in the body of a cypress tree. If it hadn't been for the tree, the car would be resting at the bottom of the ravine and whoever was inside would have no chance of survival at all.

Urgency shot a lance of fear through him. As far as he knew, he was the first on the scene. There could be a family down there. A mom. A dad. Kids. They needed him.

Worry shoved him down the cliff. Moving as quickly as he dared, David picked his way over the uneven terrain, his pulse pounding hard, sweat beading his brow and upper lip.

By the time he reached the driver's seat, his body was at a ninety-degree slant and he had to grab on to roots and foliage in order to maintain his balance.

He could see a man slumped over the wheel but there was no one else in the vehicle. His heart rate kicked up another notch. He wrenched open the door.

The man groaned.

David spoke to him first in English, then in French, telling him to hang on, that help was on the way.

Dammit. Why hadn't he called for an ambulance before climbing down the hill? He had been trained better than that. Why was he so scattered, so muddled these days?

Maddie.

No. He wasn't going to blame her for his recent rash of bad decisions. This was his responsibility, no one else. David reached into his jacket pocket for his cell phone. He peered at the numbers.

Funny, the back light wasn't coming on. He punched the power button again.

And felt two heavy, hammy fists circle his neck and squeeze tight.

Startled, David jerked his head up to find himself nose-to-nose with a bruised and bloodied but very much alive, Jocko Blanco.

"You came after me, you saved me." Cassie snuggled next to Peyton on the front seat of the ice cream truck after they'd climbed down the hill and taken the El Greco out of the trunk while Blanco was still unconscious. She nestled her head against his shoulder and savored his masculine aroma.

"Don't read too much into it. I also rescued the El Greco."

"But you could have left me with Blanco and you didn't. That means you like me."

Would he have done the same thing if the El Greco had been alone in the car with Blanco or if the painting hadn't been there at all? She knew the answer. The painting was primary; she was the afterthought.

"You came awful close to getting left in the car along with Blanco," he said.

"Oh?" She ignored the uncomfortable ping in the pit of her stomach. Maddie was the worrier, not she. "Why's that?"

"I thought you had betrayed me."

"Why would you think that?" *Don't let him see you sweat.*

"When I saw you in Paris, I thought you'd gone to Levy behind my back."

"But I was never in Paris."

"I realize that now, but it took me a while. Until I remembered you had a twin sister. I had no idea you two looked so much alike."

"You saw Maddie?"

Peyton rubbed the back of his head and winced. "Yeah, I met her. And is she ever a bitch."

"Hey, that's my sister you're talking about."

"If it hadn't been for that necklace I would have thought for sure you were still working with David Marshall. Actually, he's the one who showed up to rescue me from your twin."

"I don't understand."

"I was dressed as a mime, casing the Louvre. When I came out of the museum, I spied you in the crowd. Except it wasn't you, but I didn't know that at the time."

"Maddie hates mimes."

"Tell me about it. I started mimicking you . . . I mean her . . . because I was mad that you'd come to Paris when

you were supposed to be currying favor with your curator friend in Madrid. Then I saw the necklace. It was the
right half of the heart. Your necklace is the left side."
Peyton reached over and fingered the gold charm at her
throat. "That's when I knew she wasn't you. That's also
when she attacked me and Marshall had to pull her off."

"Maddie attacked you?" Wow. She knew her sister
hated mimes but this was beyond the pale.

"Like a lioness. The necklace chain broke off in my
hand and she thought I was stealing it."

Ah, that made sense. Maddie had been rabid about
their necklaces ever since the frozen pond incident. "It
means a lot to her."

"So I gathered."

"David Marshall didn't recognize you?"

"I was disguised as a mime, remember, and I ran off
quickly." Peyton paused. "Plus, I think Marshall was
drunk."

"Weird. That doesn't sound like David."

"Do you know him that well?"

"Are you jealous?" She teased, doing her best to
charm him.

"Not jealous. Just worried about your loyalties."

Peyton eyed her speculatively and Cassie knew she
had to do something to reassure him that she was on his
side. Which meant now was as good a time as any to let
him in on a small segment of her plan.

"Peyton," she whispered in a singsong voice, leaning
in closer and blowing softly into his ear. "Just to show
you how committed I am to making this relationship
work, I'm going to tell you an idea I have for doubling
your take on the Cézanne and the El Greco."

"Doubling my take?" That perked him right up. "Now you're speaking my language."

Cassie nibbled his earlobe. "It's dead simple."

"I'm listening."

"We hold a silent auction."

"I don't understand."

"We get Jerome Levy and Cory Philpot to invite all the wealthy collectors they know to bring their . . . ahem . . . ill-gotten works of art that they'd like to sell or trade to our underground equivalent of an afternoon at Sotheby's. We charge a broker fee and let Philpot and Levy split the take."

"That makes no sense."

Cassie raised a finger. "Hear me out. This would put you back in good graces with both Philpot and Levy. We could hold it at one of those elegant five star hotels in Venice. Since it's Carnevale, a lot of their clients are likely to be in the city already."

"But what about me? How do I get my money?"

"You tell Levy and Philpot that the impetus for the auction is to unload the red hot Cézanne and El Greco. Get them to tell their collectors that since there is so much heat on us, we're willing to let the paintings go for bargain basement prices."

Cassie's heart quickened as she waited for him to take the bait. Do it. Go on. Say yes.

"But if we let the paintings go at a bargain basement price how am I going to double my money?"

"Simple. We make copies of the paintings. We show the real paintings to the authenticators, and then pull a switcheroo, keeping the originals to ransom back to the museums for a hefty sum."

"But where do we get someone we can trust to make forgeries so quickly?"

"You're looking at her."

"You?"

"Me."

"No kidding?"

"Hey, I spent months in bed as a kid with nothing to do but draw and paint. I loved working with watercolor and started imitating artwork I saw in picture books. I was quick and accurate. But, I was mightily disappointed to discover I had zero talent for creating anything original. However, I can copy like a Xerox."

"How long would it take to replicate the paintings?" Peyton asked.

"Give me lots of chocolate and coffee, canvas and paint and then get out of my way. I can have them done in twenty-four hours."

"Really? You're that fast?"

"And that good," she bragged shamelessly.

"You're brilliant, luv." Peyton kissed her on the cheek.

"Aren't you glad you saved me?"

"Completely. We'll go to Venice. You concentrate on making the copies and I'll set up the auction."

"Deal," Cassie said and they shook on it.

She settled back against the seat and inwardly sighed with relief. Thank heavens he'd gone for her plan. Everything was falling into place. She would replicate the Cézanne twice and the El Greco again, thereby ending up with two sets of forgeries. She would keep the second set a secret from Peyton. It would be her ace in the hole.

Shriver would get Levy and Philpot to lure in the collectors and art dealers interested in picking up cheap masterpieces to Venice. Then in the meantime, she would call

David Marshall and tell him exactly when and where to arrest Peyton, Levy, Philpot and the greedy collectors.

What could go possibly go wrong?

David lay battered and bruised on the side of the hill, the steep canyon looming below him, the road stretching far above his grasp. With one eye, he stared up at the blanket of clouds crowding the Mediterranean sky and knew he was truly screwed.

He lost all track of time. It seemed he had lain here for days. His throat was parched from hollering for help, his lips were dried. His right wrist was broken and his left eye was swollen shut and he couldn't seem to muster the energy to crawl up the hill.

Blanco had pistol-whipped the crap out of him.

"You're the world's biggest schmuck, Marshall," he growled under his breath, and then decided he needed to stop talking out loud. The vibrations made his head throb even harder.

Good God, he was no better than impulsive Cassie Cooper, shimmying down the hill, throwing open the wrecked car door without once stopping to think that Blanco might be behind the wheel.

And you call yourself an FBI agent. For shame.

He closed his eye and swallowed. And speaking of Cassie, he hated to even wonder about her whereabouts. She hadn't been with Blanco, that much was clear. But had she escaped? Or had the thug done away with her?

What would he tell Maddie when he saw her again?

Correction, *if* he ever saw her again.

An overwhelming sense of loss washed through him. He'd made such a mess of things. He'd fallen down on the job, disappointed himself and placed not one, but two women in jeopardy.

All his life, he had feared being a loser. Of not being able to measure up to his father's high standards and the lofty Marshall name. And now, his greatest fear had just come to pass.

He'd blown it. Big time.

Yep. He was screwed. His single-minded pursuit of Shriver, his blind determination to win at all costs, was to blame for his graceless downfall.

So now what? He had left Maddie at the Prado after giving Antonio strict instructions not to let her leave until he returned, so there was no hope of rescue from that resource.

After beating him senseless, Blanco had taken both his duty weapon and his car. He stood no chance of driving or shooting his way out of this situation.

And when he'd tried to call for help on his cell phone he'd realized he hadn't remembered to recharge the batteries since this whole thing began back at the Kimbell museum three days earlier.

Had it only been three days since Shriver had heisted the Cézanne?

So what now? Lie here and wallow in self-pity or do something about it? He opened his good eye again and studied the distance from his perilous perch on the steep hillside to the road above.

Two hundred yards minimum. Straight up.

He had one option. Scale the incline in the rain with a broken wrist, a black eye and a brain-stabbing headache. Not a particularly cheery thought.

Still, it was better than waiting for the buzzards to find

him. Taking a deep breath to bolster his courage against the pain, David began to crawl.

"You've gotta drive faster," Maddie told herself. "I know you hate exceeding the speed limit but if you have any hopes of catching up with Cassie and Shriver you've got to jam the pedal to the metal."

Tentatively, she pressed harder upon the accelerator of the car she had rented in Nice after she'd flown there from Madrid. That project had been almost as big an undertaking as getting past Paulo. At least she hadn't had to start another fire. Now she was finally on the road and free of that infuriating David Marshall.

Thank God. She prayed Cassie and Shriver were still in Monaco. Of course, she had no idea how she was going to find them once she got there.

Try not to fret about that yet. Take it one step at a time.

Good advice, but could she take it?

She turned on the radio. Julio Iglesias was belting out a song. The music got on her nerves so she switched it off. She tried isometric exercises but found she couldn't concentrate. She turned on her headlights against the gloomy sprinkles of rain and flicked on the fan to bring fresh air into the car. Her clothes smelled like cigar smoke and charred paper and travel funk.

For the first time all day she realized she had no notion where her luggage was. When was the last time she had seen it? The train? Yes, that had to be it. But never mind. Her luggage was gone now. She could buy new clothes later. Hell, once she found Cassie, she would take her on a shopping spree.

"Cassie," she whispered. "Hang on. I'm coming. I

know you were forced to rob the museum. I believe in your innocence."

The lights of Monaco twinkled in the distance and Maddie urged the car even faster.

There. She was going a full eight miles over the speed limit. Not so cautious now, huh?

See, I can take risks.

She rounded a curve on her way up a hill. There was something up ahead. Maddie slowed and squinted through the rain. Her headlights caught a man staggering into the middle of the road.

"Eeek!" Maddie screeched and trod the brakes, coming to a stop just in the nick of time to keep from plowing over David Marshall.

Chapter

♥

FIFTEEN

"MADDIE?" DAVID BLINKED against the headlight glare at the ethereal form of the woman hurrying toward him in the rain.

Was she a mirage?

If she was a mirage, she was the most beautiful mirage ever to be conjured by a delusional brain.

But how did she get here? How did she get away from Antonio Banderas? Had she talked the policeman into letting her go? Or had she escaped? She was a pretty good escape artist. Maybe she'd challenged Antonio to a drinking contest. If that was the case, he felt sorry for Antonio.

Maybe you're dead and living out a sexual fantasy.

No, that couldn't be. His sex fantasies centered on his masculine prowess and pleasing Maddie within an inch of her life. In his current condition, he couldn't satisfy a sock puppet.

"David!" she cried and reached him just as his knees gave way.

His nose filled with the wonderful smell of her. It was Maddie. No mistaking her aroma. He had no idea how she'd found him, but she was here.

Thank God.

She caught him under his arms and he almost bit through his lip to keep from screaming in pain. He grunted and fell against her.

"Are you all right?"

"My arm," he managed to pant.

"Omigod, your wrist is broken."

"Yeah."

"And your face! Oh!" She hovered, just dying to mother him. He couldn't say he minded. "Your poor handsome face."

She thought he was handsome? He would have smiled if his lip didn't hurt so much.

"Oooooh." She touched his left eye that was swollen shut.

"Easy."

"Poor baby." Tenderly, she kissed his cheek.

In a million years David would never have suspected he would enjoy being made a fuss over. He'd lost his mother at a young age and he'd toughened up quick, eschewing mushy emotions, going so far as to make fun of boys who cried on the playground. But Maddie's concern made him want to wallow in his wounds. He wanted more touching and kissing and caressing.

"What happened?" she whispered.

"Can't talk now," he mumbled through gritted teeth. It was all he could do to stay conscious.

"Yes, yes, you're right. I'm sorry. Here. You grab on to me so I won't hurt you."

He wrapped his good hand around her upper arm. "Let's get to the car."

"Are you sure you can make it?"

"I'll be fine, woman, unless I end up catching pneumonia from standing here in the rain."

"I'm sorry," she apologized again. "I'm just so flustered at seeing you beat up. It hurts me here." She touched her heart with her fingers and David felt something inside his chest flip.

Shake it off.

Determinedly, he put one foot in front of the other and ignored the sappy feelings stirring inside him. At last, they made it and Maddie helped him ease slowly into the passenger seat.

He was soaked to the skin and the eye that was swollen shut throbbed like an ingrown toenail. His teeth chattered—tick-tick-tickety-tick—like loose rice in a tin cup. He was cold and dizzy and his body hurt like the blazes in a dozen different places.

Buck up. You can't look weak in front of her.

"Breathe deeply," she coached. "I'll get you to the hospital as quickly as I can."

He nodded, just barely. Her calm competency reassured him. He lay back against the seat and concentrated on dealing with the pain.

She didn't ask any more questions and he was glad for that. He wasn't ready to tell her about Blanco yet, or the stupidity that had landed him in the canyon.

"Maddie," he said. "I left you behind with Antonio for your own good. I shudder to think what would have happened if you'd been with me."

"Shh," she said. "No talking. We can talk later. You hang in there."

In that moment he knew she'd forgiven him for ditching her. She wasn't going to hold a grudge or pick a fight.

What a woman.

The car smelled of her. Nice. Womanly. Uniquely Maddie. They rumbled along in the rain.

"Move over, step on the gas, Grandma," Maddie grumbled to a slow moving vehicle in front of them. "We have an emergency here."

She was adorable in her urgency. David gazed at her with his one good eye. She drove with both hands on the wheel, eyes trained on the road, her chin set with serious intent. Right now, he loved her take-charge attitude. Sometimes, the way she tried to muscle in and take over infuriated him, but for the time being, he loved that she was in the driver's seat.

"Outta my way, sucker," she said and slammed her palm into the horn. "Hey, that jerk flipped me off. Well, up yours too, buddy."

He almost smiled. If his damned wrist didn't hurt so much he would have.

She was colorful. He had to grant her that.

"Here we go, here we are. It's the hospital."

Maddie left the car running and dashed inside the squat white building with a large red cross over the door of the emergency entrance. Sisters-of-something-or-other hospital. He couldn't read the lettering too clearly. Having just one eye played hell with a guy's visual acuity.

But his eye was still sharp enough to notice the sweet sway of Maddie's hips as she hurried inside. Watching her hips made him think of when he'd touched her on the train. And thinking of the train made him remember that after Henri's phone call, they'd forgotten to retrieve their luggage.

Too bad. He had condoms in his bag. Not because he'd been planning on getting lucky. The rubbers had been tucked in the side pocket ever since an unfruitful vacation to a singles resort last year.

Yeah, Mr. One-Armed Cyclops. As if you could even do anything if you had condoms.

But the lack of protection didn't stop him from thinking about making love to Maddie. Damn if he wasn't working on a woody, in spite of his plentiful aches.

You've made enough mistakes this trip. Stop thinking about sex.

Still, it was better than thinking about the pain.

Maddie returned shortly with a nurse and an orderly. They helped him out of the car and into a wheelchair.

The orderly wheeled him into an exam room, while Maddie stayed at the reception area to answer the desk clerk's questions.

The nurse assisted him onto the gurney and asked him if he was allergic to anything. She started an IV in his good hand, and then left the room. Later, she returned with an injection.

He was grinning two minutes after the drug hit his veins. Ah, sweet freedom from pain. The nurse departed again, but left the door ajar.

"Payment?" He heard the desk clerk ask in French.

"No par-lay fran-say," Maddie replied. *"Habla español? Habla ingles?"*

Maddie and the clerk began a cobbled conversation of French, Spanish and English he couldn't really follow as he drifted in and out on a sea of morphine relief. What he did follow, was the soothing lilt of Maddie's voice. The sound of it grounded him, kept him from completely floating away.

"Psssstt."

Huh?

"Pssssstt, David," Maddie whispered from the door-way.

Reluctantly, he pried open his eye. He thought he said, "what is it?" but it came out more like "mphmlottamut."

"You got insurance?"

He nodded.

"Can you give me the info? They were making a big deal out of getting paid so I had to pretend to be your wife. Until I told them we were married they weren't even going to let me see you. But now they want this money situation taken care of."

"Wife?"

Now there was a pleasant thought. Maddie as his wife. He imagined coming home from work to find her cooking dinner. No, scratch that image. Maddie wasn't the domestic goddess type. Let's see. He envisioned them getting up at dawn every morning, running five miles together before coming home to make love in a sweaty heap on the floor. Ah, much better.

"Don't blow my cover, okay? I'll get freaky if they won't let me in to see you. I need to see you to know you're okay."

Aw, but that was sweet. "I'm okay."

"Just play along, please?"

"Sure. When did we get married?"

"I told them we were on our honeymoon after a whirl-wind courtship."

She approached the gurney, her gaze sweeping over him. A look of concern worried her cute little face but when she caught him watching her, she forced a smile.

"Our honeymoon, huh?"

"It was the only thing I could think of to explain my ignorance of your medical history. The nurses think you're terribly romantic, proposing to me during a gondola ride in Venice with us both in Regency era dress."

"Great. You make me sound like a doofus."

"It's always been my fantasy marriage proposal from the time I was a kid, so sue me."

"I knew it." He smiled.

"Knew what?"

"You're much more romantic than you let on."

"It was a childhood fantasy. Luckily I had one, it made the lie more convincing."

"So how did I perform on the wedding night?" He tried to wink but being one-eyed, it didn't come off very debonair and his words were definitely slurred.

"David! You're drugged."

He gave her a thumbs up with his good hand.

"Terrific," she muttered. "Just what I need. A stoned FBI agent with a broken wrist."

"Wallet," he said.

"What?"

"My insurance card is in my wallet. Take my Mastercard too, just in case they won't take American insurance. I'm not sure how their health care system works. Maybe you have to pay and your insurance company reimburses you."

"Where's your wallet?"

"Right hip pocket."

She glanced around the room. "Where's your pants?"

"I'm still wearing them."

"Why haven't they taken your pants off yet?"

"I dunno." David felt as placid as a marshmallow rid-ing around on a magic carpet. "Maybe they decided to leave the task for my young bride."

"You're a lot friendlier when you're looped. You know that?" Maddie complained. "I'm really starting to miss the old, grouchy Marshall."

"Why? He's an egotistical asshole. Stick with me, kiddo, and I'll make sure to always put you first."

"That's what I'm afraid of."

"Why are you afraid of a little TLC? You can dish it out but you can't take it?"

"Could you just lift your butt off the gurney?" She was running her hand underneath the back of his thigh.

He laughed. "That tickles."

"Raise your butt."

"You know, that's the nicest thing anyone has ever said to me."

"Poor you. Butt in the air."

He dug into the gurney with his heels and arched his back. "How's that?"

She was skimming her hands over his backside, grappling for his pocket. "Quit squirming."

"I can't."

"Are you purposely trying to make a fool of me?"

"No." David clamped his mouth shut to keep from laughing. Damn, but those were sure good drugs.

"Ahem!" From the doorway, the nurse cleared her throat. "May I help you?" she asked in French.

"My wife, she . . ." Simply saying the words made him chuckle. Or maybe it was because Maddie's long slender fingers were still tickling the hell out of his butt.

"This is your wife?"

"*Oui.*" David said, cheerful.

The nurse marched over to the gurney and stuck a small plastic cup in Maddie's hand.

"What's this?" She gaped at the cup.

The nurse spit out instructions in French before breezing out the door.

"What did she say?" Maddie asked, still staring suspiciously at the cup.

"You still wanna be my pretend bride?"

"Yes, why?"

David grinned. "Because the nurse said you have to help me get naked so I can pee in that cup."

Chapter
♥
SIXTEEN

THANK GOD, DAVID had finally fallen asleep. If she had to hear him call her his sweetie pie or snooker doodles or make smooching noises one more time she could not be held responsible for her actions.

Who knew he was such a sentimental fool when he was loaded on painkillers?

They'd been at the hospital for over six hours and now it was just after eleven o'clock at night. After running tests, casting his wrist and giving him a dose of antibiotics, the doctor had dismissed him with a prescription of Vicodin and orders to get plenty of rest.

Plenty of rest. Ha.

She drove through the darkened streets of Monaco looking for a hotel. David snored softly in the back seat. She really didn't want to stop for the night. She wanted to keep searching for Cassie, but David was counting on her to take care of things and she wouldn't let him down.

Plus, she needed some sleep herself. And food and a bath.

The thought of a hot bath was what tipped her over the edge. Besides, Cassie and Shriver had to sleep too. She stopped at the first hotel she found.

Since she'd been masquerading as his wife all night, she went ahead and checked them in as Mr. and Mrs. Marshall because she was honestly afraid to leave David alone for the night. He was so snockered she feared he'd pitch face first into the pillow and smother himself. But she did request a room with two beds.

"David," she said, after she'd procured their room and went back to the car to roust him.

"Hmph."

"Come on, wake up. Time for bed."

"Huh?"

She repeated herself.

"You're waking me up to put me back to sleep?"

"In a bed."

"With you?" He gave her the same sly, sexy grin he'd been throwing her way ever since they'd gorked him at the hospital.

"No, not with me. I have my own bed."

"Rats." He reached up to finger a strand of her hair that had swung loose from her ponytail. "I love your hair. It's so soft and pretty."

"Come on, Lothario. Give me your good arm."

After several failed attempts, she finally got him out of the car, onto his feet and into the hotel. David leaned heavily against her and by the time they made it to their room, Maddie's entire left side tingled with radiant heat from his body.

She propped him against the wall while she opened the door and turned to find him sliding slowly to the floor.

"No, no, no, none of that. Stay on your feet." She

caught him just before his legs gave way and got a shockingly good look at the depth of the bruising on his face. She cringed in sympathy.

"Hey there," he said brightly. "Where have you been all my life, beautiful?"

"Avoiding guys like you."

"How come?"

"How come what?" she said, getting her shoulder under his left arm and jacking him up.

"How come you've been avoiding me?"

"Shhh," she said.

"Why?" He glanced up and down the hall. "Is someone coming?"

If she hadn't been so tired and hungry and worried, this whole fiasco might have been comical. As it was, she couldn't wait to get him inside and into bed.

Once over the threshold, Maddie was unsettled to discover there was only one bed. The thought of having to complain and get switched to another room this late at night was so daunting, she simply blew it off. David would be passed out cold in no time flat and she could sleep on the covers in her clothes. No problem. Especially after being handcuffed to him last night.

But last night you were mad at him.

So?

Tonight you're feeling sorry for him. It's a whole other thing.

As if anything sexual was going to happen. The man was a walking—albeit barely—pharmacy.

After dumping David on the bed, she stepped over to the phone to call room service.

"We stopped serving at ten," the woman on the other end told her.

"Please," Maddie begged, lying through her teeth. "We're on our honeymoon and my husband broke his wrist and our luggage got lost and I'm just at my wits' end."

The woman murmured sympathetically. "I could send up something simple," she relented. "Soup, crackers, cheese, fruit."

"Perfect, thank you, you're a lifesaver." Maddie hung up and turned to find David eyeing her with a seductive gleam in his eyes.

"Hey babe."

"Room service is on the way. I'm going to hop into the shower."

"Can I come with you?" He was peering at her with cocky, Cary Grant charm.

"No."

"You're no fun." He pretended to pout.

"Do you think you can let room service in if they show up while I'm still in the shower?"

"Sure thing." His speech was still slurred. She wondered how long it would be before the shot wore off.

"How's your wrist?"

He stared down at the green Fiberglas cast. "Looks okay to me."

"Does it hurt?"

"Nope." He pulled open the drawer to the bedside table and leaned so far over to peer inside that Maddie feared he'd topple into it.

"What are you looking for?"

"A comb. My hair is mussed up."

"Your hair is always mussed up. I like it that way."

"Really?" He ran his good hand through his hair and grinned again.

"I love it. Now can you behave for five minutes?" God, it was like having a toddler.

"Uh-huh."

She went to the bathroom, leaned against the door and let out a sigh before slipping off her sweater. That's when she caught a glimpse of herself in the mirror.

Egad! She looked horrible. More proof that David was out of his head if he could flirt with her when she looked like this. Her hair was lank and stringy, dark circles ringed her eyes and dots of David's blood were splattered on her cheek.

Idly, she wondered how he'd managed to drive his car off the cliff, but the time had never been right to ask. She undressed and stepped into the shower.

The hot water was pure heaven and while she yearned to luxuriate under the pulsing spray, she didn't dare leave him alone for too long. Her legs were hairy but her razor was in her bag and only God knew where that was. She'd just have to live with prickly legs.

Maddie got out of the shower, wrapped her hair in a towel, put on one of the two white terrycloth robes hanging on the bathroom door and stuffed her underwear in the sink to soak. After David fell asleep, she would wash her things out by hand and hang them over the towel rack to dry.

She returned to the bedroom to find David munching on bread and sipping champagne.

"What are you doing?" She marched across the room to snatch the glass from his hand.

"Drinking champagne and feeling no pain."

"Are you nuts? Mixing alcohol and barbiturates? You're not some sixties rock star."

"Ah, what's it gonna hurt?"

"For starters, it could put you into a coma." Maddie eyed the bottle. "How did you even get that opened?"

"Room service did it for me."

"How efficient of them."

"Wanna cracker?" David extended his plate of crackers and cheese toward her. "I'll share."

"Stop eating on the covers. You're getting crumbs all over," she said, but what she was thinking was, Honey, you can eat crackers in my bed anytime.

"You sound like my father."

"Your father? I'd have thought I sounded like your mother."

"Nope. Dad was the perfectionist. Military man. Toe the line or suffer the consequences. Do you have any idea how many push-ups I can do?"

She shot a glance at his broken wrist. "Right now?"

"Well, maybe not right this minute. But normally, I can do five hundred and seventeen."

"Why not five hundred and eighteen?"

"Dad's record was five hundred and sixteen."

"Ah. Right. Competition. I guess your Dad was impressed when you broke his record."

"He was dead by the time I broke his record."

"I'm sorry to hear that."

David shrugged and wobbled a little. "Aw, he was an s.o.b."

Something about the way he said those words tore at her heart. "Made your life difficult, did he?"

"He made me the man I am today." There was pride in his voice.

"What happened to him? If you don't mind me asking?" Henri had said David didn't like talking about himself but the pain medication had loosened his lips and Maddie was going to take full advantage.

David shrugged. "He and my mom were killed when I was twelve. They were gunned down in the streets of a Third World country. My father was a four star general in town for a peace treaty." He laughed harshly at the irony.

"That's awful." Maddie put a hand to her chest. A lump of sympathy crowded her throat and her heart ripped for the poor little boy he'd once been.

"The embassy was in chaos and I was in shock. I just walked out the back entrance and ended up wandering the streets for three days, living as best as I could before the authorities found me and sent me to New York to live with my mother's older sister."

"Your Aunt Caroline."

"Yeah." He looked surprised. "How did you know?"

"Henri blabbed."

David rolled his eyes. "That crazy Frenchman. He thinks if he tells you something personal about me you'll fall in love with me."

"Really?"

He waved a dismissive hand. "You know how the French are about romance. From the minute we stepped off the plane together he's been convinced you're my lover."

Maddie felt breathless. "Whatever gave him that idea?"

"He says it's the way I look at you."

Flustered, Maddie changed the subject. "Did they ever catch the people who murdered your parents?"

"Nope."

Well, that explained a lot about him. She understood

now why he was so dogged, so determined. Why he had such a strong need to see justice done, to win at all costs.

She didn't know what to say. Any words she could dredge up sounded silly or misguided or patronizing. Instead, she ended up telling him how her mother had gone a bit crazy after their dad left. How she drank too much, forgot to pay the bills or buy groceries. How she hopped from one inappropriate guy to another, dragging her and Cassie along with her.

"I mean here I was fifteen and waiting up until three o'clock in the morning for my mom to come home from the nightclubs when it should have been the other way around. I never really got to be a kid, you know."

"Wow," David said. "That's pretty heavy duty."

"Not nearly as heavy duty as your story. And mine does have a happy ending. My mother met her current husband, Stanley, and he snapped her out of the funk she was in. Stanley's a rock solid guy. She's tried pretty hard to make up for those years she fumbled. I don't hold anything against her. She did the best she could."

"I appreciate you sharing that with me." He traced a finger over her cheek. "It took a lot of courage for you to open up."

She cleared her throat, eager to retreat from the intimacy of their shared confidences. "Do you need some help with the soup?"

"Normally I would say no. I'm an independent bastard." David raised his casted wrist. "But, considering that I have no depth perception with one eye swollen shut, I'm right handed and so hungry I could eat a mastodon raw, I'll take you up on the offer."

She sat beside him on the edge of the bed and her heart beat crazily.

He leaned over to sniff her neck. "You smell soapy clean."

"Thank you," she said primly, desperate to ignore the thrill of pleasure his warm breath generated as it raised the hairs on her nape.

"And you look really cute with your hair all twisted up in a towel. How do women do that?"

"Ancient feminine secret. If I told you I'd have to kill you." She dished up a bite of chicken soup and held her palm under the spoon so she wouldn't spill any on him. "Open up."

"I feel like a fool."

"Don't let that stop you. Come on."

Reluctantly, he opened his mouth and she touched the spoon to his lips.

Her gaze met his one good eye.

Feeding an invalid should not have been provocative or seductive or erotic.

But heaven help her, it was.

When he flicked out his tongue to accept the soup something hot and melty ran through her.

"Hmm," he moaned. "I didn't know soup could taste so good."

Hell, she never knew that the noise of a man appreciating his soup could sound so sexy. Even the slightest touch, the briefest glance, the smallest sound took on heightened significance.

A drop of wet liquid glistened on his lip and she had the most irresistible urge to kiss it off.

Help me! Help me! Help me! she prayed. She was rapidly losing control.

Maddie gulped and with a trembling hand, went back for the next spoonful. What was happening to her?

"Too bad I'm so busted up," he said.

"What?" she sounded panicky even to her own ears. Why did she have this overwhelming desire to get naked and rub herself all over him?

"If I weren't banged up, you wouldn't have to feed me. I notice you're having a little trouble."

"If you weren't banged up, I wouldn't be snuggled up next to you in bed."

"I was simply making an observation. Our little dinner *tête-à-tête* seemed to be turning you on."

"I am not turned on."

"Your nipples are poking through your robe."

Dammit! They were.

"Stop looking at my nipples."

"I didn't mean to make you mad."

"You didn't."

"You seem mad."

"I'm not." *Mad with desire for you is what I am and it had nothing to do with your sexual healing and everything to do with mine.* "Here's another bite." Hastily, she shoved the spoon toward his mouth.

"Whoa, slow down. Let's take this nice and easy."

The way he said *nice and easy* was clearly a come-on. He lowered his voice on those two words. Maddie refused to look at him. Refused to acknowledge the power of her own needs just aching to be sated.

This was too weird. Rattled, Maddie forgot to hold her palm under the spoon and ended up dumping soup on him.

"Oh damn." She snatched up the napkin from the tray and dabbed at his shirt. "I'm so clumsy."

"You're not clumsy. It's hard feeding someone else."

Especially when that someone else was rife with sexual innuendo.

"Here," she reached for the spoon once more. "Let's try again."

"I think we better just stick with the crackers and cheese and apple slices," he said huskily.

"Good idea."

They ate in silence, nibbling their snack, neither of them looking at the other. When they were finished, Maddie put the tray in the hallway. She turned back to find David standing beside the bed.

"I'm afraid I'm going to have to ask you to help me get undressed," he said.

"Sure. No problem."

Liar.

She reached up and began unbuttoning his shirt. Might as well start with the least threatening item.

"Hey," he said. "I just now noticed. There's only one bed in here."

"I know. I asked for two beds, but this is what we got."

"Is this going to be a problem? Sleeping in the same bed with me?"

"I slept with you last night."

"Yeah, but I was drunk."

"And tonight you're drugged."

"So we're cool?"

"It's not a problem for me if it's not a problem for you. Just as long as you don't try any funny business."

He inclined his hand toward his busted wrist. "I'm not exactly a threat."

"That's why it's not a problem." Maddie finished unbuttoning his shirt, revealing the broad expanse of his thick, muscular chest.

Talk about a six-pack! A dorm full of sorority girls could get falling down drunk off this guy's belly.

Swallowing hard against her rising desire to rake her fingers along the dense, compact ridges, Maddie reached instead for his belt buckle.

And she accidentally brushed her knuckles against his fly.

Immediately, he hardened.

Wow. Compliment accepted.

"I'm sorry, Maddie," David apologized and darned if, beneath all his black and blue marks, he wasn't blushing.

"It's all right," she lied. This was the last straw. She'd been barely holding it together from the moment she'd almost run over him on the highway.

"I don't mean any disrespect. Forgive me for the boner. It's just that you're so darned sexy and I've been dreaming of making love to you for days and you smell so good and I feel so damned rotten and . . ."

"Shhh." She laid a finger over his lips.

"No seriously, I'm really sorry. I'm embarrassed and ashamed over my lack of control. I have no excuse for my behavior. Absolutely none."

"Will you just shut up?" Maddie said and kissed him.

Chapter
SEVENTEEN

As an athlete, Maddie listened to her body and right now, it was telling her to go with the flow. Her skin sizzled with heightened warmth, her muscles quivered fluidly, her breathing, though controlled, lifted her to a whole new level of experience.

David tasted like champagne and chicken noodle soup and Camembert cheese and sesame seed crackers. He ran his wicked tongue along her lips and down her chin. She tossed her head, exposing her neck and waiting for his heated kisses to find her pounding pulse point.

With unerring accuracy, he homed in on that erogenous region and nibbled like a Pharaoh at his wedding feast. He cupped the back of her head in his left palm, holding her still while he devoured her scorching flesh.

"Are you giving me a hickey?" she asked.

"Do you want one?"

"No. Yes. Oh, just keep doing what you're doing. It's making my toes curl."

"Good answer." He wrapped his good arm around her waist and drew her closer.

She knew he was still flying high on the drugs they'd given him at the hospital. Knew she was skimming along on adrenaline and no sleep and the very real fear that David could have lost his life tonight. It seemed a sacrilege not to celebrate his survival. And while Maddie knew better than to trust this sweet freefall into the abyss of pleasure, she followed it anyway.

Where in the hell is your infamous common sense? Where's your caution?

Out the door, out the window, out of this world. Who knew? Who cared? Not she. Not at this moment. She had plenty of time for remorse and recrimination tomorrow. For once, she was going to do something impulsive, totally out of character and completely irresponsible.

He loosed the belt on her robe and it fell open. When the cool air hit her heated skin, she sucked in her breath. Glorious!

But not half as glorious as what David was doing to the hollow of her throat.

Flick, flick, flick, went his tongue.

Sizzle, sizzle, sizzle went her groin.

Had she ever felt so desperate, so achy, so out of control?

While her intense feelings scared her, they also liberated her. Here she was, in Monaco with a man she barely knew, taking a walk on the wild side.

Cassie would be proud.

Her mother would be proud.

Okay, she was even proud of herself. Never in a million years would she have guessed herself capable of such complete abandon. She nestled against David, absorbing his body heat, enjoying the pure physical sensation. They were alive. That's all that mattered.

He lowered his head and lightly kissed a trail down her cleavage. Maddie drew in a long, shuddery breath. Oh yes.

Dipping his head lower still, he took one beaded nipple in his mouth and she almost screamed, it felt that exquisite.

Her practical side was getting scared. She could almost hear her knees knocking.

Before she had time to reconsider her rash rush to intimacy, David was kissing her again with an urgency that French-fried her wary voice and short-circuited the last wire of her resistance.

They fell onto the bed together, careful of his broken wrist, but not much else. David pawed at her robe, roughly thrusting the lapel out of the way. Maddie grappled with his belt, tugging the smooth flat leather free from the loops and tossing it across the room.

He pushed her into the mattress, kissing her all over. Her lips, her eyes, her cheeks, her chin. He swept her away on wave after wave of erotic emotions.

Joy and fear. Lust and tenderness. Excitement and trepidation.

They were breathing hard, breathing in tandem, inhaling the same air, inhaling each other.

She fumbled with the hook and eye on his trousers. He ran his fingers across the fine blond hairs on her chest.

He groaned.

She moaned.

She slipped her hand past the waistband of his pants and into his underwear. She sucked in her breath, daunted by the heat of him, hovering on the verge of generous discovery.

At the same time she was investigating him, he was investigating her.

"You've got the flattest, tautest tummy I've ever seen," he marveled, strumming his hand over her abdomen.

"Two hundred sit-ups a day on an incline board," she bragged shamelessly, thrilled that he loved her body. Some men thought she was too muscular, but apparently not David.

He slid his fingers slowly between her thighs and Maddie thought, *I can't believe I'm here, doing this. Letting myself go without overanalyzing things.*

While his fingers explored below, he let his tongue do the walking above her waist, licking her like a lollipop.

Her nipples bloomed under his attention and her breasts grew heavy with need. If he was this good when he was chock full of painkillers, she shuddered to imagine what he was like when he was up to full speed.

He's vulnerable. You're taking advantage of him.

That thought brought her up short and she stopped rummaging in his underpants.

"What is it?" he gasped, raising his head to gaze into her face. At the sight of his swollen eye guilt kicked her in the gut. "What's wrong?"

"You're wounded and I'm acting like a sex fiend. I should be taking care of you, babying you."

"Hush." He laid an index finger over her lips. "I need sexual healing."

"But—"

"Not a word."

"You don't really want sex," she mouthed around his finger.

"Be quiet."

"What you really want is some good old fashioned TLC and I started . . ."

He clamped his hand over her mouth. "What part of stop talking don't you understand?"

"Daydid," was how his name sounded from behind his salty palm.

"What I really want is to make love to you, Maddie, so don't ruin it by over-thinking things, okay?"

"Okay."

"Now, where were we?" He lowered his head again.

Maddie tapped him on the shoulder. "We can't do this."

"Why not?"

"I don't have a condom. Do you have a condom?"

"In my bag."

"And where's that?"

"Probably on the supersonic train shuttling back and forth from Paris to Madrid."

"My point exactly."

"I'll go get a condom. Just hold that pose."

"You can barely walk and it's after midnight."

He sighed and rolled over onto his back. "So that's it?"

"This was a bad idea from the beginning."

"It was a fine idea."

"No it wasn't. I should never have kissed you. Why did I kiss you?"

David groaned and this time not with pleasure. "Do you have to analyze everything to death? We were both horny. Things got hot and heavy. Common sense prevailed. End of story. Now let's go to sleep."

"You're right. I should just let this go. We'll forget all about it. Yes. It's forgotten."

Apparently so. David was already snoring.

Great. He was cattywampus in the bed, crowding her out. Fine, she'd just go blow dry her hair and wash out her lingerie. Let him sleep. He needed the rest.

In the meantime, however, what was she supposed to do with the throbbing ache he'd created between her legs?

He couldn't forget all about it.

David listened to Maddie puttering around in the bathroom while he pretended to be asleep. The drugs were wearing off and his numerous pains were returning to needle him.

She was humming softly under her breath and he caught himself straining to recognize the tune and finally identified it as a song by Faith Hill about the rapture of a mind-blowing kiss.

He smiled at the ceiling. He had gotten to her whether she would admit it or not.

Trouble was, she'd gotten to him too.

In a way nobody had in a very long time. Maybe even never. He thought about Keeley, about how he'd felt when he was around her and he had to confess his feelings then were nowhere near as intense as these strange and inexplicable emotions he was having for Maddie now.

The delicious smell of her remained in his nostrils, a tantalizing ghost scent. The honeyed flavor of her lips lingered on his tongue, rich, full, promising. He shook his head, remembering how quickly he'd grown hard when she'd barely touched him.

He couldn't keep lying to himself. He wanted Maddie more desperately than he had ever wanted any woman. Keeley included. He found her, quite simply, irresistible.

Some men might think she was too muscular or that her chin was a little too pointed. But he appreciated the contrast of that determined chin in juxtaposition to her soft, bow-shaped mouth. He admired the richness of shadow in her cheekbones, the clarity of light in her emerald eyes. He loved studying the geometry of her form. Her lines and curves, the angles and circles that made up her womanly body.

But his feelings for her went far beyond her physical attractiveness.

He respected how she was warm, supportive and compassionate with those she loved. He admired her work ethic and her steady reliability. She enchanted him utterly and he had never expected to be so smitten, but here it was.

He loved her loyalty, her no-bullshit outlook on life and how she fought the good fight. He enjoyed being around her. She sparked his interest with her clever sense of humor and her pragmatic approach to problem solving.

He even found her worrywart tendencies endearing. It showed she truly cared. And while he sometimes found her cautiousness a challenge, she challenged him in a good way. After what she'd told him about her family, he understood why she had trouble trusting other people to be there for her the way she was there for them.

Which was kind of weird when you thought about it, because he'd never been big on offering his trust indiscriminately. But if he ever got Maddie to put aside her doubts and trust him completely—what a precious gift that would be.

Did he dare hope for such rewards? Was he expecting too much?

He also knew it was no coincidence she'd been the one to find him after he'd been beaten up by Blanco. Even though David wasn't a big proponent of destiny, he believed something had placed her on that road at just the right time. She had an instinct for being there whenever you needed her. He probably owed her his life.

And to think he'd ditched her at the Prado.

He felt guilty and misguided and ashamed of himself for not having more faith in her. He should have told her about his suspicions that Blanco had kidnapped Cassie away from Shriver. He should have told her what Isabella had told him about Cassie's plan. He should tell her now.

She would want to know.

Yes. Maddie was a tell-it-like-it-is kind of woman. She didn't play games and she liked being informed about what was going on around her. She didn't stick her head in the sand and ignore reality.

And man, how he wanted her.

David swung his legs off the bed, grabbed his discarded shirt and headed for the door. He was going after condoms and he wasn't coming back until he found them.

He returned twenty minutes later with a box of square foil packets in one hand and a grin on his achy face. He dry swallowed a pain pill to help him see this seduction through. He was going to make love to her tonight, broken wrist, blackened eye and all.

"Where have you been?" Maddie demanded, hands on her hips, worry pulling her brows into a frown. "When I came out of the bathroom and found you gone, I almost had a heart attack."

He held up the box of condoms.

"You didn't?" Her frown dissolved into a shy Mona Lisa smile.

"I did."

"David . . . I . . ."

"Getting cold feet?" He stalked across the room and wrapped his good arm around her waist.

"I've just been thinking . . ."

"Stop thinking, babe, and just feel," he murmured.

The thing was, he'd been thinking too. He had the notion they were standing on the verge of something truly monumental but he had no idea how to articulate his feelings, so he would just show her.

With fingers full of hungry, aching need, he peeled off her robe until Maddie stood completely naked before him.

He forgot to inhale. God, but she was gorgeous. He'd never seen anything sexier. He gazed into her eyes and his chest knotted. This was his Maddie, looking at him as if he'd created the sun and the moon and the stars.

Her nipples beaded taut and her disheveled hair curled provocatively about her slender shoulders. She was completely exposed to him, vulnerable, all her protection gone, but she did not shy away. She did not shrink back.

She was so brave to trust him.

David drank her in. Every dazzling inch of her. From the hollow of her throat, to her rounded breasts, to the flat smoothness of her belly to the sweet blond V at the juncture of her thighs.

Her cheeks flushed rosy at his perusal. Her eyes sparkled, reflecting his expanding excitement. She wet her lips and never took her gaze from his face.

He clenched his fists to keep himself from grabbing her and taking her right there on the floor. He wanted their first time to be nice and slow and easy. He wanted it to last. He wanted to please her beyond her wildest expectations.

His cock throbbed and his throat tightened as she reached out to unbutton his shirt for the second time that night. Her touch was soft, yet stimulating. It was incredible.

He was without a doubt the luckiest bastard on the face of the earth. To have this warm, strong, supple woman caressing him as if he were pure gold, when she was the find, the treasure, the glistening diamond. He was just an old chunk of coal.

Doubts suddenly flooded his mind. What did he have to offer a woman like her? The FBI was his life. He craved excitement, the thrill of the chase. It was the reason Keeley had left him. Secretly, he feared the quiet stability of a loving relationship. Feared it because he just knew he'd eventually screw it up. He had no idea how to be the kind of solid, rock-steady man someone like Maddie needed.

She leaned into him and softly brushed her lips against his. "Stop thinking," she whispered. "You're thinking too much. Enjoy the moment."

Here she was, turning the tables on him. Just when he thought he had her figured out she did the unexpected.

He kissed her, putting all his long-dormant emotions into it.

Several minutes later, she pulled back to take a breath. "Wow," she said. "Wow."

"You ain't seen nothing yet," he teased.

Eagerly, she peeled the shirt off his shoulders, over his cast and then let it drop to the floor. Her fingers went to his zipper and he hissed in his breath. He wrapped his hand around hers.

"Let me."

David shucked his pants in record time, almost tripping as he kicked them into the corner. Maddie turned, displaying the creamy curve of her delectable fanny and walked toward the bed.

He followed.

Chapter

EIGHTEEN

THE PRESSURE BUILDING inside Maddie's body was low, deep, and hot. It was a heavy liquid flame, denser than mercury, more flammable than gasoline.

She wanted him inside her, filling her up, easing this intense, throbbing ache. She wanted to fly into a million pieces and lay breathless forever. Her need was as desperate as a wild animal, thrashing to get free from its cage.

"I need you," she said. "I don't want to wait anymore."

"Oh babe," he groaned.

He pulled back the covers and eased her down onto the cool sheets. He hugged her close and she could hear the steady thumping of his heart.

"Close your eyes."

She did and he kissed her eyelids. First one, then the other and back again. No one had ever kissed her eyelids before and it felt amazingly erotic.

He ran his good hand through her hair and that was an erotic sensation too. He kneaded her scalp. Back and forth, soft and slow.

Then he planted kisses down the length of her nose until he got to her lips. He paused.

"Don't stop, you wicked man." She opened her eyes and found him staring at her.

"You ready for this?"

"I've been ready since the moment I first saw your naked chest in that motel room in Grand Cayman."

"No kidding?"

"Don't get egotistical on me now."

"I thought you didn't like me."

"I didn't like the feelings you stirred in me."

"You were turned-on that day?"

"You couldn't tell?"

"No."

She nudged him in the ribs. "I'm turned-on now. Or at least I was. Get to it, man."

"Yes, ma'am," he said and claimed her mouth.

He tasted wonderful.

Maddie moaned as his wicked tongue flicked across her palate, the sound of her pleasure humming against his mouth. She felt weak and dizzy, strong and steady all at the same time. A carousel of sensation, spinning her around and around.

He tightened his grip, his masculine hands reassuring her that she wasn't making a mistake. His excited touch sent a thousand minuscule infernos fanning out down her abdomen, scorching her, rousing her higher and higher until her body was nothing more than a trembling, molten core.

His mouth left hers, and he tracked his sinful tongue over her eager flesh, forging a channel of ripe heat to her throat where he sketched erotic triangles along the length of her collarbone.

He seemed to know her body more intimately than she knew it herself. With unerring accuracy, he found her every erogenous zone and used his discoveries to full advantage. Massaging the underside of her jaw, stroking the smooth area between her elbow and her armpit, nibbling the back of her knees, blowing lightly on the spot just below her navel after he'd licked it.

When he blew warm air gently into her ear, she giggled at the tickly sensation and felt younger than she had in years. She felt lighthearted. He made her want to play.

He used his tongue to maximize her pleasure, dispatching shuddering waves of chilly thrills throughout her body and when he stroked her inner ear with his tongue, she literally quaked.

His touch was magic, making her forget everything but this moment. She breathed him in, inhaling his masculinity, savoring the uniqueness of their joining.

Ah, the power of his fingertips. The mystery of his tongue.

He stretched his body over hers, lying atop her but propping his weight on his elbows. She worried about his broken wrist but it didn't seem to bother him. His erection throbbed hot and hard against her belly. He stroked her cheek with a hand and gazed into her eyes.

She hiccupped against the intensity of emotion written on his face. She telegraphed her own feelings to him, staring deeply into his soul.

You're special.

She knew him. The way she'd never known another. Not even the connection she had with her twin could rival this bond, this link, this nexus of meaning so intense there was no need to speak. In fact, words would have lessened the impact of what they were both feeling.

He dipped his head, breaking the visual bridge between them, but where his gaze left off, his lips took over. Gently, he sucked one of her pebble hard nipples into his red hot mouth.

Maddie hissed in her breath. Chills peppered her body like buckshot, searing the root of every single nerve ending she possessed.

Her breasts swelled and ached against his mouth and she whimpered. "Please, please."

"Please what?"

She was swept away by this mounting hurts-so-good pressure, she couldn't even speak.

"Do you want me to stop?" He pulled back leaving her damp nipple bereft.

"No, no, don't stop."

"You want more?"

She nodded.

"More of this?" He lightly flicked her nipple. "Or would you rather have some of this?" He made his penis bounce against her belly.

"I'm greedy," she admitted. "I want it all."

"And you deserve it all," he said.

He shifted, positioning himself with one hip pressed into the mattress.

And then he began to explore, trailing his fingers from her breastbone downward on a treasure hunt that soon had her quivering from her feet to her head.

"Wait," she said, fighting off the deliciousness of it all. "I have to tell you something."

"This isn't the part where you tell me you used to be a man?" he teased. "Because babe, I don't believe it for a minute."

"Don't be silly, I'm serious."

He propped himself on an elbow. "All right, Serious. I'm listening. So what's the big secret?"

"It's not that it's a secret, it's just something you don't tell a guy until things advance to a certain point."

"I take it we've reached that point."

"Passed it actually."

"I'm listening. You can tell me anything," he assured her. "I don't want any secrets between us."

"You really mean that?"

"Absolutely." He nodded, grinning impishly. "If you really did used to be a guy I'll just learn how to deal with it."

"David, stop teasing."

He forced away his frown and cleared his throat. "Do I look serious enough?"

"Oh you." She shook her head.

"Okay, I'll settle down." He took her hand and gazed into her eyes again. "What do you have to tell me?"

"I've never . . . um . . . I'm not sure how to say this."

He blinked at her. "Maddie, are you trying to tell me you're a virgin?"

"No, I'm sorry, I'm not a virgin. Are you terribly disappointed?"

"Don't be ridiculous. You're twenty-seven years old and damned attractive. I'm glad you haven't been waiting just for me to show up. The pressure would be intimidating."

"Oh."

"That didn't come out right." He pressed a palm to his forehead. "What I mean to say is, I'm certainly not a virgin. How could I expect you to be one?"

"Whew," she giggled. "That's a relief. And here I was worrying I'd have to teach you all about making love."

"I'm not saying I don't have a lot to learn. I want to memorize every inch of your body. Just tell me what feels good to you, babe."

"You've been doing a great job so far."

"We've gotten sidetracked. Let's go back to whatever it is you wanted to tell me." He rubbed his thumb against her palm.

"Well, it's along those lines. Of knowing my body I mean."

"Yes."

"I'm . . . I've never . . ."

He arched an eyebrow. "Had an orgasm?"

"Not with a partner."

"All right."

"I'm just telling you so you won't be disappointed or upset if I can't come with you inside me."

David touched her cheek. *Maybe you've just been with the wrong partner,* he thought but what he said was, "That's okay. Thanks for telling me."

"I'm so glad you understand."

"I'll tell you what," he said, rolling over onto his back. Now that she'd told him she'd never had an orgasm with a partner, he was more determined than ever to make sure she did. "From here on out you're in control."

"Really?"

He thrust his hands over his head. "I'm tied up. Can't move unless you tell me I can. I'm yours for the taking, do with me what you will."

And please don't make me come before you do.

She straddled his waist and leaned over him, her breasts rubbing provocatively against his chest. She kissed him with a passion that filched his breath and left him at her mercy.

Her tongue plunged deeply into his mouth. She saucily bit his lower lip. With a feral, pressing need, her hands clasped his body. His breath was coarse and jagged in his throat as he clutched her hips to his.

"No hands," she admonished and reluctantly, he raised his arms over his head again.

She sat up and he gloried in the sight of her above him, in the diffuse light from the bathroom, coupled with the moonlight shining through the bedroom window.

Damn! She was a goddess.

Her knees were flush against his flanks, her bottom pressed against the top of his penis. She was so close. His body cried for her to take him inside her warm moistness, but at the same time he wanted to wait.

"Show me," he said. "How you like it. How you pleasure yourself."

Maddie hesitated a moment, then she reached for his left hand. Totally mesmerized by her sensual movements, he gave her his hand and waited, trancelike for her to make good use of it.

She moved his hand downward, and placed his fingers against her velvet opening.

Oh yeah. Gently, he began to stroke her with his index finger.

"That's right," she cooed.

While his first finger stayed busy carefully strumming her straining hood, he slipped his second finger past her warm, milky lips and into her moist secret cave.

Excruciating excitement flashed through him and he groaned. "You're so wet and hot."

"For you," she murmured. "All for you."

Her words brought a sense of pride to his heart and he

experienced love for her so strong it pushed at the back of his eyelids.

He clenched his jaw and swallowed hard.

Without warning, she pulled away from him.

"Whaaa?" He stared at her dumbstruck and pained. She wasn't turning back now. No.

She slid down the length of his body, gliding her hands nimbly over his skin. She undulated with catlike grace, her motions supple. Her hot probing tongue licking down his belly.

"No, if you go down there, I won't last a minute."

"What's your recovery time?" She winked and he came undone. Groaning, he shoved his hand through his hair and reminded himself to breathe.

She kissed his body with promises of unimaginable ecstasy. She rolled her tongue over his navel, teasing and cajoling.

Her breasts dangled provocatively above his penis. His gazed fixed on her jiggling, rosy-pink nipples. His penis stiffened, straining as if trying to reach up and touch those gorgeous nubs. Reaching down, she lightly tangled her fingertips in his hair.

"Please, I want to be inside you."

"All in good time."

"You're loving this. Torturing me."

"Uh-huh." She winked.

"Tease."

When she cupped his balls, he hissed in a scalded breath and when her hand traveled up to stroke his shaft he had to close his eyes and fight to keep from coming in her palm.

"You're so big and thick," she said, with awe in her voice. She made him feel like a million bucks.

Then she blew a stream of hot breath on the throbbing head. Involuntarily, he lifted his hips off the mattress, straining for her.

"Enough," he said.

He couldn't take the teasing one more minute. Grabbing her around the waist, he rolled her over, tumbling them both to the edge of the mattress. He dropped his feet to the floor, pulled her hips close to him.

"Wrap your legs around my waist," he growled.

She obeyed.

He liked this position. It was his turn to tease.

He caressed her tender, feminine flesh, inhaled her musky womanly scent and breathed in pure pride. She was with him!

She quivered and pulsed against his hand and he knew he could make her come with his fingers, but he wanted to see if he could take it higher. If he could be the one to give her an orgasm during intercourse.

Then he dropped to his knees and kissed her sweet inner lips, drinking up her warm, womanly flavor. No one on earth tasted like her and the essence that was Maddie branded into his brain. He would never forget this moment, this taste, this woman.

On and on they played the game, on and on. Touching and stroking, licking and nibbling, bringing each other to the brink of orgasm many times but never tumbling over the precipice, until they were breathless with need, their eyes shiny with feverish desperation.

"I can't . . ." Maddie whispered.

"I know," he answered.

"Condom, please, now, hurry."

"Okay." He tore into the box of condoms, grasped a corner of one foil packet in his teeth and ripped it open.

He rolled the condom on with the speed of an Olympic athlete going for the gold.

"Take me," she said, the minute he positioned himself beside her on the bed.

He could no longer resist. David knelt between her thighs and spread them wide.

The core of her womanhood welcomed his throbbing tip with a tightening twinge. He eased in gently, not wanting to cause her any discomfort.

She arched her hips upward, wrapped her arms around his shoulders and pulled him down, forcing him in deeper, spearing herself with his body.

"Ooh." She sighed, her warm breath feathering his hair. "Aah."

His heart pounded in a wild, frenzied rhythm. Go slow, he told himself, but he could not. She felt too good, this felt too right.

She writhed against his movements, eyes closed, head thrown back, hair spilling over the pillow like golden sunshine.

You are my sunshine, he thought recklessly.

He reveled in her soft coos of pleasure. He could feel her body responding to every precise, sensual stroke he delivered. In the quivering of her buttocks, he felt her bliss. She was close, so very close. He grinned.

While he stroked her with his body, he also stroked her with his hand, tenderly tweaking her trigger spot. The small, hooded button surged against his attention, begging for more.

His lungs shredded with the effort of breathing past the intensity of his desire for her.

"I'm on fire," she moaned. "I'm on fire."

"I know, sweetheart, I know."

"David, David," she cried his name and he'd never heard a more precious sound cross a woman's lips. She clutched his shoulders with both hands and rocked her pelvis like a mad woman. "I'm close, I'm close."

Ah, he thought, for the *coup de grâce*.

He angled his head and took one burgeoning nipple into his mouth, never stopping his slow, steady stroking. His left hand stayed busy, gently caressing her hood. He suckled her. Cautiously at first and then picking up the tempo.

She writhed and thrashed, bucked and moaned. He never let up even though he was getting a cramp in his calf. To hell with his discomfort, this was about giving Maddie the pleasure she so justly deserved.

She raked her fingernails over his back, she tugged at his hair. He closed his eyes to fight off his own release, knowing that if he could just hold out for a few more minutes, he could take her with him.

He raised his head and peered into her face. Her eyes were closed, her face twisted into a mask of sexual anticipation. Her breathing was incredibly shallow, her face flushed.

"Look at me," he said. "Open your eyes and look at me."

Her eyes flew open and they tumbled into each other. The world fell away. Monaco did not exist. The hotel room did not exist. The bed did not exist.

It was as if they were floating in a separate universe. They were the only two people occupying this deep, vast space. Just he and Maddie and their beating hearts.

Lub-dub, lub-dub. Beating as one cosmic force.

She started to close her eyes.

"No, no, keep looking at me."

She stared into him.

He stared into her.

And then they were one being. One force. There was no separation.

They cried out in unison when their simultaneous climax hit. Their gaze never separated as they were mirrored back to each other.

He was she. She was he. Yin and Yang in perfect harmony. Two halves of the whole. One.

Wave after wave of sensation washed over them, sending them hurtling together on the shores of sexual release. But with the deceleration of tension, came a quiet, soft, incredible peace.

This was right. This was perfect.

"David," she whispered his name on a reverential breath. "Thank you, David."

He smiled tenderly at her, his heart so full he could not speak. He did not move. He never wanted this moment to end.

Maddie. Maddie. Maddie. Had any name ever sounded so sweet?

She smiled back, reached up and lightly traced her fingers along his lips. "I love being joined to you like this."

He nodded, the emotions so thick in his throat he feared he might actually cry if he started talking. He had never known such connection with another human being was possible. Had never dreamed he'd find such a woman. He'd always viewed love as a dark mystery that struck others but had somehow left him unscathed. That was probably why he hadn't been heartbroken over his breakup with Keeley. The love had never really been there.

But now he knew the truth. Love was mysterious, oh

yes. But he was not immune. He'd once thought he was too idealist to fall for the earthy, helpless trap of love, but he'd been wrong.

He'd been wrong about so many things.

What he thought was a heedless swirl of foolishness was instead the pinnacle of life itself. He wasn't a poetic man, although he'd always admired beauty in art. But this feeling made him want to spout Wordsworth and Browning and Teasdale until he had no breath left.

His heart sang like a bird.

His heart bloomed like a cherry tree in spring.

His heart refracted like a rainbow, full, vibrant and unashamed.

He, David Marshall—the man who'd immersed himself in his work, the man who played to win at all costs, the man who was never quite sure where he belonged— was in love.

Maddie lay in the dark listening to David's soft snores, her body still quivering from the effects of their stupendous lovemaking.

She wanted to cry with joy but she was too overwhelmed for tears. She'd never had an orgasm with a partner. She figured she never would.

But David . . . ah David. She hugged her pillow to her chest and grinned in the darkness. Thank you, David, thank you.

Her body was sated and her heart was full. She felt peaceful, relaxed and wonderfully reckless. Maybe that's what it took for her to have an orgasm. To simply relax and let go of her fears. To turn loose and fall headlong into passion.

Careful. That old naysaying voice was back, ruffling

the waters of her newfound serenity. *Don't jump to con-clusions. Don't assume you have a relationship just be-cause he pushed all the right buttons.*

So what should she assume? That they'd had one great night of unbridled passion and that was it?

Protect yourself. Hold back. This was just fabulous sex. You can't forget that David is ultimately your enemy. No matter how much you like him, he's out to jail your sister.

Right.

The last thing she needed was to go soft in the head over a man who was married to his job.

She had her sister to think about and the vow she'd taken on that cold December night oh so long ago. Cassie came first. Always

So here was her plan. She'd play it cool. Act like noth-ing monumental had happened. If their joining had meant more to David than mere sex, then he was going to have to be the one to make the first move. He was going to have to open up and talk to her. She'd bravely taken the physical risk, opening her body to him. Only time would tell if he was brave enough to let down his steely guard and take an emotional gamble on her.

Until then, Maddie was making darned sure she kept her own heart well out of the fray.

Chapter

NINETEEN

"So where do we go from here?" Maddie asked David over an omelet the following morning.

She'd been unusually quiet, waking him not long after dawn with a gentle nudge and a nod at the bedside clock.

They'd avoided talking or even looking at each other as they got dressed and left the room. For his part, David was pretty fuzzy on the details of the night before. He remembered making love to her. Remembered her orgasm quaking around him. Who could forget that?

But he didn't remember what he'd said. Or what she'd said. Or if there had been any expectations for the future on her part. Hell, he didn't even remember how he felt about all this. Everything beyond their explosive physical connection was pretty much a blur.

How did she feel about what had happened? Should he ask?

But fear of learning more than he could handle held him back. He elected to go with the closed mouth policy Maddie seemed to have adopted. If she wanted the sex to be casual, he was cool with that. The fewer complications, the better.

Right?

Don't ask. Don't tell. Best policy.

She'd put up the wall, he wasn't inclined to scale it. Not now anyway. Not until the investigation was over and he knew where they stood.

"Pardon?" He pretended to be highly interested in his croissant, buttering it with elaborate intent.

"There are no more clues from Cassie," Maddie said. "We've run into a dead end. You're the detective. Where do we go from here? Do you suppose she and Shriver are still in Monaco? Why do you think they came here? Is there a famous art collector or something that lives nearby?"

"Maddie . . . I," he started.

"Yes?" She leaned forward, her gaze fixed on his face and she clucked her tongue. "Your eye looks awful."

"Don't worry about me. I'll live."

"We never discussed your accident last night. What happened? Did your car fishtail in the rain?"

David cleared his throat. "I didn't have a car accident."

"No?" She looked confused.

"I came upon an accident and went down the hill to see if I could help. I pulled the driver from behind the wheel. He turned out to be Jocko Blanco. He took me unaware, beat me up, stole my car and my gun."

"Oh, David." Concern swam in her eyes and she raised a hand to her throat. "Jocko Blanco is here? In Monaco?"

"I'm afraid it's worse than that."

"Worse?" Her bottom lip trembled. He tried to keep his face impassive, neutral but somehow she picked up on his body language. She already knew something was wrong.

Steeling his courage, he told her what he should have told her back at the Prado.

"No." Her face paled.

"I'm afraid so."

"So I was right. Cassie didn't willingly rob the Prado."

"She did not."

"You think Blanco kidnapped her away from Shriver and used her as a pawn to gain access to the museum?"

He nodded.

"So where is Cassie?" she whispered hoarsely.

"I don't know."

"Where do we go for answers?" She gazed at him intently, her bottom lip caught between her teeth.

She was depending on him to find her sister and he would not let her down. David had the oddest sense that helping her was the most important thing he'd ever done and at that moment he knew he had to make a choice. Stay on Shriver's trail or go look for Cassie.

Four days ago, he would have snorted in derision if anyone had told him that anything could get in the way of his single-minded focus on collaring the art thief. For ten years, ever since Shriver had cruelly robbed his beloved Aunt Caroline of both her dignity and the Rembrandt, he'd lusted to see the man behind bars.

He'd even changed his major to law enforcement and joined the FBI just so he could hunt Shriver down and make him pay. He'd lain awake at night, imagining just how satisfying it would feel to clamp handcuffs on the thief who'd glibly used dozens of women to make his ill-gotten fortune. He'd dreamed of recovering the Rembrandt and returning it to his aunt. He'd spent a decade envisioning the happy smile on her face when he broke the good news. He wanted so badly to repay her for everything she'd done for him.

He had yearned for justice, yes, but he'd also longed for revenge. No one treated his loved ones badly and got away with it. He'd been determined to win at all costs.

But that was four days ago. A lot had happened. Exactly when had his priorities shifted from bringing in Shriver to saving Maddie's sister?

When he'd realized Blanco was the masked man at the Prado.

Even now, a cold chill passed over him. Cassie's life hung in the balance and a life, anyone's life, would always be more important than stolen art.

But, maybe, if he was lucky, he could save Cassie *and* send Shriver to prison for a long, long time.

"I'll call Henri," he assured Maddie and then he made a vow he would spend his last breath trying to keep. "And I promise you, whatever it takes, I won't stop until I find your sister."

"I believe you," she whispered and he was gratified by her trust. "But will we find her alive? Or dead?"

They wandered around the streets of Monaco waiting for Henri to call David back, not knowing where else to go or what else to do. All Cassie's breadcrumb clues had dead-ended in this quaint little country. Maddie tried her best not to imagine the worst, but fighting her instincts was a losing battle.

David reached over and took her hand. "Stop visualizing disaster."

"How do you know that's what I'm doing?"

"Whenever you're thinking scary thoughts, you screw your forehead up tight."

"Do I really?" She reached up to smooth her forehead with two fingers.

"Yes, really."

Maddie inclined her head at him. In spite of the broken wrist and black eye and the cut along his jaw, he looked dashingly handsome in the early morning sunlight. Strong and reliable and there.

That was the most important part.

He was there. Holding her hand.

She remembered what he'd sworn to her in the restaurant and she held it close to her heart. *And I promise you, whatever it takes, I won't stop until I find your sister.*

She realized she was counting on him to keep his promise. Somewhere along the way, she'd started believing in him.

And that terrified her.

Be careful. Don't let him know how you really feel about him.

They stood on the sidewalk, studying each other and Maddie was struck hard by the intensity of her feelings. *I could fall stone cold in love with him if I let myself.*

That notion scared her even more.

But you won't!

She'd never been in love, never wanted to be in love, had avoided anything that remotely looked like love.

Because she didn't trust it.

Her parents had once been wildly, madly, crazily in love and poof, a sick kid had ended it all. If you couldn't trust a wedding vow, what could you trust?

"Stop it." David rubbed her forehead with his thumb. "No more dark thoughts."

She had to admit this was pretty handy. Having someone monitor her inner negativity. He was good for her.

But was she good for him?

"No, no." he rubbed her forehead harder. "You're too young and pretty for frown lines."

The cell phone he'd just recharged in the cigarette lighter of Maddie's rental car blasted the *Dragnet* theme.

They both jumped.

David reached for the phone with his right hand but the bulky cast stopped him in mid-reach. The phone rang again.

"Hurry, hurry, before he hangs up," Maddie said.

He fumbled in his jacket pocket with his left hand and ended up dropping the phone.

"Let me do it." Maddie grabbed for it at the same time David bent down and they ended up cracking their heads together.

"Ouch!"

"Ow!"

Frowning, David answered it on the fifth ring. "Marshall here."

Nervously, Maddie gnawed a thumbnail. He listened intently, nodding occasionally but never once letting his expression give any clues about the information he was receiving.

"Okay, Henri, thanks." He rang off and shifted his gaze to Maddie.

"Well?"

"They found my rental car with Blanco's prints all over it."

"Where?"

"At the Piazzale Roma car park outside Venice."

"Any word on Cassie?" She clasped her hands. Please, please, please let her be okay.

"I'm sorry, sweetheart, no."

Venice was architectural poetry.

A floating fantasy. A dozy reverie of mist and sunshine. A winding labyrinth of walkways and waterways of complicated beauty.

All her life, Maddie had daydreamed of visiting Venice. She'd pictured herself strolling along the cobblestone streets, gliding through the canals in a graceful gondola, shopping in the Rialto district. She'd longed to watch artisans blowing exquisite glassware. She'd thirsted to drink Bellinis at an outdoor café.

And she'd blushed to think of kissing a handsome stranger under the Bridge of Sighs.

To think she was in the city of her dearest fantasies in the midst of Carnevale and she could not enjoy a minute of the experience. All she cared about was finding Cassie.

They arrived on a vaporetto sardined with tourists. By the time the waterbus arrived at their stop, Maddie was yoga breathing to ward off claustrophobia.

At least she told herself it was claustrophobia. What she really feared was that among the maddening throng, in the narrow pathways of this ancient city, she would never find her sister alive.

Venice in February was an overwhelming jumble of sights and sounds and scents. The weather was chilly but not uncomfortably cold. Maddie snuggled deeper into her denim jacket and eyed the throng of people—many dressed in colorful Carnevale garb—streaming through the streets.

Faces were hidden behind elaborate masks. Hair was

secreted beneath decorative wigs. Excited shouts of pleasure and rich laughter filled the air.

A woman in a huge bustle waltzed with a man wearing a startling codpiece along the edge of a piazza. Roaming troubadours in Renaissance attire strummed mandolins or lutes. Young women wore feathers and lace and an abundance of jewelry.

Maddie stopped and stared, unable to absorb it all.

"This way," David said.

Getting a hotel at the last minute in Venice during Carnevale would have been impossible if it weren't for Interpol. Henri had pulled some influential strings, grabbing them a VIP suite at the exclusive Hotel International near the Piazza San Marco.

David took her hand and while she appreciated the comfort of his touch, she couldn't help bristling. She was still upset with him for not telling her his suspicions about Blanco back at the Prado. He claimed he hadn't told her because he'd wanted to protect her, but Maddie couldn't help wondering if he'd kept silent because he was too hardheaded to admit he'd been wrong about Cassie.

They edged their way to the middle of the bridge but once there, discovered they couldn't move any farther.

Up ahead, something had captured the crowd's attention and no one was budging. From above, the noonday sun cast a festive glow over the city. Below them, gondolas, waterbuses and barges cruised the canal.

"You know," she said to David, "if someone had a heart attack right here, right now, they'd die before help could get to them."

David shook his head and smiled wryly.

"What?"

"Do you always have to imagine the worst case scenario?"

"It helps prepare me for any eventuality," she said, defensively. "I like being prepared."

"Well, you can stop worrying so much. I'm here."

Maddie snorted. "As if I would rely on you."

"You still don't trust me?" He sounded hurt. "Not even after all we've been through together?"

"Don't take it personally, you're a little busted up." She waved at his broken wrist.

"Didn't get in my way last night."

She felt her cheeks color. She didn't want to talk about last night. She'd lost her head, lost her mind, lost every shred of common sense. She didn't want to be reminded of her mistake.

"You're a hard nut to crack, Maddie Cooper," he said, his unblackened eye snapping with an intelligent light.

She glanced away, not knowing how to deal with her feelings. Did he think it was good or bad that she was distrustful? Did he admire her prudence or believe she was just a nervous Nelly?

Maddie shifted her attention to the surrounding mob. It was an eclectic mix of old, young and in between. She heard several languages bandied about: French, German, Italian, Japanese.

David asked a Frenchman if he knew why everyone was stopped on the bridge.

"The Spectacle of Angelo," the man answered. "It starts in ten minutes."

If she'd been on vacation Maddie might have been able to relax and enjoy the pedestrian traffic jam but as it was, she felt as jittery as if she'd just downed ten cups of strong coffee.

Everyone was watching the Campanile several hundred yards ahead, waiting for the performance to begin. Everyone that is, except for Maddie. She was busy scoping out her environment, and searching the crowd for any signs of Cassie.

A young mother dressed in a T-shirt emblazoned with the British flag stood several feet behind them. She was scolding an older child who'd been misbehaving, not paying attention to her toddler trying to climb onto the bridge parapet. One slip and the boy would plunge into the canal.

Maddie's heart leaped into her throat and she could think of only one thing.

The day Cassie fell into the pond.

Maddie slipped free from David's grasp and wound her way through the crowd.

"Ma'am," she shouted. "Your baby!"

But apparently the woman couldn't hear her over the crowd noise.

"Maddie," David called her name. But she was utterly focused on what she was doing. All she could think about was getting to that little boy before he fell. She elbowed people aside, hurrying as best she could.

"Ma'am, ma'am," she kept hollering.

Dear Lord, don't let me be too late.

The toddler was marching along the top of the narrow ledge, wavering on his chubby little legs as he peered down at the water.

She was so close.

Desperately, Maddie lunged forward at the same time a woman with an oversize handbag turned sharply to see what was happening.

"Oops," the woman exclaimed in a British accent.

The swinging purse caught Maddie off guard, smacking her squarely in the back. She tripped over the cobblestones and fell awkwardly across the bridge railing right beside the toddler.

"Look!" the boy said and grinned at her.

"Oh my," gasped the mother, finally realizing what was happening.

Maddie shoved the boy toward his mother who safely caught him. But the motion knocked Maddie completely off balance.

The next thing she knew, she was falling over the edge.

Chapter

♥

TWENTY

$\mathcal{M}$ADDIE DIDN'T TUMBLE into the canal.

Just as she toppled over the bridge, a barge loaded with several large vats glided by. David reached the edge of the bridge where Maddie had been standing at the same time her feet ruptured through the plastic cover of one of the vats.

He jumped off the bridge after her, aiming for a flat empty spot on the barge near the vats. The crowd on the bridge hollered instructions. He landed with a hard splat and stumbled to his knees. Quickly, he swung around, and saw Maddie's head disappear under the rim of the vat.

What was in those containers? Toxic chemicals? Petroleum products? Battery acid?

Adrenaline had him sprinting for the vat. Fear had him praying she was all right. Worry had him ignoring the pain shooting through his right wrist.

He reached the vat, which was taller than he. He clambered atop a stack of wooden pallets beside the vats. With his heart in his throat, he peered inside, not knowing what he would find.

He saw Maddie slowly sinking into a thick tub of raw honey. Honey. Just plain old honey.

"I've gotcha, sweetheart." David grabbed a fistful of Maddie's hair just before her nose submerged.

She was thrashing around, apparently trying to swim, but there was no swimming in the thick, brown syrup.

"Help!" she sputtered.

"I'm here," he murmured and their eyes met. He saw relief on her face and felt his corresponding relief relax the tension knotting his gut. "I'm here."

"Get me out of this before I attract ants."

"Yes, ma'am." He tried his best not to laugh.

She tried to swipe honey off her face with a hand thick with the sticky stuff. "Oh bother."

"Now we know why Winnie the Pooh always says that," he said.

"Did you see that little boy on the bridge? Can you imagine what would have happened if he'd been the one to fall in here?"

"He would have been all right. You'd have jumped in after him," David said. "When it comes to protecting other people you're braver than a firefighter."

"You think so?"

"Nobody else in that crowd ran to rescue the boy."

"I don't think anyone else saw him."

"Trust you to notice someone in trouble, Miss Mother Hen."

The two-man barge crew picked that moment to stroll over and investigate the commotion. They helped him pull Maddie from the honey.

The men struggled not to laugh. They kept turning their

backs to snigger and chortle, before turning around again and with straight faces offering clean-up suggestions in Italian.

David had to admit that she was a pretty comical sight. Her clothes were plastered to her skin and with every step she took honey rolled off her.

"Don't you laugh at me, too!" She shook a finger at him and a big blob of sweet goo smacked him squarely in the chest. He had to slap a hand over his mouth to hold back his own laughter.

"It's not funny," she growled.

"Yeah, it is."

"You're a horrible man, you know that?"

He could tell from the tiny upward pull at the corners of her mouth that she was beginning to see the humor in the situation. "Insult me all you want, sweetheart, I'm the one who pulled your fanny out. Without me, you'd be breathing treacle."

"So what do you want? A merit badge?"

"A kiss would be nice."

"You're serious? You want to kiss me? Now?"

"Yep."

"You're taking a risk. I could wallow all over you, suck you down to my level."

"But you won't."

"How do you know?"

"Because I'm the one who can get you cleaned up."

"You're so smug."

He moved toward her, his mouth itching to capture hers. He was just so damned happy to discover she was all right that he had to kiss her, no matter how inopportune the moment.

Maddie tilted her head toward him, presenting her cheek.

"That's not going to cut it, babe. I want the lips."

She relinquished and puckered up.

David leaned in and pressed his mouth to hers. He'd never tasted anything sweeter and he wasn't talking about the honey. His naughty libido wished they were somewhere private so he could lick her clean to the last drop.

David imagined that they resembled a very peculiar version of the Bavarian couple who emerged from Aunt Caroline's cuckoo clock at midnight to steal a quick kiss before popping back into their respective houses. Him with his blackened eye and busted wrist and Maddie dipped in bee spit.

The Venetians clapped and cheered.

"Our audience approves."

"That's all fine and dandy, but what am I supposed to do now? I don't have a change of clothes and I don't think the concierge is going to let some honey-glazed American go traipsing through their chichi hotel lobby."

In his rudimentary French, David asked the men if they had something onboard he could use to drape over Maddie. One man nodded, disappeared and returned with a newspaper. Not exactly what he had in mind, but it would do.

"What are you planning?" Maddie asked, eyeing the newspaper suspiciously.

"I'm arranging it so you can at least walk around without enticing the local wildlife." David opened the newspaper, separated the pages and then pasted them to Maddie. "What's black and white and read all over?"

"Hardy-har-har."

"I'm betting this is one worst case scenario you never anticipated."

"You got me there."

When he finished covering her clothes, he wrapped her feet with newspaper. In the end, he was almost as messy as she, with honey and bits of newspaper sticking to his cast and printer's ink decorating his skin. He started to shove his hand through his hair, but stopped himself just before he got a head full of honey.

The bargemen let them off at the nearest dock and they had to walk back to the Piazza San Marco. Poor Maddie was struggling valiantly to keep from sticking to the ground with every step.

"This is just fabulous," she muttered and glowered at the passersby staring openly in her direction. "As if I'm more interesting than Carnevale?"

"You are pretty eye-catching," he said.

"I don't want to talk about it anymore."

"You never let *me* get away with avoiding uncomfortable topics."

She bared her teeth and growled.

"I'm on to you, Maddie. You don't scare me."

"You forget. I'm covered in honey. I can wreak much sticky havoc on you." She shuffled forward, arms outstretched zombie-style.

He held up his tacky hands. "You already did."

"You think that's bad, you ain't seen nothing yet."

"Oh," he said. "Here we are. The Hotel International." He gave Maddie the once-over. She was the cutest darned newspaper mummy he'd ever seen.

"What should I do?"

"I'll go check us in, then I'll come around and let you in a side entrance."

"Hurry up. I'm starting to draw flies."

He checked them in and then slipped out a side door to find Maddie pacing and muttering to herself behind the hotel.

"Psst." He dangled their room key for her to see. "This way."

"I feel like I'm in a bit from *I Love Lucy*," Maddie grumbled.

"I guess that makes me Ricky."

"More like Ethel."

He chuckled. "Insult me all you want, sweetheart. I can take it."

They ascended the staircase to their room, Maddie leaving bits of honeyed newspaper sticking to everything she touched. David opened the door, stepped aside and bowed with a flourish.

She tramped over the threshold, then stopped and stared.

"Wow," she said. "Fancy shmancy."

David moved through the suite, opening doors and checking the premises. He didn't want any ugly surprises like Jocko Blanco hiding under the bed. Maddie trailed after him, taking it all in.

"This place is almost as big as my condominium in Fort Worth."

It was decorated in an elegant Old World style that combined vintage furniture with new pieces, but David hardly noticed. Instead, he was checking the security. There was a large sitting area, two separate bedrooms and a private bath.

He ambled over to open the drapes and revealed French doors. They were on the second floor with a balcony overlooking the Piazza San Marco.

While it might seem romantic, the balcony and the trellis of vines growing up the side of the hotel posed a security problem. Anyone with the desire could scale the trellis and break into their room.

He tested the locks. "Make sure you keep this door locked anytime you aren't on the balcony."

"Okay."

David stepped back and jerked a thumb toward the door. "I'm just going to go call Henri, let him know we've arrived."

"Hey!" She sounded panicky. "You're not leaving me like this!"

"I thought you'd want some privacy."

"Wait, wait, wait."

"Yes?"

"How do you expect me to get out of these clothes by myself?"

"Come on." He grinned. "Say it."

"Say what?"

"You need me."

"I'm not saying that."

"Okay." He knew he was cruel to tease, but he just couldn't resist. "I'll see you later."

"All right, come back. I need you," she said through clenched teeth. "Now get in this bathroom and help me out of my clothes."

"Oooh, I like it when you get all dominatrix on me."

She stuck out her tongue.

"Now that's an interesting thought, but let's wait until you're cleaned up."

"What lit your fire, Sparky?"

"I don't know. Maybe the excitement of you almost drowning in a vat of honey."

"Maybe it's that knock on the head Jocko Blanco gave you yesterday."

"Don't underestimate yourself, Maddie." David said. He didn't know why he was feeling so damned giddy.

"Well, don't just stand there looking all googly-eyed, help me get this sweater over my head."

He fished around between the layers of newspaper and goo to find the hem of her sweater. Gently, he peeled the garment up over her head.

It got stuck halfway, giving him a perfect full-on view of her breasts.

"Ahem, David," she said in a muffled voice. "I can't breathe."

Snap out of it, Marshall.

What was happening to him? What kind of erotic spell had this woman woven? He finished tugging the sweater from her head, but it got caught in her hair.

"Ow, easy. You're pulling my hair."

"Sorry, sorry."

He worked to free her hair and several minutes later finally disentangled her from her sweater and dropped the soiled mess to the floor. That's when he realized his breathing was labored and sweat was pooling under his arms.

Their eyes met and the resulting jolt of electrical response had them both turning away. David reached for the porcelain knobs on the white claw-foot bathtub at the same time Maddie started peeling strips of newspaper off her blue jeans.

He added a squirt of bubble bath to the water, and then backed toward the door. "You should be able to take it from here."

"Wait." She pointed a finger at him.

Damn. If he didn't get out of here soon, something was going to pop up. Briefly, he closed his eyes and willed himself not to get aroused.

It didn't work.

He wanted her so much and that desire terrified him. No woman, not even Keeley, had ever been able to distract him from his work.

Until now.

Until Maddie.

Startled, David realized he hadn't thought about Cassie or Shriver or the stolen artwork since Maddie had tumbled off that bridge.

The realization disturbed him.

He was different around her, less competitive, more laid-back. He had changed. She was changing him.

Why and how it was happening, he had no idea, but he didn't like this feeling. Not at all. It was too close to losing control.

He inhaled sharply.

"David? You okay?"

Maddie's eyes were wide with concern. Steam from the hot bathwater curled around her face, dampening her hair. She looked like some nurturing yet naughty nymph just waiting for him to come play with her. He kept his eyes trained on her face and purposely avoided looking at her body.

But he knew that amazing figure was there, calling him with a powerful lure. Last night he'd made love to her, but he'd had an excuse for his behavior. He'd been drugged, out of his head, wounded and vulnerable.

Today was different. He was lucid and sober and impervious to his body's sexual response.

Yeah, right, his penis taunted, poking hard against the zipper of his pants.

He had to get out of here. Now.

"Um," he said, edging for the door. "Why don't I just go ahead and give you that privacy? Looks like the only way you're going to get the rest of that gunk off is to soak."

"Okay."

"I'll just go buy you some new clothes. What size do you wear?"

"A six. And I'll need new shoes. Those sneakers are beyond salvaging. Size nine. Don't say it. I know I've got big feet." She grinned.

"Gotcha, size nine clothes, size six shoes."

"No, no, the other way around. I'd have to chop off my toes to fit into a size six shoe."

"Right, right." He stared at the ceiling, at the floor, at anything but her. It was all he could do to keep from tossing her in the bath, jumping in beside her and doing incredibly sexy things to her.

"Are you sure you're all right? You're acting weird."

"Great. Terrific. Be right back."

And then he ran out the door as fast as his legs would carry him.

Chapter

♥

TWENTY-ONE

$\mathcal{D}$AVID NEVER MADE it into a dress shop for Maddie's new clothes. He'd no sooner left the hotel than his cell phone rang.

"Marshall here," he'd barked into the phone but he could barely hear over the noise of the Carnevale merry-makers. He was expecting Henri, but the voice on the other end was female.

"David?"

Jamming his index finger against his other ear, he said, "Hang on. I can't hear you. Let me get inside somewhere."

"Hurry, I don't have long to talk."

Someone chose that moment to blast a noisemaker behind him. He winced and ducked into a tobacco shop that looked relatively quiet.

"Who is this?" he asked.

"It's me, Cassie." She sounded exasperated that he hadn't recognized her voice.

"Cassie!" The hairs on the back of his neck lifted. "Good God, woman, where are you?"

"I'm in Venice."

"Me too. At the Hotel International."

"Wonderful, I was praying you'd tracked me here."

"You're in serious trouble, you know that?"

"Tell me about it. This undercover FBI stuff is a lot harder than it looks."

"Are you with Jocko Blanco?"

"Not anymore. Thank God. Peyton rescued me. And none too soon, let me tell you. I shudder to think what might have happened if . . ."

"Where is Shriver?" he interrupted.

"That's what I'm trying to tell you. He could come back any minute and he doesn't completely trust me. Which is good since I'm double-crossing him and to tell you the truth I'm starting to feel kind of bad about it. He's not really a rotten guy, David. He's just misguided."

"Where in Venice are you?"

"We'll get to that in a jiffy. Just hear me out."

"I'm listening." He forced himself not to sound cross.

The man behind the counter was giving him the once-over. "Pipe tobacco?" he asked in English.

David shook his head and turned his back on the guy. "Cassie?"

"You probably should give up smoking."

"What?"

"If you're thinking about romancing my sister. Maddie hates smoking."

"What? I don't smoke and I'm not romancing your sister!"

"Sure, uh-huh."

"Could you get to the point?" he snapped.

"Testy. Maddie must be giving you a run for your money. She can get on your nerves with that overly cautious stuff, can't she?"

"I thought you said you didn't have much time to talk."

"You're right. Here's the deal. Shriver is about to dispose of the paintings."

"Why the hell didn't you say so in the first place?"

"Don't yell at me."

"Okay. I'm sorry. I won't yell." David took a long, slow deep breath so he wouldn't yell at her again. "Tell me about the paintings."

"I set it up."

"Set what up? The fence?"

"No silly, the sting."

"What sting?" She was nuttier than a macadamia farm. No wonder Maddie watched over Cassie as if it was her life's mission. The woman needed a keeper.

"I made forgeries of the El Greco and the Cézanne."

"Why?"

"Here's the plan I talked Shriver into. We hold an underground auction. He gets Levy, Philpot and all the collectors he can find willing to bid on stolen art together in one room. We have the real paintings authenticated to everyone's satisfaction and then we do the old switcheroo with the forgeries. After we pull the scam, I told him that we would ransom the paintings back to the museum and double our haul."

Stunned by the level of her cleverness, David could only mutter a disbelieving "What?"

"Don't misunderstand," she said hurriedly. "I wasn't actually going through with this scheme."

"But you made forgeries?"

"Just for Shriver's benefit. But listen, at five o'clock this afternoon he's holding the auction at the Hotel Vivaldi in room 617. If you want to catch Shriver red-handed, along with the unscrupulous potential buyers, be there."

"All right." He nodded to himself. Maybe Cassie wasn't so crazy after all. "I'll be there. Is there anything you want me to tell Maddie?"

"I've gotta go. I heard Peyton in the hall." She rang off.

David snapped his phone shut, adrenaline pumping through his body. He didn't know what to make of Cassie's call, but he did know one thing, his lust to bring Shriver to justice had returned with a vengeance. Grinning to himself, he turned to the shopkeeper behind the counter and asked him how to get to the nearest police station.

"Who's on the phone, luv?" Peyton asked Cassie. He was standing in the doorway, disappointment on his face, resignation in his voice.

"Um . . ." Cassie slipped the receiver into its cradle, her heart pumping fast. "Wrong number."

"You're going to have to do better than that." He stepped into the room, suddenly looking very menacing and kicked the door closed behind him. He pulled the gun she'd taken from Jocko Blanco out of his pocket.

Uh-oh. Trouble.

"What's with the gun?" she asked, giving him her best wide-eyed innocent expression. "You don't like guns."

"I decided I needed to learn to like them."

"How come?"

"I thought I could use this one for protection."

"Against what?"

"My enemies."

"I'm not your enemy, Peyton."

"You're certainly not my friend. I've been listening at the door for quite some time."

Gulp. "It's not what you think."

His smile was wistful but the look in his eyes was deadly. Cassie took a step back and eyeballed the door. He stood squarely between her and freedom.

"Don't lie to a liar, luv."

"Peyton . . . I . . . I . . ." Cassie sputtered, at a loss for words.

"You called David Marshall," he said flatly.

Come on. Concoct a likely story. You're good at thinking on your feet.

Cassie wracked her brain but came up with zip in the good excuses department.

"And here I was thinking we might have a real future together." He clucked his tongue and stepped closer. Cassie drew a deep breath and forced herself not to back up. "Serves me right for getting these romantic ideas."

"The phone call was not what it seemed."

"It's exactly what it seemed. You planned to rat me out to Marshall all along, but only after you convinced me to set up this auction so you could take my connections down with me."

"Are you terribly mad?" she asked, wrinkling her forehead. "It really wasn't personal. I just wanted to prove to my irritating twin sister Maddie that I could do something useful."

"Like catching an art thief?"

"Not just any art thief," she flattered, "but the world's best."

"You've put me in a difficult position. I'm going to have to do things I wouldn't usually do."

"Hey, your problems are your own fault. If you hadn't targeted me as your next mark, none of this would have happened."

"My mistake," Peyton said. He came closer until they were nose to nose.

Cassie struggled to control her fear, forcing herself to breathe normally, to smile cheerfully. She had no idea what Peyton was capable of. "Do you forgive me?"

"If you forgive me for what I'm about to do to you."

"What's that?" Her voice rose an octave.

"Open my suitcase."

"What?" Was he going to chop her into little pieces and ship her home in his luggage?

Peyton nodded at his suitcase resting on the luggage rack at the end of the bed. "Open it."

Nervously, she obeyed because he was bigger and stronger and he had a gun and she was still hoping she could flirt her way out of this. She released the snaps and unzipped his suitcase. His clothes were carefully folded. She gave him extra credit for neatness.

She glanced at him. "Now what?"

"Under the clothes." He motioned with the gun. "I was hoping I wouldn't have to use it but you've left me no choice."

"Peyton . . ."

"Shh. Under my shirts."

She slipped her hand beneath his shirts, her fingers making contact with a coil of rope.

Oh boy.

"Let's have it."

Slowly, Cassie pulled out the rope.

"Good girl, now bring it here."

What was he going to do? Goosebumps lifted the hairs on her arms and her mouth went spitless.

He took the rope from her. "Take off your clothes."

What! Was he going to rape her? In spite of all her efforts to control her fear, Cassie felt her legs tremble.

"Take off your clothes."

"I won't." She notched her chin upward.

"I guess I'll have to do it for you." He reached for the buttons on her blouse.

She slapped his fingers. "Hands off. I can do it."

He smirked, watching her with half-lowered lids. "Too bad we never had a chance to make love. I can tell I missed something special."

"Yes you did," she said tartly, standing before him in her bra and panties.

"Those too."

"What?"

"Your knickers."

"Aw, come on."

He waved the gun, not pointing it at her, but threatening her with it. "Off with the underthings."

"Why?"

"Just do it."

"Peyton . . ."

This time he did point the gun at her. "Please don't make me hurt you."

"Okay. Okay. No shooting." She shimmied out of her panties and then unhooked her bra and let it drop to the floor. How friggin' humiliating.

"Hands behind your back," Peyton said.

She complied, waiting with bated breath to see what he would do next.

"Now turn around."

"Oooh, sounds kinky," she teased, desperate to lighten things up and get him to change his mind.

"I'm not playing. Turn around."

Cassie did as he asked; grateful at least that he couldn't see the expression on her face. She knew her eyes would give away her fear.

"You're lucky I'm just going to tie you up and leave you here," he said, wrapping the rope around her wrists.

She didn't know what he'd done with the gun while he was tying her up but she was too big of a wimp to fight him at that point. He would only win and she would end up getting hurt in the process. She wasn't strong and physically fit like Maddie.

"That's so terribly sporting of you, thanks," she said sarcastically.

"Could be worse. I could give Jocko a call and tell him where to find you."

"You wouldn't." Her heart thumped.

He traced a finger along her jaw. "I would."

"I thought you two were at war with each other."

"We negotiated a peace treaty."

"Hey," she said, narrowing her eyes in suspicion. "How come you packed rope? You intended on ditching me all along, didn't you?"

"It crossed my mind."

"Stop acting so betrayed. You're not any more honest than I am."

He sighed wistfully. "I had such high hopes that the rope wouldn't be necessary. But alas, we obviously weren't meant to be." He tightened the bindings. "Now, into the bathroom."

"The bathroom?"

"I'm going to tie you to the toilet."

"Oh, that's really rude. Taking my clothes and tying me to the john."

"Would you rather me lash you to the bed with no access to the water closet?"

She thought about it for a moment. "No."

He marched her into the bathroom, made her sit down and laced her hands around the back of the toilet bowl.

"By the way," he said, once he'd finished tying her up. "Just to let you know, I'm taking all your clothes with me. In case you get any crazy ideas about escaping."

"That's really low."

He shrugged. "All's fair in love and war."

"We were never in love."

"True enough. Oh, and by the way, your phone call to David Marshall isn't going to ruin the auction."

"What do you mean?" Cassie frowned, trying her best to look cool, calm and collected without any clothes on.

"I told you the wrong time on purpose. The auction isn't set for five o'clock."

"It's not?"

"No." Peyton grinned, leaned over and placed a kiss on her cheek. "It's in thirty minutes."

What was taking David so long?

The soap and water had dissolved the honey long ago and bits of newspaper floated around her. And even though she'd twice let out some cold water and refilled it with hot, the bath had gone cold and the bubbles dissipated.

She'd been in here at least an hour, her hands and feet shriveling into pale prunes. Leaning over the edge of the tub, she peered at her clothes plastered on to the bathroom tile. There would be no salvaging those garments without a heavy-duty washing machine and that was still an iffy proposition. Her luggage was lost in the wilds of Europe. Essentially, she was naked in a foreign country, dependent on a man she didn't even trust all that much.

Come on, Maddie, David is an FBI agent. He's not going to abandon you. He's probably just having trouble finding your size.

When the going gets tough, men take off. The old refrain that had formed her belief system about the opposite sex circled in her brain.

That's utter nonsense. Why would David leave you stranded in a tub?

Same reason he'd given her the slip at the Prado, to find and arrest Cassie on his own. He had a perfect opportunity and he'd seized it.

No he didn't.

How about the way he ran out of here?

Don't jump to conclusions. Remain calm.

But even as she was giving herself a pep talk, Maddie was reaching for the towel. That's it. If he didn't come back within the next fifteen minutes she was never ever trusting another man again.

Briskly, she toweled herself off and marched into the bedroom. Too bad he didn't have any luggage either. She would have borrowed his clothes.

Maddie stood in the middle of the room, assessing her options. Hmm, perhaps she could fashion a toga for herself out of a bedsheet, pretend it was a Carnevale costume, slip down to the hotel gift shop and pray that they sold apparel.

Not the best plan in the world, but it was the only one she had.

She searched the bathroom, found a sewing kit and spent the next fifteen minutes fashioning a toga from a sheet. Once she was certain the makeshift garment would stay on, she opened the French doors and stepped out onto the balcony. She'd give David one last chance to appear before taking matters into her own hands.

Below her window Carnevale was in full swing. Loud riotous music played. Delicious aromas filled the air. Revelers danced in the streets, wearing all manner of costumes and masks. She would fit right in.

Part of her was angry with David, but another part of her was worried. Maybe he hadn't ditched her. Maybe something bad had happened.

Maybe he'd run across Blanco again.

Either way, she needed clothes. She turned to go back into the room to retrieve her Mastercard from her honey-coated shoulder bag when she saw something in her peripheral vision that rooted her to the spot.

Was that Peyton Shriver moving through the crowd on the other side of the square? Maddie stepped farther out onto the balcony and narrowed her eyes.

Come closer, she mentally willed him.

He must have picked up her vibes, because he did walk in her direction.

Yep. It was indeed Shriver. His plain beige coat amid the colorful Carnevale costumes was what had snagged her eye. She searched for Cassie in the crowd around him, but Shriver appeared to be alone.

She had to get down there, had to follow him.

What if he spots you? What if he and Blanco aren't at odds as David contends but working together? What if . . .

To hell with *what ifs*. Where had caution and prudence gotten her? Shriver was out there right now. She had a chance to do something about it. Was she going to stay here and cower in a hotel room hoping David would come back and take care of things? Or was she going to plunge ahead, take a chance and sally forth after Shriver.

Go, Maddie, go. She heard Cassie's voice, clear as if her sister was standing beside her.

She stared at the crowd, intimidated by the thought of waltzing around in a bedsheet. You can do it. She raised her chin. Yes. She would do it.

Glancing around, she realized she'd lost the beige coat in the mass of humanity. Oops! Where had Shriver gone?

Panicking over the thought that her indecision might have lost her only link to Cassie, Maddie desperately scanned the people for Shriver.

Ah, there he was, going into a church not far from the hotel.

She wasn't about to let him escape now. Resolutely, Maddie squared her shoulders, marched out the door, down the stairs, through the lobby and into the Piazza San Marco.

She moved through the costumed throng, her gaze beaded on the church where she'd seen Shriver disappear only minutes before. No one gave her a second glance in her makeshift toga, and for that she was grateful to Carnevale.

What she wasn't so thankful for was the wave of humanity keeping her from her target.

You can't let him get away.

She elbowed aside a drunken Marco Polo who was leering openly at her breasts and dodged a man on stilts juggling orange glowing balls. The air was ripe with enticing aromas—freshly baked pastries, roasted turkey legs, generously spiced pan-seared fish—but Maddie barely noticed.

She vaulted over a two-year-old sitting on the steps of a shop eating gelato. She zigged past strolling young lovers holding hands and zagged around slow-moving tourists gawking at the sights.

The trip across the Piazza San Marco seemed the longest trek of her life—much longer than any race she'd ever run—although it probably took less than three minutes. Finally, she pushed through the door of the church and blinked against the contrast from the bright sunshine outside and the dimly lit interior.

She stepped away from the door and stood there a moment getting her bearings and letting her eyes adjust. A few people sat in the pews praying. She swung her gaze up and down the aisles.

No sign of Shriver.

He was gone. She'd lost him.

Dejected, she sagged against a pillar.

What now?

And then she saw him pass by the window. He was outside the church. His head was down as if he was talking to someone either shorter than he or someone sitting down.

As quickly and quietly as she could, Maddie padded through the church in her bare feet to the door at the other end of the building, her pulse spiking in irregular blips.

She went through the exit to a narrow walkway between the church and the canal.

A shadow fell across her. She looked up and gasped.

An ominous figure in a long black robe stood before her in the most sinister costume she'd ever seen. He wore a breastplate of mosaic mirrors and he was carrying a large, evil-looking scythe. His head was a skull mask, covered in the same small reflective glass as the breastplate. She could see herself fractured into a hundred tiny, bedsheet-wearing Maddies.

His deep laugh was wicked and menacing.

The Grim Reaper.

She froze, trapped in the surreal moment, wondering if it was a nightmare.

Then the Grim Reaper simply shouldered his scythe and stepped around her, his knee-high black leather boots echoing sharply on the cobblestones as he headed for the Piazza.

Clutching a hand to her heart, she heaved in a shaky breath. The man had scared her. More than she cared to admit.

Settle down. It's just Carnevale. Forget the guy in the Grim Reaper outfit. What about Shriver?

Still unnerved, she looked to the left where she'd last seen Shriver and spotted a gondola stand but no art thief.

She'd lost him.

Dammit.

But no, wait. There. Out on the canal. Shriver was in a gondola headed away from her. As she watched, the gondola disappeared around a corner.

What to do now? She had no money to hire a gondola to follow him, she was barefoot and in a makeshift toga.

She was defeated. Time for Plan B.

You have no Plan B.

Well, she'd better get one, pronto. Maddie gnawed a thumbnail. She really only had one option. Head back to the hotel and hope David had returned in her absence.

Unhappy with her plan, but not having a viable alternative, Maddie pivoted on her heel to return to the hotel but found herself staring down the barrel of a very wicked looking handgun.

Chapter

♥

TWENTY-TWO

THIS WAS A fine mess.

Cassie sat perched on the toilet, her naked body covered in goose bumps, the rough rope gnawing nastily at her tender wrists as she listened to the echoes of the door slamming behind Peyton. When she got out of this predicament, boy, was she going to make him pay.

In the meantime, how was she going to get out of this?

Think, Cassie, think.

Bad idea. Thinking was not her strong suit. What would Maddie do?

Wrong question. Maddie would never get herself into such a snafu.

Okay, but what if by some wild stretch of the imagination, Maddie *had* gotten herself into this situation. What would she do then?

Knowing her Wonder Woman twin, Maddie would probably just bust through the ropes with her superpowers.

Ha, ha, this is serious. Concentrate.

She had less than thirty minutes to get free, call David and tell him what happened. Otherwise, when he showed up at the Hotel Vivaldi at five and found no one there, he would think she really *was* in cahoots with Peyton and had just set David up.

And she'd end up going to jail instead of getting on the cover of *Art World Today.*

Not good. She would look ghastly in prison stripes. If that wasn't an impetus to get on the ball, she didn't know what was.

Think, Cassie, think.

She scanned the bathroom. Her makeup and beauty supplies were strewn all over the counter but what good could an eyelash curler or a tube of lipstick do at this point?

And then she spied her trusty battery-powered travel curling iron peeking provocatively at her from behind a bottle of Opium perfume.

Aha!

Now for the hard part. Reaching it.

David was returning through the Piazza San Marco when his cell phone rang again. He'd just completed a long discussion with Henri and the chief of the Venice police. He had also gotten a new duty weapon issued to replace the one Blanco had stolen. Both the local authorities and Interpol were preparing to join him at five o'clock to raid the Hotel Vivaldi and catch Shriver in the act of auctioning off the paintings.

"I've gotcha now, Shriver," he murmured gleefully under his breath, just as the phone did the *Dragnet* thing.

He flipped it open. "Marshall."

"David, it's Cassie again." She sounded breathless, anxious.

"Hang on, I'm in the Piazza San Marco and I can barely hear you. Let me get someplace out of the way." He cornered a church and ducked onto the narrow side street running along the canal. "Go ahead."

"Shriver caught me on the phone and he heard me talking to you and he made me take off my clothes and he tied me to a toilet and . . ."

"Whoa, whoa, slow down."

"Can't. No time. Listen carefully."

"I'm listening."

"Shriver gave me the wrong time. The auction isn't at five o'clock but in ten minutes!"

"What!"

"I know. I'm sorry. Apparently he didn't trust me so much and fed me the wrong info."

"Is it still at the same hotel?" David asked, wondering if Cassie was jerking him around. Maybe she'd realized how much trouble she was in and she was trying to get herself out of hot water.

"Yes, yes. At least I think so. I hope so."

He had ten minutes to get to the Hotel Vivaldi on the opposite side of the city in the middle of Carnevale. Even a superhero couldn't have made it, but he had to try. He'd spent too many years and too much of himself in pursuing Shriver. He wasn't going down without one hell of a fight. If he didn't win this one, he'd become the laughingstock of the FBI.

David's face flushed with embarrassment. No dammit. He was going to win. He was going to catch Shriver and Philpot and Levy and get his Aunt Caroline's Rembrandt back.

A woman's sudden screams drew his attention. Was someone getting mugged?

He jerked his head in the direction of the sound. About a quarter of a mile farther down the narrow street, a bald man was trying to pull a struggling woman—who looked as if she was wearing a bedsheet—into a waiting motorboat.

"Take your hands off me if you value your testicles, bub!" the woman hollered.

There was no mistaking that voice. Or that nerve.

Maddie.

A chill of fear squeezed his spine when he realized the bald man was Jocko Blanco.

"David? David?" Cassie asked from the phone. "What's going on? You don't have time to waste. You've got to get to the Hotel Vavaldi or Shriver's going to get away!"

"To hell with Shriver, Blanco's got Maddie." He snapped the phone shut and took off at a dead run.

But he was far too late. Long before he could reach her, Blanco had successfully dragged Maddie into the motorboat and they were zipping off down the canal, headed toward the Venetian lagoon.

"I like the toga," Jocko Blanco said, keeping one hand on his gun and the other on the speedboat's steering wheel. "And the no-bra look. By the way, your headlights are on. Does that mean you enjoyed our tussle or are you just cold?"

"I'm cold," she said haughtily.

"Should have thought about that before you decided to go boating in a bedsheet."

"I didn't decide to go boating. You kidnapped me."

"Serves you right for escaping. How did you escape by the way? Shriver said he tied you buck naked to the toilet." Blanco wagged his tongue lasciviously. "I was looking forward to seeing that."

What? Maddie stared at him, not understanding one word of what this cretin was saying. She sized him up. Beefy, shaved head, skull and cross bones tattoos on his hand. She'd seen this guy before. At the top of the Eiffel Tower talking to Jerome Levy.

"You're Jocko Blanco."

"Ah, babe. Don't tell me you forgot me already. I thought I made a pretty strong impression on you back in Madrid." He pursed his lips in a pout. "Now here I find you barely even remember my name. And after all we shared together."

Oh!

Realization dawned. He thought she was Cassie. Shriver must have tied Cassie up to a toilet somewhere and told Blanco to go fetch her. But why?

He winked at her and clucked his tongue. "Don't worry, sweetcheeks. I'll make sure you won't forget me again. My name is going to be the last one to pass those luscious lips of yours." He ran the nose of his gun along her jaw and laughed when she flinched. "Put your hands out in front of you."

"What?"

"Don't give me no crap, just do it."

Rolling her eyes, Maddie extended her hands.

He grabbed a roll of silver duct tape sitting on top of a shovel in the bottom of the boat and then wrapped it around her wrists, binding them together.

"Ow, not so tight."

"Quit whining."

I've got a third degree black belt in karate. I'm not taking this crap.

A week ago fear would have frozen her to the seat, but a lot had changed in seven days. She'd gone without adequate food and sleep. She'd been knocked off a bridge and dunked into a vat of honey. She'd been forced to run nearly naked through the streets of Venice. Frankly, she had reached the end of her tether.

You've picked a bad day to mess with me, pox-face. With a well-aimed kick, Maddie planted her foot in Blanco's crotch.

And made contact with something toe-crunchingly hard.

Yeow! Startled, she glanced at Blanco's face.

"Special made jock strap with an aluminum alloy cup." His grin was wicked.

"I take it women kick you there a lot."

"Provides one hundred percent protection. Don't believe me?" he bragged. "Go ahead. Kick me again."

"That's okay. I'll pass."

"Good, then just sit back and behave."

Yeah, right. Desperate to escape, she searched the lagoon. "Help!" she cried out to a passing vaporetto. "Help!"

"Save your breath. It's unlikely they understand English."

"Help! He's trying to kill me!"

"Lover's spat," Blanco sang out to the passengers, smiled, waved and goosed the speedboat faster.

Once they were out of sight of the waterbus, Blanco cocked the gun and pressed it against her temple.

"I could just kill you now," he said. "Think about it. The only reason you're still alive is because I don't want to have to scrub your blood off the boat. I'm lazy that way."

Maddie tried to swallow, but she was scared spitless. All right, racking him hadn't worked. What now?

Maybe she could reason with the guy. Find a way to buy some time.

"So one way or the other, you intend on killing me?" she said.

"That's pretty much the plan."

"But why?"

"You're an inconvenience to Shriver."

"How much is he paying you? I'll pay more."

Blanco snorted. "On a museum employee's salary? I don't think so."

Think of a good lie. Come on, come on. Bluff. Be outrageous. What would Cassie say?

"What if I told you the Cézanne and El Greco are fakes," Maddie babbled, saying the first thing that popped into her head. Cassie was extremely gifted at copying great works of art quickly. It was within the realm of possibility that she could have made forgeries. Cassie loved showing off her talent.

"I'd say you were lying in order to save your hide."

"But what if I wasn't?"

He studied her a moment. "I'm listening."

"It's all part of a sneaky plot I concocted to outwit Shriver." Maddie was grasping at straws, embellishing as she went along and praying like hell Blanco's greed was greater than his knowledge of artwork masterpieces. She was probably okay on that score. He looked like a velvet-Elvis-dogs-playing-poker aficionado. "And he's setting you up as the fall guy."

"What do you mean?"

"Shriver's been planning these robberies a long time. He hooked up with me because he knew I could create identical replicas of the Cézanne and El Greco." Please don't let him ask me why, Maddie prayed. She really hadn't thought this thing through.

"Why?"

So much for thinking on her feet.

"Well?" Blanco raised both eyebrows.

"Er . . . umm . . . because Shriver loves the paintings so much he wanted to keep them for himself but he also wanted the big bucks." Maddie held her breath and tried not to visibly wince at the lameness of her *faux* explanation.

To her amazement, Blanco nodded. "He does love those damn paintings. Me, I never got the attraction: What's the big deal about some old dead guys slapping paint on canvas and everyone calling it great art? Personally, I prefer photographs. Much more real."

"Ansel Adams," Maddie said.

"Yeah." Blanco nodded. "He's pretty good. I like Richard Avedon too, although they have completely different styles."

"What about Annie Leibowitz?"

"Naw. She's the one who does all the babies in pumpkins and shit like that, right? Too schmaltzy for me."

"No, that's Anne Geddes. Annie Leibowitz photographs celebrities. A lot of her work has appeared in *Rolling Stone*."

"Oh yeah. She's cool." Blanco snapped his fingers. "Hey, have you ever seen that guy who takes photos of naked people lying down in city streets and bizarre places like that? Now that's compelling."

Gee, they were actually bonding. Maddie decided to

push it. "You know, Jocko, Shriver's just using you. Getting you to do his dirty work. You kill me, and then he calls the cops on you. Next thing you know, you're in the big house marking time."

The hoodlum chortled, but he looked unsure of himself. "Big house? Marking time? You've been watching too many old gangster movies."

Maddie shrugged, trying her best to appear nonchalant. Her bid to turn Blanco on Shriver had better pay off or else she and Cassie were in deep swamp water.

And she would never see David again.

No more sneaking through coconut groves together. No more cutting up in hospital emergency rooms. No more rescuing each other from their misadventures.

She would miss the taste of his intoxicating mouth, the sound of his deep, sometimes stern, but always caring, voice and the smell of his manly scent.

Why her first thought was of David and not her twin she could not say. What she did know was that the idea of never seeing David again tore at her heart with razor-sharp tiger claws.

And where was her sister? Without Maddie to look after her, track her down and save her, what would happen to her? Maybe she could trust David to take care of Cassie when she was gone?

No. She couldn't depend on that. She'd never been able to depend on anyone except herself. She had to get out of this mess. Had to save her sister.

But she was in serious trouble. No one knew where she was. When David returned to the hotel to find her gone, he would have no idea what had happened to her. No clue where to look for her body.

*   *   *

Cassie had to do something. David had gone to save Maddie. She paused a second to savor that image. For once in her life Maddie was the rescuee instead of the rescuer. But with David in hot pursuit of Blanco, there was no one to stop Shriver. No one except herself.

But how?

She was at least thirty minutes away from the Hotel Vivaldi and what was she going to do when she got there anyway? Shriver had hired security guards and he wasn't dumb enough to let her fool him again. If she went to the police, they would probably arrest her as a fugitive.

She'd exhausted her charm and her luck.

The jig was up.

That is, unless she invented something completely creative.

Think. How could she marshal a squadron of police to the Vivaldi pronto?

Think, think, think. Quick, quick, quick.

Then inspiration struck.

She hurried to the phone and called the police. The dispatcher answered in Italian. Cassie asked for someone who spoke English. After a wait that seemed agonizingly long but was probably only about three minutes, a man with a sexy sounding voice came on the line.

"This is Dominic Salveto. I speak English."

Cassie swallowed hard and forced herself not to flirt. This was serious business. She couldn't let herself get side-tracked by sex appeal.

"Dominic," she said sternly and then lied through her teeth. "There's a bomb in the Rialto room of the Hotel Vivaldi and it's set to go off in fifteen minutes!"

*   *   *

David zipped through the Grand Canal in a borrowed police boat. Blanco had a good ten-minute lead on him and he could only pray his suspicion that the thug was headed out to sea was a correct one.

If the bastard so much as breathed germs on Maddie and gave her a cold, David would hunt him down and squash him like the cockroach he was. The vivid intensity of his bloodlust took him aback, but he couldn't help his feelings. His gut squeezed, his head churned, his heart thundered with fear and concern and something much, much more.

At this point, right and wrong didn't exist. All that mattered was Maddie.

You should never have left her alone in the hotel room. If you'd stayed you would have made love to her and you know it.

And she would be safe in your arms at this very moment.

But he hadn't stayed. He'd let both his fear of emotional intimacy and his almost maniacal need to capture Shriver, drive him away from her.

Just when she needed him most.

He picked up a pair of police issue binoculars, brought them to his eyes and scanned the horizon. Straight ahead of him several boats bobbed together in the distance, most of them in a cluster.

Blanco would shy away from witnesses or potential rescuers. David swung the glasses to the right, saw two or three boats motoring along in that direction. He looked left. Only one boat over there.

Knowing he was taking a calculated risk by changing his course, knowing Maddie's very life lay in his hands, David headed north, following his gut.

"Hang on, Maddie, I'm coming," he said aloud, refusing to believe he was on a wild goose chase. This was the right direction. It had to be. He was going to rescue her.

Unless she was already dead.

Chapter

TWENTY-THREE

BLANCO WASN'T BUYING her art forgery story, even though Maddie kept bargaining, elaborately embellishing the lie.

"What kind of idiot do you take me for?" he snapped.

A big one, she hoped. Maddie batted her eyelashes at him. "I don't think you're an idiot."

"Then you must be as big an airhead as Shriver says you are."

"He called me an airhead?"

"He said killing you would be easy because you're too much of an airhead to even see it coming."

Maddie was insulted on Cassie's behalf. "Like you and Shriver are nuclear scientists. For your information, you don't even have the right woman."

Blanco narrowed his eyes. "What do you mean?"

"Weren't you supposed to go to a hotel and find me chained to a toilet?"

"Yeah."

"Then why do you suppose you captured me out on the street?"

"Because you got loose. Peyton's notoriously terrible at tying people up. He's not too good at anything that messes up his manicure."

"No. That's not the reason. It's because I'm not Cassie." She shifted uncomfortably. The only thing between her bottom and the hard wooden bench was one thin layer of bedsheet.

"Okay, I'll play along. Who are you?"

"I'm her identical twin, Maddie. Kill me, you kill the wrong sister and Shriver will be highly ticked off at you."

"Your forged painting story was more plausible," he said. "I'd stick with that one if I were you."

"You don't believe me?"

"Not for a minute."

"Okay, it's your funeral. Don't say I didn't warn you. When you get back to Venice and find Cassie got free and called the cops, you're going to feel really stupid."

"Blah, blah, blah."

"You were with my sister when you forced her to rob the Prado. Can't you tell she's twenty pounds heavier and soft as a marshmallow?" Maddie flexed a bicep. "You're saying you can't tell a difference?"

Blanco glanced at her muscle. "Well, Miss Smarty Pants, if you're not Cassie, then how do you know I was the one who robbed the Prado? The news media is blaming Shriver. And you. Nobody's even mentioned my name."

"What was that all about, anyway?" Maddie asked. "What's going on with you and Shriver? How come sometimes you're working together and sometimes you're fighting each other?"

"It's complicated. Besides, you already know the answer."

"No I don't."

"Hmph."

"What's so complicated about your relationship with Shriver? You guys gay or something?"

"No!" Blanco scowled. "He's my half-brother. We got the same old man. Except he was married to Peyton's mama but not mine."

Ah. Sibling rivalry. That explained a lot. She could tell Blanco resented his brother's legitimacy. "So what happened between you two?"

"Jerome Levy paid Peyton and me to heist the Cézanne from the Kimbell for a high-powered collector. Except Peyton got a better offer from Cory Philpot. He had the hots for you and was thinking of quitting the business, so he double-crossed me."

"That was rude."

"Thank you."

"Hey, I understand completely about thoughtless siblings," she said, still frantically trying to figure a way out of her predicament.

"To get even with him, I horned in on his deal with you at the Prado. I figured I'd steal the El Greco out from under him and we'd be even."

"When did you guys kiss and make up?"

"When Peyton found out you were still working with the Feds and he knew he was going to have to get rid of you." Blanco's lip curled in a snarl. "Pretty Boy doesn't have the guts to do his own dirty work so he calls me and says he'll cut me in for half on this auction deal if I do away with you."

"What auction deal?"

"Stop playing ignorant. You're getting on my nerves with that." Blanco waved the gun in her face. "Shut up."

He stared out over the bow of the boat. Maddie turned in her seat to see what he was looking at. Up ahead loomed a small island with what appeared to be a crumbling, abandoned monastery.

Uh-oh. This looked like the place where he planned to put a bullet between her eyes and stash her in a shallow grave.

Over my dead body.

Well, yeah, Maddie, that's sort of the general idea.

Blanco killed the motor and slowly beached the boat on a pebbly shoal. The gravel grated against the hull and the air hung thick with the odor of dead fish. Maddie tasted the coppery flavor of her own fear.

Don't panic. Stay calm. No worst case scenarios. She was living a worst case scenario. No need to obsess about one.

She wondered how much time had passed since Blanco had abducted her and if David had gotten back to the hotel yet. She imagined his rugged handsome face, drawn with concern and her eyes misted with tears.

Would she ever see him again?

A deep longing filled her heart. The longing for all the things she'd missed out on. The feeling was so intense she lost her breath. She felt a monumental stirring inside her, a sharp shift, a cagey change. She wanted so badly to live, to see how things turned out between her and David.

Face facts. There's not much hope of that.

"Get out of the boat," Blanco commanded.

"Screw you," she said, not to Blanco, but to the nagging, worrisome voice that had dogged her for years. The doom and gloom voice that kept her from taking a chance on life, on intimacy, on love.

"Get out," he repeated, cocking the gun and for one dizzying moment she thought he meant to shoot her right then and there and leave her body floating in the sea.

But then he swung one leg over the edge of the boat and stepped out onto the wet rocks. She shivered, the damp chill invading her bones.

"Move it," Blanco said. "And no more smart-mouthed backtalk."

Stumbling a bit, she managed to climb onto shore in front of him, even though having her hands bound threw her off balance. She had to think of some way to stall him until she could come up with a plan to save her life.

"Walk."

"Which way?"

"Toward the monastery."

Nice. He was going to murder her in a church. Obviously, he wasn't Catholic. Neither was she, but there had to be some rule against killing someone in a place of worship.

Maddie decided to balk. She stood her ground, refusing to move.

"Get going," Blanco growled and pushed the gun against the back of her head. She smelled the ominous scent of gunpowder.

An odd serenity stole over her and Maddie realized Blanco could do whatever he wanted to her and it didn't matter. The sudden stilling of her fretful voice was liberating.

"I'm not moving," she said calmly and turned to face him.

The end of the gun was pointed straight at her nose but she didn't flinch. Blanco looked confused.

"I've got a gun," he said unnecessarily.

"So I see."

"I'll shoot you if you don't move."

"Go ahead. You're going to shoot me anyway. What difference does it make?"

"I want to keep you out of sight. In case a plane is flying over or sumthin'."

"Sorry. I'm not going to make it easy for you."

He growled. "Go!"

"No."

Blanco gritted his teeth. "I've met stubborn women before, but none as stubborn as you."

"I'll take that as a compliment."

"It was meant as criticism."

She shrugged.

"March!" He howled.

She shook her head.

Blanco cocked the gun.

Maddie stood her ground. She didn't even blink. She had no idea what weird mental Valium her body had defensively churned into her brain, but she was not afraid.

All these years she'd spent worrying and fretting and agonizing over every small hazard, every tiny danger, every minuscule risk. For what?

"You're not her, are you?" Amazed, Blanco stared open-mouthed. "You *are* the twin sister."

"I tried to tell you."

"Shit!" He stamped his foot. "Shit, shit, shit. Peyton is going to have a fit."

Just then, the sound of a speedboat tearing through the water at full throttle drew their attention to the water.

Maddie was already facing that direction, her bound hands clasped in front of her, but Blanco had to turn to see what was happening.

The sight of the blue and white police boat raised her spirits. Was that . . . ? Could it be . . . ? She squinted. David at the controls?

When the going gets tough, men take off.

But not David. There was her man bigger than life, coming to her rescue.

Maddie's heart soared.

But only for a fraction of a second. Blanco swung the gun around.

"David! Look out! He's got a gun!"

Blanco got off a shot at the same time David hit the deck. He ducked his head and rolled to the back of the boat.

Oh God! She thought Blanco had missed but she couldn't be sure. Please let David be okay.

Blanco fired again.

David jumped overboard, disappearing under the water's surface.

The water was ice cold. He would get hypothermia in a matter of minutes. She had to dispatch Blanco's gun. Now.

The time for calm passivity had passed. Blanco could shoot her if he wanted, but she'd be damned if she would let him hurt the man she loved.

Maddie whooped a loud war cry and with a well-aimed kick, sent Blanco's gun jettisoning to the bottom of the Lagoon.

David popped to the surface of the icy water, his lungs crying for air. Salt water burned his eyes. He blinked, trying to locate Maddie and Blanco on the beach.

The boat blocked his vision. He couldn't see them, but the shooting had stopped. Why? Where were they? He heard his own raspy breathing as harsh and loud as a ticking clock.

His feet touched bottom. He slogged ashore, crouching low, attempting to stay down in case Blanco was waiting in ambush.

He crept around the edge of the motorboat and cautiously raised his head. He spied Blanco dragging Maddie by the neck in a macabre dance, heading for the aged monastery. Beside the monastery, at the very edge of the water on the opposite side of the island loomed a crumbling campanile.

The minute he saw the bell tower, David knew what Blanco intended.

"Sonofabitch," he cursed, shook off the excess water weighing down his clothes and took off at a dead run.

By the time he reached the monastery, he was out of breath and shivering like a malaria victim. Blanco and Maddie had already disappeared inside.

He burst through the door into the empty church. A rat scuttled in front of him, rose up on its haunches and chattered angrily. David grit his teeth. He hated rats.

Shrugging off his revulsion, he plunged through the church, kicking up dust and pushing through the serpentine tendrils of cobwebs. From the direction of the bell tower, he heard the steady clump-whump, clump-whump of Blanco dragging a reluctant Maddie up the stairs. He also heard Maddie's muffled voice either bargaining or arguing with her captor.

Fear chilled him deeper than the cold water. White fingers of dread wrapped icily around his heart. He had to get to her before Blanco threw her off the tower.

No time to waste. Urgent. Urgent. Maddie needs you.

He took the steps to the bell tower two at a time, barely registering that the stairs shifted and swayed beneath his feet. He was busy fumbling for his gun even while knowing it probably would not fire in its waterlogged condition.

By the time he reached the top step, he was shaking so badly he could hardly stand. He'd never been so cold. Ahead of him was the closed door leading into the bell tower.

Hurry, hurry, get to her.

He was desperate, but his policeman's instincts warned him not to charge ahead. He knew untold dangers lay behind closed doors. He hesitated, gun drawn, listening.

The silence echoed deep and disturbing.

Perhaps he'd been wrong. Perhaps Blanco had not taken her into the bell tower. He wet his dry lips, thinking what to do next.

Then someone screamed.

Chapter
TWENTY-FOUR

$\mathcal{M}$ADDIE BIT DOWN hard on the sweaty hand Blanco clamped over her mouth. He tasted like dirty feet smelled.

Ptui. She spit.

Biting him was risky. He was holding her with one hand around her waist, the other plastered over her mouth, at the very edge of a gaping hole where the floor of the bell tower used to be.

If he took one step forward, she would be dangling in empty space. The boards had rotted away years ago and it was one long drop to the jagged rocks poking from the water below.

She heard David charging up the stairs on the other side of the closed door and a terrible image flashed through her head. She could see him barreling through the door, propelled by his high-minded need to win at all costs and momentum shoving him through the open pit.

She had to warn him!

If she bit Blanco there was a good chance he would

drop her. But she had no choice. She wasn't about to let David die.

When her teeth cut through his flesh, Blanco yelped like a girl.

Wimp.

He jerked his hand from her mouth and staggered backward, blessedly taking her with him. He landed heavily against the stone wall and Maddie fell onto his thick chest.

The entire tower quaked with the impact and a fine dusting of sand and mortar rained from the ceiling.

Maddie gasped.

The campanile was ready to collapse. Any sort of scuffle could do the trick and send the ancient structure crumbling into the water.

Blanco scrambled to his feet, never letting go of Maddie's waist.

The tower trembled again.

Her ribcage ached where his fingers dug in and her wrists burned from the chafe of the duct tape. But the pain was inconsequential considering they were on the verge of plunging to their deaths.

She and Blanco stood on the south side of the open hole, directly opposite from the closed door.

The stone walkway on either side of the hole was less than two feet wide. No bell remained in the recess above them, but there was a ratty old rope dangling from the empty cavity. She eyed it speculatively, just in case she was driven to desperate measures.

Dream on. That decomposing rope wouldn't hold a rag doll's weight. Not that she could even grab for it with her hands bound.

Slowly, the door creaked open.

Maddie held her breath and waited for David to appear.

He spoke before he stepped into view. "Let her go, Blanco."

"Let her go down the hole? Sure. No problem." Blanco waltzed her to the edge again. Briefly Maddie closed her eyes, fighting nausea.

"You drop her and I'll kill you."

There he was.

Her lover.

Filling the doorway with his reassuring broad-shouldered presence, his duty weapon clutched in his good hand. He was soaked to the skin, his hair plastered to his head, his cast dark with dirt, but he was still the most incredible sight she had ever seen.

David's gaze met hers. Are you all right? he telegraphed with his eyes.

She nodded.

Blanco used her as a shield, ducking his head behind hers in case David took a notion to play sharpshooter. "You wanna see your girly alive again, I suggest you go back down those stairs, get in your boat and cruise away. Give me breathing room and I'll leave her here on the is-land."

"No can do, Blanco."

"Why not?"

Yeah, why not? It sounded like a terrific plan to Maddie.

"For one thing," David continued, "there's a jail cell reserved in a United States federal prison with your name on it. You've got a nonrefundable one-way ticket to jus-tice, pal, and I'm your travel agent."

Maddie rolled her eyes. Dandy. Just dandy. Was

putting people behind bars the only thing David ever
thought about?

Not that Blanco didn't deserve to get socked away for
the rest of his life. Personally, she could really get into
locking the cell door, incinerating the key and performing
a celebratory clog dance. Yee-ha.

But she was all for letting the creep get away if his escape spared their lives. Where did winning get you, if in
the end, you were pushing up petunias?

"Looks like we've got ourselves a Venetian stand-off,"
Blanco said.

"Looks like," David replied tightly.

"I think I'm going to call your bluff."

"How's that?"

"I want you to toss your gun into the sea," Blanco said.
"Or I'll throw her down the hole, I swear I will."

"You're not going to do that. Once your hostage is
gone, you're mine for the taking. And while I prefer to arrest you, killing you wouldn't trouble me too much. I'll
take justice any way I can get it."

His hostage? Well that wasn't a very romantic way to
refer to her. She had a name for heaven's sake. Why not
use it?

"And I don't believe for one second you would jeop-
ardize her life in order to get me." Blanco sneered.

"Why not? She's been nothing but a royal pain-in-the-
ass," David said evenly.

What? Now that wasn't nice. Not nice at all. Maddie
glared at him but he didn't make eye contact. Why was
he saying such things about her? She thought he liked
her. She thought she liked him.

Oh, who was she kidding? She was in love with him.

But now, he was acting as if he didn't care about her at all. She was going to have one helluva broken heart.

Unless she ended up with a broken skull first.

Blanco moved suddenly, yanking Maddie forward until her feet left the precarious perch and she was hovering directly over the abyss.

Gulp!

"No!" David shouted and lunged for Maddie as if to catch her.

Ah, maybe he really did care. Her heart leaped.

"Throw the gun away," Blanco repeated.

David's gaze met Maddie's. His jaw tightened. She saw the war of conflict in his eyes. This was a lose-lose situation and nothing could be worse for a guy who loved to win.

"She's getting awfully heavy lawman. Better make up your mind before I lose my grip."

"Put her feet back on solid ground."

"No."

David cocked the gun. The click of the hammer sent icicles through Maddie's veins. "By dangling her over the hole you've left your head exposed. I have a clear shot."

"You kill me, she dies."

"She's going to die anyway."

Blanco pondered this a moment. "Okay. I'll pull her back, but you throw the gun away at the same time."

"All right."

"Step over to the right and pitch the gun through that window arch."

David sidled right and Blanco danced left heading for the open door, all the while holding Maddie over the opening. He had to be getting tired. What if he dropped her accidentally? Her mind raced. How to get out of this?

"Keep going," Blanco said and David inched farther away from the only means of escape.

The tower shivered against their movements.

This was bad. Really bad.

"Now," Blanco said.

Simultaneously, David threw his gun over his shoulder while Blanco settled her feet onto the ground. The gun tumbled through the window arch and disappeared from view. A second later, they heard a distant splash.

Blanco shoved her at David and bolted for the door.

Maddie cried out as she fell, the yawning chasm waiting to gobble her up.

"Maddie!"

David grabbed for her and caught her by the ankle with his one good hand. Fear shoved his heart into his throat. She was dangling above a thirty-foot drop. He was the only thing between her and definite death. A nasty premonition of certain doom crawled over his scalp.

He could not drop her, but already his fingers were growing numb from the effort of holding her up.

"I've got you, sweetheart," he said, surprised to hear how calm he sounded. "Don't worry. I've got you."

But for how long?

The tower rumbled.

Chunks of the structure broke off. More rubble dusted them from above.

"The stairwell's pulling away from the tower!" she yelled. "We'll never get down."

At that moment, the stairway separated from the tower and fell in upon itself. In the clamor of collapsing stone, they heard Blanco scream. The sounds daggered into his brain.

He peered over the edge of the hole; saw that the bedsheet Maddie wore had peeled down over her head. Her hands, bound with duct tape, dangled below her head. She swung in the wind, trusting him. He was nauseous with fear. He could not let her go. He would not.

You've got to do something now.

His fingers cramped while his mind frantically searched for a solution. He reached into his back pocket with casted wrist and found his handcuffs. Grimly, he cuffed his left wrist to her ankle.

"David! What are you doing?"

"Sweetheart, I'm shackling myself to you. If you go down, I go down too."

"Don't be a fool, save yourself."

"I don't run away from trouble," he said and reached out with his casted wrist to grab her other leg when it swung past.

Now what?

The pressure of her weight caused the handcuff to gnaw into his wrist so tight it was all he could do to keep from groaning in pain. His casted wrist wasn't in much better shape. He gnashed his teeth.

"How many incline sit-ups did you tell me you could do?" he asked, willfully numbing his mind to the agonizing pain in his arms and hands.

"Two hundred."

"Well here's the good news, sweetheart, you've only got to do one. I've got your feet, I want you to sit up all the way. When you reach the level of the floor, I want you to slip your arms around my neck. Do you think you can do that?"

She *had* to do it. It was their only chance.

The pain in his wrists intensified as Maddie curled her elbows into her chest and rolled up. The fierce ache spread up his arms, through his shoulders and into his back until he was one throbbing mass of hurt.

David heard her grunt over the exertion and he knew she was hurting too.

"Come on, you can do it," he said as much to himself as to her.

He clenched his jaw, locked his legs around the stone pillar. She was close now. Almost through the opening. But the look of pain on her face matched the searing burn in his muscles.

"Almost there."

Her skin was flushed red from the effort, the veins on her neck and forehead bulging.

What if she couldn't do it?

Don't think like that. She'll make it.

"Come on baby. Two hundred sit-ups. That's it. You're almost here."

She was breathing as hard as he was when her head came back through the hole and their eyes met.

Instantly, they were one. One force, a team, lifting together.

"Arms around my neck," he whispered, scarcely able to breathe. He was hurting that badly.

She separated her elbows as far apart as she could with her hands bound. She dropped her wrists behind his head, encircling his neck with her awkward embrace.

Gathering the last bit of strength he possessed, David gave a mighty cry and rolled them both backward.

Maddie cleared the hole.

They lay on the stone floor, gasping for air. His hand was handcuffed to her ankle. Her arms were locked around his neck. Every muscle in their bodies twitched. They were covered in sweat and dust.

"I'm okay, I'm alive," Maddie keep repeating joyfully as he gently unlocked the handcuffs and then peeled off the duct tape. Her wrists were raw and bleeding and so were his. Their blood mingled.

"Yeah." He laughed, giddily. "Yeah."

"You saved me. You chained yourself to me." She gazed deeply into his eyes and then he was kissing her with the most soulful kiss in the world, branding her with his lips.

"You nearly died," he whispered, burying his face in her hair and holding her close against him. "I almost lost you."

He was overwhelmed not only by what had just happened, but also by the intensity of emotion surging through him. Did she feel what he felt? Could he trust the power of their connection or was it merely a manifestation of surviving the worst together?

Was this love?

Boom, boom, boom went his heart.

Creak, creak, creak went the bell tower.

"We're not out of the woods yet," he murmured. "The stairwell collapsed. The tower is crumbling and we have no way down."

Maddie pulled back and stared at him, as if recognizing for the first time what a truly dangerous predicament they were in.

David shifted onto his knees, grasped the wall to pull himself up. As he did, more stones broke free and the tower bobbled like a rocking horse.

"Easy," Maddie cautioned.

He glanced over the edge of the window arch. "There's only one way down."

His eyes met hers. He looked grim.

"The water," she whispered.

He nodded. "We're going to have to jump. Can you do it?"

"I have a fear of drowning. Ever since Cassie's accident."

"It's our only chance," he said. "I wouldn't suggest it if we had a choice."

She rose to stand beside him, her body swaying along with the tower. On one side they could see the jagged rocks lying under the water. No jumping off there. She shifted her gaze to the other side.

"What if it's not deep enough?" She gulped.

"We'll be killed."

"Together."

"Yes."

"And what if we're not killed? What if I drown?"

"You won't drown. I won't let you," he said gruffly.

Maddie placed her right hand in his left. "I'm trusting you."

She couldn't have paid him a grander compliment.

"I swear I won't let you down."

"This is big for me."

"I know."

"I'm scared."

"So am I."

"You'll be there for me?"

"Have I ever let you down?" He kept his voice tender, his gaze steady.

She looked deep into his eyes, peered far deeper into him than anyone had ever peered.

More stones broke loose, smashing and bumping as they fell. The tower was going. If they waited much longer, the decision would be out of their hands.

"Ready?" David whispered.

Maddie took a deep breath and nodded.

Together, they moved as close to the ledge as they could.

"Arc your body outward," David said. "Then roll your legs up and tuck your head down. A cannon ball isn't the most graceful, but it's our best chance for survival."

"All right."

She stood beside him, poised to jump. She glanced down. "I can't."

"Don't look at the water. Look at me." He squeezed her hand tightly.

Maddie wrenched her gaze from the water and met his eyes again. She was so brave! His heart wrenched with the intensity of his feelings for this courageous woman.

"Atta girl. We're just going to step off. We're taking a stroll. That's all. No big deal. You can do this."

"Uh-huh."

Chapter
TWENTY-FIVE

AFTER CALLING IN the bomb threat, Cassie called the front desk and talked the concierge into buying her an outfit from the gift shop and charging it to Peyton's account. The preppy black slacks and white wool sweater and sensible loafers were more like something Maddie would wear but she shrugged it off. Beggars couldn't be choosers.

Besides, she felt more responsible, more in control, more reliable these days. She might as well look the part. Once she'd acquired her new threads, she took the originals of the El Greco and the Cézanne that she'd hidden under her mattress after she'd made the double set of forgeries, rolled the canvases up in cardboard tubing and went to the Hotel International. Pretending to be Maddie, she claimed to have lost her room key. Once she had access to the room, she stashed the paintings in the open wall safe—good thing David hadn't found a reason to use it yet—assigned the lock a combination code and sashayed out again.

Mission accomplished. No one could accuse her of being in cahoots with Shriver now. Then she hurried over to the Vivaldi to find out what was happening over there.

And she arrived just in time to see Levy and Philpot being taken from the hotel in handcuffs.

Not wanting to be recognized, she dodged behind a statue and waited until the art brokers had been led away in handcuffs before slipping inside the building. Her heart hammered with excitement.

Had they nabbed Shriver? Was he already in custody? Or had the elusive thief managed to give them the slip?

The place was in chaos with cops and news media and hotel personnel running willy-nilly. To think she'd caused all this bedlam.

Cassie grinned and tried to look inconspicuous as she slinked down the corridor toward the Rialto room.

So far so good.

She was almost there. She quickly skirted past a jani tor's closet that stood slightly ajar. She craned her neck, trying to get a peek around the burly door guard into the Rialto Room.

That's when a hand clamped over her mouth and an arm snaked around her waist and she was yanked backward into the janitor's closet.

Floating. Drifting dreamily. Maddie was aware of the cold water, but oddly enough the frigid temperature didn't register against her skin. Nor was she panicked about being face down in the water.

Her eyes were closed and she didn't try to open them. She didn't want to see. She simply wanted to embrace this light airy feeling where nothing seemed hurried or dangerous or even real.

Was she dead? Had she been killed by the fall from the disintegrating tower?

Hmm. Well, this wasn't so bad.

Only one thing bothered her. Just one tiny flaw marred her peaceful flow. She was dead and she'd never told David that she loved him.

Such a shame.

That's what you get for holding back. You had a chance for true love and you blew it.

Then she started thinking of all the times she'd held back, afraid to take a risk, afraid of getting hurt, afraid to trust.

And now here she was finally figuring out that dying was no big deal. Her biggest worst case scenario had come to pass and all she had were regrets for the opportunities she'd lost. The things she had never tried.

I should have given it my all at the Olympics. I should have stopped playing cleanup for Cassie years ago and concentrated on taking care of myself.

If she had her life to live over, knowing what she knew now, she would make some very different choices. She would dye her hair punk-rocker red just to see what it looked like. She would eat a doughnut now and again. She would strip off her clothes and dance naked in her backyard during a summer rainstorm.

If only she had a second chance!

Then she thought of the things she was never going to get to do. She'd never be able to apologize to Cassie for not letting her stand on her own two feet. She wouldn't get to tell her father how much he'd hurt her when he'd abandoned the family. She wouldn't see her mother one last time or teach another aerobics class or walk in a garden with the sun on her face. She'd never sing lullabies to her babies. Never send them off on their first day of school with a hug and a wave. She would never worry when they didn't make curfew the day they got their driver's license.

Something inside her heart ripped. Babies made her think of being married and being married made her think of being in love and being in love made her think of David.

She would never be able to tell David she loved him.

This realization brought a raw, intricate pain, shredding her earlier peace. She didn't want to be dead. She couldn't be dead. She had so very much to live for.

"Maddie! Maddie!"

Who was calling her? Was that Cassie? She frowned. Or at least she thought she frowned. She couldn't really tell. Did dead people frown?

She felt herself being yanked around.

Ow! Who was pulling her hair?

So much for the quiet dignity of death.

She tried to struggle, to fight the water, to fight for her life but her hands seemed leaden and reluctant. Was she dead or not? She couldn't seem to move or open her eyes, but someone kept yelling her name. A rough, frightened masculine voice.

David. It had to be David.

Her heart gave a crazy little hop and she wondered when she would get to float out of her body so she could see him.

"Don't you dare leave me, Maddie Cooper," he raged. "Breathe, dammit, breathe."

It sounded like he was getting mad. She tried to obey, tried to breathe, but her lungs didn't want to expand. The languid ease of the water was gone and her back was pressed against something hard. The ground?

"I gave you my word I wouldn't let you drown," David was babbling. "And I never go back on a promise. Never. So you can't drown. Get it. You won't drown. Don't give up on me. Fight. Fight. Fight for your life."

He might have slipped a hand under her neck, but she was so numb she couldn't really tell.

"Breathe." She thought he might have been stroking her face. "Breathe."

She felt pressure against her lips. Heat against her cold flesh. Her lungs, which had been peaceful in the water, now ached and burned. She heard more sounds. A seagull's caw, a fish breaking the surface of the water, a helicopter rumbling overhead.

And she experienced the heavy rush of David's life-giving breath forcing its way into her narrowed airway. Her stomach churned. She was going to be sick.

With a sudden gasp, Maddie sat up. David rolled her onto her side and held her tenderly while she purged the seawater from her body.

"That's my girl," he soothed, gently running his fingers through her hair, stroking her forehead. "Cough it all up."

She opened her eyes and looked into his face.

Not dead. Not by half. David had given her the precious second chance she'd mourned so woefully. She was reborn.

"David," she croaked.

He clutched her to his chest, rocked her back and forth in his arms. The helicopter flew above them, blades whirling. The force of the air sent dirt and debris blowing over them. Luckily the bedsheet was so wet and tangled around her legs, that the breeze from the helicopter couldn't raise it.

Maddie tilted her head and saw it was a police chopper. Henri Gault was half hanging out the door. He waved to them.

"The cavalry is here," she whispered.

"Late as always," David murmured.

"Where's Blanco?"

"Don't know, don't care. All I care about is you." His eyes shone with the truth of his statement. His words and the concerned expression on his handsome face warmed her in the way nothing else could have.

The helicopter touched down. Henri and a Venice police officer hopped out and hurried toward them in a running crouch.

"You all right?" Henri shouted over the noisy chopper.

David nodded.

Henri pointed to the rubble of the campanile. For the first time since David hauled her from the sea, Maddie looked back at where they'd been. The sight of the demolished building struck her like a slap. If they hadn't jumped they would both be dead. No one could have survived. She gasped and David tightened his grip around her.

"From the air we could see a man crawling over the rocks," Henri said.

"It's got to be Blanco," David said.

Henri clamped a hand on his shoulder. "Relax, *mon ami,* we'll take care of this one for you."

"Thanks."

Henri and the policeman took off after Blanco and the helicopter pilot came over with blankets. David wrapped Maddie warm as a papoose and although she protested, he insisted on carrying her to the chopper, his casted wrist be damned. She wrapped her legs around his waist and allowed him to tote her like a toddler.

"There are clothes in the helicopter you could change into," the chopper pilot said in heavily accented English as he eyed their sopping wet garments. "They are costumes my wife and I wore for a Carnevale pageant this morning and I was supposed to take them back to the costume shop but didn't have time. You can wear them. I wait out here while you change inside."

"Thank you," David said.

They found the costumes, wriggled out of their wet things and into the new outfits.

"I look like Jane Austen," Maddie said.

"Lucky you. I look like Lord Dandy."

They blinked at each other. They were both wearing Regency era dress. Just like her fantasy. Maddie gulped. Stupid, stupid fantasies.

"I guess we're both lucky it's Carnevale. No one will take a second glance," she said.

"Yeah," he agreed huskily and she couldn't help but wonder if he was thinking what she was thinking. "It's better than being wet."

Henri and the policeman returned, supporting a hobbling Blanco. They loaded him onto the police boat David had shown up in and the policeman motored Blanco back to the mainland while Henri rejoined them in the chopper.

"Love the costume," Henri grinned at David as he climbed into the helicopter. "Shall we waltz?"

David shoved a hand through his hair and the shirtsleeve brushed against his cheek. He was expected to believe manly men in the nineteenth century wore crap like this? And to think Maddie's dream proposal consisted of her beloved dressed up like a pompous ass. Women. Who could figure 'em?

"I'm grateful for your help," he growled at Henri. "So I'll ignore that comment."

"Better be nice to me. I have more news."

"News?" David tensed and leaned forward. "Good or bad?"

"Is it about my sister?" Maddie interjected.

David shot her a glance. If she didn't look so cute in that pageant dress, he would have been irritated with the interruption. Now on her, the Regency thing worked. Especially the way the cut of the dress emphasized her assets.

Henri nodded. "Your sister called in a bomb threat to the Vivaldi. At least we suspect that it was her. We traced the call and it came from Shriver's room at the Hotel Polo."

Maddie groaned and dropped her head in her hands. "Why would she call in a bomb threat?"

"To get the police to the Vivaldi in time to foil Shriver's art auction," David said.

"I don't understand. Is Cassie with Shriver or against him?" Henri asked.

"Neither do we," David muttered darkly. "Did they succeed in stopping the auction?"

"They stopped the auction," Henri confirmed.

"And they caught Shriver?" David fisted his hand and his gut clenched. Was this it then? The compilation of ten years' worth of police work. Was his dream about to come true? His hand trembled. He was that moved by the notion of finally, *finally* winning this thing.

Henri shook his head. "Shriver disappeared."

David cursed. Not again!

"But what about Cassie?" Maddie asked. "Where is she?"

"There is an all points alert out on her for calling in the bomb threat," Henri said. "No one knows where she is."

"Did the police at least nab Levy or Philpot?" David snarled.

Henri smiled. "They did even better."

"Oh, yeah?"

"They arrested both Levy and Philpot, almost a dozen collectors and they recovered seven stolen paintings including your aunt's Rembrandt."

"No kidding? They've got Aunt Caroline's Rembrandt?" David slumped against the back of his seat. Well, at least that was something. He imagined the joy on his aunt's face when he returned the painting to her and his spirits lifted. This wasn't over yet. He would get Shriver too.

"Levy brought the Rembrandt to the auction to dump it. Apparently the pressure we've been putting on him was too hot. He was desperate to ditch it."

"High five," David held up his left hand.

"You Americans with the victory celebrations." Henri grinned and smacked his palm.

"Hey, it's been a long time coming. I'm due a little victory dance."

"Not so fast, *mon ami*. I'm afraid there's more unpleasant news."

"What's that?"

"The Cézanne and the El Greco are still missing. The ones we found at the Vivaldi auction were forgeries."

David sucked in his breath. Cassie had been a busy girl. "Where are the originals?"

"That's what your supervisor wants to know," Henri said.

David swallowed. "You called Jim Barnes?"

"No, he came to Venice after receiving your telegram."

"I didn't send him a telegram."

Henri shrugged. "Someone did. And they signed your name. The telegram said you had the originals in safe-keeping."

"What? I don't have the originals!" Panic took hold of him. Calm down. Chill. You'll figure it out. You're so close to wrapping this up. Don't take a dive now. "Who could have sent Jim the telegram with my name on it? And why would . . . oh, shit."

His eyes met Maddie's and in unison they both exclaimed, "Cassie."

Henri went to the boat launch to meet the police and oversee Jocko Blanco's arrest. "Go on," he told David. "Find Shriver. This case belongs to you. After ten years, you deserve the win."

Leaving Henri behind, David and Maddie ran through the streets of Venice looking like a deranged Mr. Darcy and Elizabeth Bennet. If she hadn't been so worried about Cassie, Maddie might have seen the humor in the situation. As it was, she was desperately missing her half-a-heart necklace. Ever since she'd lost that necklace in Spain things had gone dramatically from bad to worse.

They zipped around the Carnevale crowd and clattered through the Piazza San Marco on the boards set out to provide a makeshift walkway for spanning the encroaching tidewater. They arrived at the Hotel Polo where Shriver and Cassie had been staying. An investigative team from Interpol was there, along with David's boss Jim Barnes, meticulously combing through Shriver's room for evidence.

"Marshall," Barnes barked, the minute he spotted David standing in the doorway.

Maddie saw David's shoulders tense and his jaw clench. "Yes, sir."

"You look like hell, man." The salt-and-pepper-haired Barnes was in his mid-fifties with a bulldog face, buzz cut and stocky build.

"Ran into a slight problem."

"I hope the other guy looks worse."

"He does, sir."

"And what's with the foppish outfit?" Barnes made a face at David's costume.

"Undercover at Carnevale," he said.

Maddie had never seen this side of David. All correct and by the book. It was a far cry from the usual loose cannon persona he wore in the field. He was a secret bad boy, she realized. Eager to please those in power, but deep down inside not really willing to let go of control for anyone.

Jim Barnes took the telegram from his pocket and handed it to David. "You want to explain this?"

Maddie hesitated in the hall behind him, her gaze trained on David's face. Would he tell his boss the truth? That he had recruited Cassie to spy on Shriver and she'd been the one to make forgeries of the paintings and hide the originals?

Would he assume responsibility for breaking all the rules and take his lumps? Or would he pretend that Cassie's accomplishments were his own and throw her sister to the wolves?

"Do you have the original Cézanne and El Greco?" Barnes asked.

Maddie closed her eyes briefly. Please, David, please, David, please say the right thing.

"Yes," David said and with that one word, he shattered all hope for their future.

Maddie opened her mouth to call him a liar, to defend her sister, but no words came out. She was too stunned to speak. Mind numb with the realization that David actually would do anything to win, no matter what the cost, she turned on her heel and stiffly walked away.

"Good job." Jim Barnes slapped him on the back. "Now bring in Shriver and Cassie Cooper and that promotion belongs to you."

"Maddie," David called out to her. "Wait a minute. I have to talk to you."

But she didn't want to hear rationalizations or excuses.

"Maddie!" David bellowed. "Stop right there."

To hell with that. She was one person he wasn't going to best. She ducked her head and ran. I won't cry. I won't give him the satisfaction of breaking my heart.

"Maddie, don't you dare take another step."

She flipped him the finger just before she dashed through the fire exit door and plunged down the stairs.

"Sir," David said to Jim Barnes. "I need to leave right this minute. I love that woman and I've got to straighten things out. She's misunderstood my intentions."

"Well isn't this just precious. Bullshit, Marshall. What you need to do is tell me where those paintings are."

"I don't have access to them at the moment."

"What do you mean you don't have access to them? Did you send me this telegram or not?"

"I did not."

"Then who did?" Barnes's face was a thundercloud.

"Cassie Cooper."

"Shriver's girlfriend? What's she got to do with all this?"

David blew out his breath. If Barnes got pissed, then Barnes got pissed. At this point, he didn't much care. He wasn't going to hang Cassie out to dry, no matter what Maddie believed him capable of. "She's not Shriver's girlfriend."

"What do you mean?"

"She's been working for me all along." Which was true. Cassie had been on his side whether he'd known it or not.

"You told her to call in a bomb threat?"

"I told her to do whatever she had to do to stop Shriver."

"So you went behind my back and recruited her. Just like I told you not to."

"Yes, I did. And it was a good solid plan." Until Blanco had fouled things up. "We've been working together to round up Levy and Philpot and Shriver and the stolen artwork."

"So where's the El Greco? Where's the Cézanne?"

"Cassie has placed them in a secure location."

"How do you know?" Barnes glared, his nostrils flaring.

"I just know."

"So if she's working for you, then where is she? Where's Shriver?"

"At the moment, I don't know."

"Are you sure she wasn't just scamming you, Marshall? Ever think that maybe you're the dupe?"

"I'm not a dupe."

"Bring me Shriver and those paintings, Marshall. Now. Or you're out."

"You're firing me?"

"If you go after that woman, yes. My patience with you is at an end. You've gone behind my back one time too many. Your call. Either the promotion or the boot."

David ground his teeth. He was jerked in two opposing directions. On the one hand there was his job, which was much more than just a job. It was a career. It was his identity. Once upon a time the promotion would have meant everything to him.

But now there was Maddie.

Fireworks were going off on the Grand Canal. A parade of lights on the water. A spectacle of flotillas. Maddie ran through the narrow streets along the canal not knowing where she was going, not really caring. All she wanted was to escape David and the aching pain in her heart.

She kept running until her side hurt and she couldn't get her breath. She had trusted David and he'd betrayed her. With one bald-faced lie, he'd claimed to have the paintings and he'd taken credit for the work Cassie had done. He didn't care about her or her sister. All he cared about was winning.

Her stomach twisted in knots. A rocket exploded into ribbons of colorful light overhead. The crowd oohed and aahed.

Maddie skirted a clot of people lined along the bridge and turned down the cobblestone walkway. Glancing up, she was taken aback to see she was on the steps of the Hotel Vivaldi. The place where Shriver had held his illegal auction and Cassie had called in the bomb threat. She didn't see any policemen. Had they already cleared the robbery scene?

The crowd was on the move, trailing along the canal, following the water parade away from the Vivaldi. Within minutes, the immediate area was silent, deserted.

From her peripheral vision, Maddie caught movement in the shadows of the side street. A man and woman struggling over something.

It's none of your business, Maddie. Stay out of it.

Another rocket from the fireworks display exploded into the night sky.

The couple was silhouetted in the reflected glow and she could clearly see the man had a gun.

Maddie's heart leapfrogged into her throat.

It was Cassie and Shriver.

Years of honing her protective instincts toward her sister sent Maddie hurtling straight for them. She didn't stop to think things through. Only one thing pounded in her head—the same thought that for the past eighteen years had rarely left the forefront of her mind—save Cassie, save Cassie, save Cassie.

"Get away from my sister!" she yelled and with the intensity of a wrestler intent on full body smackdown, Maddie charged into Shriver.

And knocked him into the canal.

"What are you doing?" Cassie shrieked as Shriver disappeared into the black water.

Maddie spun around to face her sister. "Are you all right?"

"Dammit, Maddie. You've gone and screwed up everything."

"What?" Cassie was mad because she'd saved her life?

"When are you going to stop interfering?" Cassie's eyes flashed fire and she sank her hands onto her hips.

"I was just trying to help."

"Well stop it! I'm tired of you always running interference for me. You act as if I'm a child. We're not nine years old anymore and I'm not your responsibility, so leave me alone."

"But I came to Europe after you."

"No one asked you to. That's the problem. You've always just assumed it was your place to take care of me. Well, it's not."

"But you're always getting into trouble."

"Maybe that's because I've never had to suffer the consequences of my actions. You were always there to catch me if I fell, so why hold back? But guess what, Maddie? I'm tired of being the airhead sexpot. I wanted to be strong and competent and capable like you."

"But . . . but . . ." Maddie sputtered, completely taken aback. She had no idea Cassie felt this way. "I vowed I'd never let anything happen to you."

"Vow, vow, vow. I'm so sick of you waving that vow in my face. Know what I think about that vow, Maddie? Here's what I think about that stupid vow of yours." Cassie ripped the half-a-heart necklace from around her throat and flung it into the canal.

"Cassie!" Maddie gasped and instantly her hand went to her own neck to finger the necklace that was no longer there.

"There! The necklace is gone. The vow is broken. You've been exonerated of all guilt. It was never your fault that I fell into that pond. It was my fault. All mine. Stop being a martyr and get a life."

"Is that what you think of me?" Maddie asked, aghast. All the times she'd resented Cassie for having to clean up her messes, Cassie had been resenting her for doing the cleanup.

"Ladies, ladies," Peyton Shriver interrupted, climbing up the side of the retaining wall with his gun pointed right at Maddie's head. "Let's not fight. Let's just go get the originals of the Cézanne and El Greco."

"I'm not afraid of you," Maddie said. "There's two of us and one of you. Your gun is wet. It probably won't fire."

"His gun might not fire," said a familiar voice from the darkness. "But mine will."

Chapter

♥

TWENTY-SIX

$\mathcal{D}$AVID PUSHED UPSTREAM against the mass of costumed tourists following the fireworks water parade. He had no idea which direction Maddie had gone. Nor did he know where to start looking for Shriver, Cassie or the paintings.

He was almost back to square one. Maddie hated him. Shriver was on the lam along with the paintings and he hadn't a clue what Cassie was up to. If it weren't for Blanco, Levy and Philpot cooling their heels in jail and Aunt Caroline's Rembrandt sitting safely in the evidence room, he would feel like a total failure.

It's not over until it's over.

He wasn't out of options yet.

Pausing in the doorway of a closed shop to let the thick of the crowd pass him by, he called the police station to see if Henri was still there. The chief officer on duty told him Henri had gone to the Hotel Vivaldi. Not knowing where else to search, David decided to hook up with his Interpol counterpart and see if he had any thoughts on Shriver's possible whereabouts.

But no matter how hard he tried to concentrate on the job, he couldn't stop thinking about Maddie.

He'd known by her shocked reaction that she'd misunderstood when he'd told his boss he knew where the paintings were. He hadn't meant to usurp Cassie's victory but rather to include her as his partner.

Maddie had immediately jumped to the wrong conclusion and assumed he was taking credit for Cassie's *coup*. He didn't know why he'd phrased it the way he had unless deep down he'd been unconsciously testing her trust in him.

She'd failed miserably.

Or maybe you were the one who failed for testing her loyalty in the first place, whispered the angel on his shoulder.

David knew it was true. Maddie wasn't at fault. He was. He had to find her. He had to apologize. He couldn't lose her. He had to open up his heart and tell her how he felt. Because until he let her in, how could he expect her to trust him?

But where to look?

Muttering under his breath, he started for the Hotel Vivaldi.

Henri hadn't told him how Shriver had managed to escape when the police had busted the auction. Shriver was a slippery bastard. David couldn't count the number of times he'd almost had him and then somehow Shriver had eluded him. Ten years of chasing. Ten years of hard police work. No other art thief could rival Shriver's incredible longevity.

In fact, Shriver had only been arrested once and that was in Paris back at the beginning of his larcenous career, long before he'd scammed Aunt Caroline. Oddly enough, Henri had been the arresting officer.

Shriver had done a short stint in prison, but he must have learned a lot while he was there. He'd come out with a more sophisticated technique. He seemed to have a knack for getting into places other thieves only dreamed of. It was almost as if he had a second sense about such things. Or as if someone on the inside was feeding him security information.

How had Shriver done it? How had he, time and again, evaded capture? How had he repeatedly bested the most elaborate security systems in the world? Courting female museum employees got his foot in the door, yes, but that wasn't enough. He had to have had access to complicated codes and knowledge of tripwires and timing mechanisms and infrared sensors.

It was almost as if Shriver knew as much about the various museums as the art task divisions of the FBI or Interpol.

Then suddenly, with the shocking stab of a lightning jolt David realized something he should have realized a very long time ago.

"Henri?" Maddie stared open-mouthed at the man who stepped from the shadows with his duty weapon drawn.

"Oui." Henri gave a regretful half-smile. *"C'est moi."*

"You two are in on the heists together?" Maddie blinked as the truth slowly sank in.

"Not this time," Henri said sadly to her, then to Peyton he said, "You've been a very naughty boy. Not keeping me apprised of what you were up to. How can I help you if you don't talk to me?"

"Don't you get it? I don't want your help anymore,"

Shriver said hotly, his gaze locked on Henri. "I'm through. I've had enough. I want a different sort of life. The El Greco, the Cézanne, they're my ticket out of this relationship."

Henri's laugh was high-pitched, almost maniacal. "What? You leaving me for the likes of her?" He waved a hand at Cassie. "You think an airhead like her can take my place?"

"Hey!" Cassie protested.

"You always knew I liked women too," Shriver countered. "But she's not the reason I'm leaving. I'm tired of doing all the work, living on the run while you get to sit back and play Interpol man. And I'm sick of your jealousy. It's annoying."

"Without me, you are nothing but a common criminal," Henri yelled. "I'm the one who gave you international acclaim. Alone, you couldn't break into hives."

"You two are lovers?" Cassie squealed.

"He loves me," Shriver said. "I was just in it for the art."

"You told me you loved me too!" Henri cried.

"So I lied." Shriver shrugged.

"Bitch," Henri said and shot him.

Shriver staggered backward into the canal, clutching his hand to his chest.

Maddie and Cassie shrieked and hugged each other.

Henri swung the gun around. "You two are next, but first take me to the paintings."

"It's over, Henri. Put the gun down," David's voice rang out from the bridge. Maddie swiveled her head, saw him crouched, ready to shoot.

"Not so fast, *mon ami*." Henri lunged forward,

grabbed Maddie around the neck and pressed his gun against her temple.

Stunned, Maddie could only blink. This couldn't be happening. Not twice in one damned day.

"Why, Henri, why?" David asked. "You were such a good cop."

"You don't understand," Henri said and that's when Maddie realized he was crying. "I loved him. It was all for him. He craved the glamorous life. I had the power to make it happen."

"All these years, whenever I was close to catching Shriver, you were the one tipping him off."

"David, forgive me. But I loved him. Surely now that you have Maddie, you understand how that feels."

What did Henri mean? Was David in love with her? Maddie's heart thumped.

"We can work this out, Henri. Let her go. Put the gun down."

"And if I say no?"

"Then I'm going to have to kill you."

"Who cares? Without Peyton I have nothing to live for." He was sobbing so hard, he loosened his grip on Maddie.

Her mind raced. If she could shift her body just a little, get enough leverage, she could flip him over her head and into the canal.

Just as Maddie was about to make her move, there was a smashing noise behind her and Henri slumped against her, heavy as a sack of lead. The weight of him knocked her to the ground.

"Umph," she grunted as the air left her lungs and she whacked her head on the cobblestones.

When she finally stopped seeing stars, she looked up

to discover Henri's prostrate body splayed across her. Above him stood Cassie triumphantly wielding a broken wine bottle left behind by some Carnevale revelers.

"That'll teach you to mess with my sister," she crowed.

"Cassie," Maddie exclaimed. "*You* saved *me*."

"I did, didn't I?" Cassie proudly puffed out her chest.

"I guess you can take care of yourself." Maddie grinned.

And then there was David, hovering over her, looking frantic and breathing hard.

"Maddie, sweetheart," he cried as he knelt to slap handcuffs on the dazed Henri and pull him off her. "Are you all right?"

"I'm fine. Thanks to Cassie."

David smiled at her sister. "Good work."

Cassie's face glowed.

"Um," Maddie said. "Shouldn't someone check on Shriver?"

Cassie peered over the edge of the canal. "He's not quite dead yet. In fact, I think he's made a miraculous recovery. If I'm not mistaken, that's him swimming off."

"Sonofabitch," David swore. "He's not getting away this time."

David ran after Shriver. When he drew abreast of him, he dived into the canal. Shriver tried to swim in the other direction but he was too exhausted.

David caught him.

He bit David's hand and tried repeatedly to kick him.

David sighed, drew back his fist and cold-cocked him. "That's for Aunt Caroline."

Shriver's head lolled back. He was out. David dragged

him from the canal, handcuffed him and left him on the bank while he hurried back to check on Maddie.

Maddie and Cassie were huddled together talking sister stuff. Henri was lying where David had left him.

"Peyton is alive? Did I kill him?" he asked David.

"No."

"But how? I shot him point blank in the heart."

"Bulletproof vest. Apparently he anticipated that you would have a wicked jealous streak."

"Thank heaven, he's alive," Henri murmured.

David shook his head and crouched beside his colleague. "How did it come to this?"

"*Amour, mon ami.*" Henri sighed. "It makes you do crazy things."

Henri was right on one score. Love could make you do crazy things.

Except what David was about to do felt anything but crazy. It might be impulsive and premature and ill-timed but nothing had ever felt so rational, so sane, so perfectly right.

It was just after midnight. He and Maddie were leaving the police station. Shriver and Henri were in jail. Cassie had retrieved the Cézanne and El Greco from the safe in his hotel room and turned them over to Jim Barnes. David still hadn't figured out how she'd managed that one. He'd gotten his promotion and he'd called his Aunt Caroline to tell her about the Rembrandt. Her tears of joy had sated the lust for justice he'd been chasing for the past ten years. He'd gotten everything he'd ever wanted.

Except for one thing.

The one thing he'd never even known he wanted, but had needed desperately.

Love.

They were still wearing the Regency costumes they'd borrowed from the helicopter pilot. They passed a gondola stand. David reached out and took Maddie's hand. "Would you like to take a gondola back to the hotel?"

She peered into his eyes and the look she gave him turned him inside out. "That would be nice," she said.

They settled into the gondola. The moon was huge. The gondolier sang a famous Italian love song. It was the most romantic damned thing he'd ever heard. A knot of emotion swelled in his chest.

Ah, crap, protested the devil on his left shoulder. *You're no good at this mushy stuff, Marshall.*

Well, advised the angel on his right, y*ou better just get used to it.*

Maddie trembled in the seat beside him.

"You're cold," he said.

"No," she denied. "Not cold."

He sucked in air.

"You're trembling too!" she exclaimed.

"Yeah."

"But you're wearing wet clothes. I'm sure you are cold."

"I am cold but that's not why I'm trembling."

"No?"

They were staring into each other's eyes, neither one daring to breathe.

And then he got down on one knee.

"What are you doing?"

"It might not be under the best of circumstances and my Mr. Darcy suit might be a bit soggy, but when else am

I going to have the perfect opportunity to give you your fantasy proposal?"

"Oh, David!"

Maddie pressed a hand to her chest. If she didn't hold it down, she feared her heart might simply flutter away.

"I know we've only known each other a week. I know you're the cautious type. I know we've been through a lot of stuff and you're probably worried that the thrill of the chase is what's got me feeling this way about you."

She couldn't talk. She could only nod.

"I know we've both had a few problems with the trust issue but I think that just got resolved tonight."

"Uh-huh."

"I'm not suggesting we rush into anything. When I want something I have a tendency to just plunge right in and bluster my way through it. But I don't want to bluster my way through life with you."

"You don't?"

"You were right about me. I like to win because it means I'm in control and I mistakenly thought that if I wasn't controlling every situation that meant I was in a position of weakness. I can see now how wrong that belief is. And I've learned that there are a lot more important things than always having to win."

"You have?" she squeaked.

"Romantic sentiment doesn't come easy to me, Maddie, but dammit, I love you. And I want to marry you. We can take all the time you need. A year. Five years. Ten. Hell, if nothing else we both know I'm determined."

He was offering her the one thing she never thought she would have. For years, she'd avoided love and commitment, telling herself she could never really become involved with someone because she had to take care of her sister. But the reality was she had used Cassie as an excuse. She realized that now. She'd been hiding behind her childhood vow. Afraid of making a mistake. Afraid of getting hurt. Afraid of taking a chance on love.

"Oh, David! I love you too. So very much." Her throat clogged with happy tears. "And I don't want to wait a long time to marry you. I've waited twenty-seven years to start my life. I've been cautious and guarded and scared to trust. But I'm not afraid anymore. I might have misunderstood you at times, but you've never let me down."

Love and moonlight shone in his eyes. He looked at her as if she were the greatest prize ever to be won. "Is that a yes?" he whispered.

"Yes, yes, yes," she cried.

Then he took her into his arms and kissed her and it was as if she'd belonged there always.

Epilogue

❤

North Central Texas
Christmas Day, ten months later

$\mathcal{I}$T WAS TURNING out to be the best day of Maddie
Cooper's twenty-eight-year-old life.

For one thing, she was about to be married to the sexiest, most self-confident FBI agent on earth. Her sassy
twin sister Cassie, who'd become a media darling after
helping mastermind the biggest art theft bust in history,
was able to get off work from her new job as PR director
at *Art World Today* magazine and serve as her maid of
honor. Her mother and stepfather had flown in from Belize and her father had driven up from San Antonio. And
David's Aunt Caroline had arrived from New York to
share their special day with them.

For another thing, she and David were spending their
honeymoon in Europe, seeing all the sights they'd been
unable to visit on their first trip. And while they were

there, David insisted she interview with a renowned track and field coach who specialized in helping retired athletes make a comeback. She was going to give the Olympics one more shot. And this time, she wasn't holding back.

She stood in front of the mirror at the church rectory in her Regency-inspired wedding dress. Her heart fluttered to think she was about to get everything she'd ever dreamed of.

"Psst."

Maddie turned her head and looked at the door. "David?"

"Yes."

"You can't see me in my dress. It's bad luck."

"I've got my eyes closed. Let me in."

"That's cheating."

"Since when is bending a few rules cheating?" He laughed.

"Oh you." She pulled open the door and he tumbled inside with his eyes squinched tightly closed. "What is it?"

"I have a present for you." He grinned. "Where are you?"

"I'm right here." She tapped him on the shoulder. "Couldn't this wait?"

"Nope." He extended a long slender jeweler's box in her direction.

"What is it?"

"Open it up and find out."

Maddie unwrapped the box. Nestled in the tissue paper was a gold heart necklace.

"David," she whispered.

"I know it can't replace the one you lost in Spain," he

said. "And I couldn't find that half-a-heart design. But this is it, babe, I'm giving you all of my heart."

"And you said you weren't any good at this sentimental romantic stuff."

"Come here, you." With his eyes still tightly closed, he reached for her.

He kissed her long and hard while his hands pushed up underneath her dress. Passion swept over them and the next thing Maddie knew, they were sprawled across the window seat breaking all the rules.

Several minutes later, breathless and sated, they lay against each other, listening to their hearts thump in unison. True to his word, David's eyes were still shut.

"I love you, Maddie Cooper," he whispered.

"Soon to be Maddie Cooper Marshall," she whispered back. "And I love you too."

"Soon to be Maddie Cooper Marshall, Olympic gold medalist," he added. "Now let's go get married."

Ten minutes later, before God and their loved ones, Maddie and David vowed to love and cherish each other and they both knew that this was a vow they would happily keep forever and ever and ever.

About the Author

$\mathcal{L}$ori Wilde is the best-selling author of more than twenty books. A former RITA finalist, Lori's books have been recognized by Romantic Times Reviewers' Choice Award, the Holt Medallion, the Booksellers Best, the National Readers' Choice and numerous other honors. She lives in Weatherford, Texas with her husband and a wide assortment of pets. You may write to Lori at PO Box 31, Weatherford, TX 76086 or e-mail her via her homepage at www.loriwilde.com.

sashayed out again.

No question about it. The mummy was following her.

Cassie Cooper slipped past King Tut who was chatting up Nefertiti beside the lavish hors d'oeuvre table and cast a surreptitious glance over her shoulder.

Yep.

There he was. Peeking from behind the Sphinx's chipped nose, his mysterious dark eyes following her around the main exhibit hall of the Kimbell Art Museum.

Stifling a triumphant grin, she readjusted her Cleopatra Queen of the Nile headdress, which kept slipping down on her forehead and messing up her wig, and then she seductively moistened her lips.

Who was lurking beneath the swaddling linen?

Her pulse quickened. She *did* have a lot of admirers. No telling who might be in that costume.

Maybe it was an old flame. Maybe a new one. Maybe it was even a stranger.

Goosebumps dotted the nape of her neck. A mystery. How exciting.

From over Phyllis's shoulder, Cassie spied the mummy again. He was waving, trying to get her attention. When his dark enigmatic eyes met hers, he inclined his head toward the exit door leading to the garden courtyard.

Her pulse revved. Was the mummy telling her to meet him outside?

Then a staggering thought occurred to her. Could Adam Hartfield be the mummy?

"Well?" Phyllis demanded, forcing Cassie to look away from the man in the mummy suit.

"Umm, yes," she lied through her teeth. No point in putting the woman into a snit before there was something to snit about. "I heard from Adam. He's on the way."

"All I have to say is that he better show up on time." Phyllis tapped her watch again. "Because if anything goes wrong tonight, you can kiss that recommendation to the Smithsonian goodbye."

"Nothing will go wrong."

"Reassure me. Locate Dr. Hartfield."

"Yes, ma'am." Cassie used the convenient excuse to retrieve her purse from where she'd stashed it in the coat closet and then scuttle out into the courtyard.

The balmy spring night air greeted her and the door snapped closed behind her, muting the laughter and voices inside the museum. Suddenly, she felt very far away.

Isolated. Alone.

Tingles raced up her spine.

Her breath came in short, raspy gasp. Anticipation escalated her excitement. She looked right, then left. Where had the mummy gone?

Maybe she'd misunderstood his intentions. Maybe he'd been signaling to someone else and she'd made a mistaken assumption.

Nah. She knew when a guy was sending signals. And the mummy had been telegraphing her big time.

Who was he? Old boyfriend? New boyfriend? Friend? Lover? Enemy? The suspense was unbearable.

The courtyard was illuminated with ambient lighting from quaint low voltage streetlamps. Well-manicured trees and shrubbery cast dark shadows over the walkway.

"Yew-hoo." Cassie wound around the maze of chest high bushes. "Anybody here?"

No sound except for the echo of her high-heeled sandals clicking against the cobblestones.

What if Adam really *was* the mummy? What if he needed to tell her something important about the exhibit? What if someone had been following him and he had dressed up like an extra from the old *Hammer Films* horror movie so that he wouldn't be recognized?

"Don't get fanciful," she growled under her breath and plopped down on a stone bench. More than likely, the mummy was just teasing her, escalating their flirtation.

Well, she would set her mind to rest. She'd just call Adam right now. She took her cell phone from her purse, along with a tin of cinnamon Altoids and hit speed dial for his number while she popped one of the curiously strong mints.

The phone rang. Once, twice, three times.

Come on, Adam pick up.

After the tenth ring, Cassie sighed, switched off the phone and stuffed it back into her purse as she crunched the remainder of the cool, arid cinnamon breath mint between her teeth.

She heard rustling in the bushes behind her. Her stomach nose-dived. She turned her head; saw the mummy silhouetted in the light.

"Adam?"

He shuffled toward her.

She stood, dropping her purse on the ground beside the stone bench. "What is it? Is something wrong?"

He made a rough, gurgling sound.

Cassie sank her hands on her hips. "This isn't earning brownie points with me. I like to be surprised, not terrified. Besides, now really isn't the time or the place, everyone is waiting for you inside the museum.

He lumbered closer. His hands outstretched, reaching for her zombie-like. He mumbled something indecipherable in a foreign language.

She was fluent in Spanish, but he certainly wasn't speaking that. Neither was he uttering French nor Portuguese. Latin maybe? Or Greek.

But why? Her heart fluttered wildly.

"Adam," she repeated. "Is that you?" Maybe she'd made a boo-boo and this wasn't him after all.

"Beware . . ." he whispered hoarsely, and then he started coughing.

"Are you okay?" She took a step toward him. "You need a glass of water?"

"Beware . . ." He raised a linen wrapped hand to his throat and coughed again.

"Beware of what?" She frowned.

He uttered the foreign phrase again.

She strained to listen. If she squinted hard and turned her head in his direction it sort of sounded like he was saying, "wannamakemecomealot."

"Pardon."

"Wannamakecomealot."

"Oh I get it. This is some kind of kinky sex game, right?"

She grinned.

During their numerous transatlantic telephone conversations over the course of the past few weeks, as they made preparations for the exhibition, Cassie had nonchalantly let it slip that she adored surprises and fantasy roleplaying games. Maybe Adam had taken her flirtatious comments to heart and decided to use the occasion of their first face-to-face meeting as an opportunity to seduce her.

Too fun.

"Let me guess," she said. "You're pretending we're in jeopardy. Bad guys are after us. Danger heightens the sexual re-sponse. Good game. You really had me going there for a minute."

"Beware of the . . ." He wavered on his feet, just inches from her.

Was he drunk? She hoped he wasn't drunk. She didn't like drunks.

"Spit it out, man. Stop being cryptic, I know it's a game

but I can't get into it if you don't move things along. I have a short attention span. Everybody says so. Beware of what?"

But he didn't answer.

Instead, he pitched forward and Cassie was forced to thrust out her arms to catch him before he smashed face first into the ground.

And that was when she saw the butcher knife protruding from his back.

THE EDITOR'S DIARY

Dear Reader,

Everyone needs a little help from their friends—just ask the Beatles. But what happens when your innocent gesture gets you into more delicious trouble than you ever could have dreamed? Jump into SCANDAL and CHARMED AND DANGEROUS, our two Warner Forever titles this July.

Amanda Quick raves, "**Pamela Britton** writes the kind of wonderfully romantic, sexy, witty historical romance that readers dream of discovering." Well, open your eyes Sleeping Beauty—your dreams are about to get even better! Rein Montgomery, the Duke of Wroxly, is being held prisoner of his late uncle's will. He must survive without his wealth or title in the meanest of London streets for one month or lose his entire fortune. Confident that he can charm any woman into doing his bidding, Rein sets his sights on Anna, a captivating market girl . . . but he never expected such a struggle. Though she offers him shelter for a night, Anna has no intention of letting this dashing stranger into her bed. After all, she may not be a well-bred lady, but she's hardly going to fall over with her muslin skirts in the air. But as Rein's defenses come down, Anna can't help but succumb to him. She knows better than to think he'll stay forever . . . but when he does leave, will he take her heart?

Journeying from the desire and deceit of securing an inheritance to the intrigue and exhaustion of trailing a thief, we present **Lori Wilde's CHARMED AND DANGEROUS**. *Romantic Times* calls Lori's last book "sexy and a hoot" so grab your passport—her next book is out and you're in for the ride of your life! Dependable Maddie Cooper has spent her life cleaning up the messes left in her twin sister, Cassie's wake. So when FBI agent David Marshall pops into her life, she can't help but sigh—Cassie's done it again. But little does Maddie know that her calm life is about to hit turbulence. Hot on the trail of an international art thief who just happens to be Cassie's newest boyfriend, David enlisted Cassie's help to catch him. But Cassie has disappeared, a painting is missing and Maddie is madder than hell. Determined to find her sister, Maddie is sticking to David like a bad suit. From the Caribbean to Paris, Madrid to Venice, Maddie and David search high and low for Cassie . . . and find love along the way.

To find out more about Warner Forever, these July titles, and the author, visit us at www.warnerforever.com.

With warmest wishes,

Karen Kosztolnyik, Senior Editor

P.S. The dog days of summer are here so why go outside? Crank up your A.C. and curl up with these two reasons to hope for a heat wave: **Susan Crandall** pens the poignant story of a man who's haunted by the death of an army buddy . . . only to find himself falling in love with his friend's wife in **MAGNOLIA SKY**; and **Julie Anne Long** delivers the touching story of a woman who's so desperate to escape her impending wedding that she runs for the countryside with the family groomsman in **THE RUNAWAY DUKE**.